NEW HARMONY

Book Four of the Go Love Quartet

Michael Gills

Published by Raw Dog Screaming Press
Bowie, MD

First Edition

Printed in the United States of America

ISBN: 978-1-947879-50-8
Library of Congress Control Number: 2022944143

RawDogScreaming.com

Acknowledgements

I'd like to thank writer and friend par excellence Rick Campbell for reading *New Harmony* in manuscript form, and his boatload of good advice which included composing a fifth novel as a sort of coda, so that the Go Love Quartet is now a quintet—more to come on that… Thank you to my editor at Raw Dog Screaming Press, Jennifer Barnes, for steadfastly seeing the project through, even though my books are neither best sellers nor especially profitable. I am grateful to the mentors I continue to look toward, notably Fred Chappell, whose Joe Robert Kirkman Tetralogy gave me license for my own quartet. I'm grateful to my novel writing students, who submit to rising at 4:30 a.m. for a solid academic year, and whose energy sustains my own efforts. And I'd like to thank Dean and friend Sylvia Torti for making novel writing happen. Thank you to my readers out there, and for everyone who had a hand in keeping me afloat, or pulling me out when I fell in—you know who you are. Finally, I want to thank my daughter, Lyra Gills, for her love and support, for telling me to keep my head up and making that exemplary acceptance letter to replace a rejection I'd received that hurt her young heart. I keep it in front of my book of submissions for good and ever. And, with all my heart, thank you Jill, whose love and belief in me is all that I've ever needed to keep going.

for Jill and Lyra, always my love

and for Captain Peter C. Peterson

#1

"Here 120 men, women and children were massacred in cold blood early in September, 1857. They were from Arkansas."

Carved in granite, Mountain Meadows, New Harmony, Utah

PART I

1.

Falling in and out of sleep, Edgar dreams of the Stepwell boy, his missing finger sewn on straight, pointing west toward the scene of the crime. The blue doors of hogans shine. East across the sage covered badland, north toward *Teec Nos Pos* to *Dinnehotso,* the *Lukachukai* to the west, Utah up there somewhere beyond Shiprock's godawful shadow, the petrified throat of a smoking volcano if the reading material back to the rest stop be trusted. It's all here—the whole goddamned world. Or so it seemed to Edgar, falling in and out of the dream of the Stepwell boy, the finger pointing west, blazing in the very real light of the rising sun. What was it with these Indians and blue doors? All faced east so the August sun made them into pieces of sky you could walk through into their dirt mound churches where they did who knows what, snake dancing and flesh piercing and praying to their warthog god. Though he doesn't know it, Edgar traces the river bed that once bore quartz crystal from the Ouachita Mountains back near Mount Ida across the breadth of what is now Oklahoma and Texas and New Mexico to this place, near the mouth of the Grand Canyon, Four Corners, the place of Hope, where he's followed his kith and kin west through the blue doors of time. He's driven to forever and ever, Edgar.

The culvert jolts him straight awake, knocks the front end of his Jimmy out of alignment, so he has to pull left to keep from hitting the derelict car with an Indian's head stuck under the hood on the side of the road. There's a woman inside, a couple kids. What the hell. Maybe it'd bring him some good mojo to help out, make the hoard of spirits chased his ass all night leave him be. May be.

Outside is sage fragrant, new light shimmering as if from an alien sun, damn sure not the same one that beat down on Pope County, which he so recently put behind his back for good and ever. July had been a hot son of a bitch in River Valley, a scorcher, so folks had dropped left and right—at the dog food plant, the pickle factory, Con-Agra, Edgar'd burned out the backhoe clutch twice digging their holes and backfilling. And the last one, a Tri-County Coon Club full penis carrier, his plot was in the same field as long-legged Tina Casteen. Even in death she rattled him, Edgar, who had such proximity for so many years with the newly departed. He'd dug his lover'shole himself, cast in the first fistful of mother earth, and still he felt her cold brown eyes from the last time he saw her, when she said that they were three. And that night of the funeral, cold dark with no moon, he'd returned to the raw dirt still wet from digging, hammered the red clay with the backside of a number ten shovel blade, the hollow wallops echoing over the field where those who'd walked down from Henry County, Tennessee lay buried at the feet of their fathers till the rapture comes, and most of them even after, especially Tina. Somehow they'd all coalesced and chased him like they wanted something, something that he alone could give, three generations of drownings and car wreck victims and heart attacks. What they wanted Edgar didn't know, but it gave him the willies, and he'd headed west, not the first of his kind to do so, nor the last.

"Need some hep?"

The Indian was fiddling with the battery cables, both the positive and negative posts corroded as all get out. Inside the car they were silent as stone. He'd been like this a good many times himself, Edgar, broke down in the middle of bumfuck.

"You got cables?" the man said, lifted his face so the sun shone in both earth-colored eyes. "Give me a jump?"

Edgar did have cables, three kinds of shovels and a pick axe. In his toolbox was the wrench they'd need, a 5/8 for tightening the connectors back onto the posts. A wire brush. WD-40. He retrieved the jumper cables, hauled out a couple icy lemonades for the kids.

"Here," he told the lady. "Here." He held them through the open window, the lemonades.

"No thank you," she said, took them both.

He could see sixty miles in every direction, wide open, this place. The two men latched up the cables, and Edgar started his Jimmy, gave it some gas. The Indian gave it a goodminute before hitting the ignition, no go. Not even a piddly clickety-clack.

"I think she's dead," Edgar said.

The cables sparked when the Indian adjusted connections. "You think?" he said, his voice hurt sounding. Inside the car, one can opened, then the other.

"I think."

"Run me to Shiprock?"

Edgar said, "Sure."

The Indian yanked his dead battery out, said a few foreign words to the woman and kids. In the cab of Edgar's truck, the man sat the battery between his feet, said, "Wife thanks you for them drinks."

Edgar said, "I've been driving all night."

Colorado reared up straight ahead, Ute Mountain and Mesa Verde, the San Juans and the Hogbacks, a land so wide flipping open it hurt to look at. The man smelled like cornbread, the Indian. He had on tennis shoes, Nikes, on either side of the battery.

Edgar'd never buried an Indian.

Of a sudden, fat rain drops thwack the windshield, then it's all out pouring out of nowhere, not a cloud in the sky five minutes ago. Tail end August, the monsoon rains blown up from the Sea of Cortez. He flipped the wipers on high, slowed down, the truck hydroplaning some. The Indian smiled, stuck his whole right arm out the open window, turned his palm up so hard rain splatted on it. "My grandmother used to do this," he said.

There was the good smell of sage and thunder; it washed through the truck's road funk. Back at the car, Edgar imagined the three Indians sticking their arms out rolled down windows.

"She lives over there," the Indian said, pointed at Edgar's chest. "In Dinnehotso."

Edgar let his hand ride the wind out by his side mirror. Wiped his face with the sweet water. "I sure could use some coffee," he said.

"On me," the Indian said. "I know a gas station."

And then the rain was gone sudden as it came.

What he didn't know, Edgar T. Paris, was that Saturday morning was the very worst possible time to drive across Navajo land, except maybe Sunday morning when all the Mormon EMTs were forbidden to work, so the ambulances were scarce. He neither knew nor suspected that Indians could be Mormon, nor that they believed Pahana, the lost white brother, was none other than the bishop who'd walked down from Salt Lake, held out his hand and showed them a tablet, the swastika sign, and the fourth world ended that second and the fifth began. Why, there's a whole boatload Edgar can't but suspect, navigating the flipped cars left and right all up Highway 64 East on a morning he hasn't realized is 8.18.18, a palindrome unto itself. Middle of nowhere on Indian land, ambulances howling who knows where. It wasn't until he came upon a flipped compact being sawed open by the three EMTs on the Rez who weren't Mormon that Edgar realized all the bashed to Jesus car wrecks he'd just driven past had people in them, men and a few women who'd tried to make it home while blitzed out of their minds, and now walked in the happy hunting ground or whatever hereafter it was for Indians to go to on the other side.

He'd been listening to Code Talker radio since Shiprock, where he'd dropped the Indian with his dead battery off at a truck stop, accepted a coffee to go and flew toward all he didn't know. It would come to him. The Indian had told him a story about how his dad used to get off work on Friday afternoon and drive them from Aneth over to Grandma's house in Dinnehotso, only they'd drive up to the river bridge on the Utah side near Mexican Water and Daddy'd pull over a hundred yards or so from the Arizona state line. It'd be way dark, after midnight on a work day in the old fields, Montezuma crude on Rez land, so the headlights would splash the highway stripes and all of them, even Mama, would hop out and footrace to Arizona, see who'd cross the line first. Edgar'd taken the gift go coffee and wished the Indian and his family well. They were good people—that car would get them somewhere. He'd forever wish to Jesus he had a story like that to tell, running with his people in the headlight splash, racing to Arizona.

There's a line of cars, a whole slew of them, nobody was going anywhere. Code Talker Radio was all about rape on the Rez, how white folks drift down to stalk the Diné, because they couldn't be prosecuted—Indian law didn't apply to them. What shit, back home the man would cuff you to his headrest, drive on out in yonder field and cut your nuts off, feed them to his dog. What good was law if it didn't apply?

The flipped car was American, a junker Chevrolet, it had skidded a football field length gouge into the asphalt. A big-bellied Rez trooper was taking a metal saw—the jaws of life, wasn't it called—to the driver's side, cutting off hunks of sheet metal. A second ambulance screeched to a stop and out hopped three medics with a hand gurney. They ran to the flipped car, got on hands and knees and looked through the busted-out windows. Still, the trooper saw-sawed.

Cars lined up in either direction. It occurred to Edgar that he was hungry. He fished an orange from the little cooler, dug nails into navel, stripped the peel off in one tangy strip. A girl got out of a truck, walked up to the car wreck, got down and peeked in. Her mama, Edgar guessed it was her mama, smoked inside the cab. The little girl walked up to the wreck, peeked in, then walked back shaking her head. *No, it's not Daddy*, she lipped.

After another ten minutes, they pulled the hugest man Edgar's ever seen out from the sawed-off roof. Six workers out there now, they rolled him onto the gurney, so small it seemed silly. They tightened straps, strained and lifted. Veins bulged as they struggled to haul this mammoth man the twenty feet to the ambulance's back door. They staggered hard left and Edgar was sure they'd drop him, this dark-haired giant would breathe his last right there in front of them all. What a hole it'd take to bury that one. But the bearers hung tight, they somehow made it. Inside, the big man was talking, moving his fingers. He was smiling, telling a joke, how him and his sisters had sprinted across the state line, maybe, pumping a fist. *Yeah!* the man screamed. Then, siren wailing, the ambulance spun out toward Teec Nos Pos, and the trooper waved them past the wreckage, on down the line, on a road west where Indians hitchhiked the highway, some holding up dollar bills, the paper money blowing between their fingers.

Truth is, Edgar doesn't know where he's going or why. When he left home, well, The Tri-County Coon Club where he was caretaker and gardener and fish fryer, he'd only known that it was time, he had a calling. It was time, Lord. He'd filled his tank and two cans at the Conoco in R-Ville and lit out on I-40, hit Fort Smith at sunset and drove on into Oklahoma, Choctaw bingo country on the Trail of Tears. And it was somewhere around there, just after dark, the spirits caught up with him in the form of a long-nose Peterbilt that blew the fuck by, shook him sideways and rattled his balls, so Edgar flipped on his bright lights, flew a birdie out the window, and immediately knew it was the wrong thing to do, bright-lighting and flipping the birdie to someone he didn't know, could be somebody like Uncle Larry who'd run you down and slit your tires, cut that finger off and make you chew on it a while, before he peed on it and fed it to the one-eyed dog in his truck bed. Best not shitkick the cardboard box full of rattlesnakes. *Wrong, wrong, wrong*, he knew it straight away, but of course that was too late.

The truck, which was black, flew past, a high-pitched whir of trailer and signal and danger lights—the son of a bitch might have been an alien space craft come down to blow the world away. He could feel their eyes, spirit wind hot through the open window. She slowed down, the semi, there on the empty stretch of highway in Oklahoma, just about midnight, dark-thirty. A face shone in the side mirror, one he knew and had once loved or known or something in another lifetime, maybe. They had bad blood, had sniffed each other out, and this was it, could go either way.

The black hole of a truck rolled to a stop, racked off, dared Edgar to pass. There was nobody out there, nobody. Stars above, earth below, and nobody to tell the story. Ain't that the shits, when there's nobody to tell the story.

Edgar's Chevy was a column shifter. He cut the trash radio and dropped her down to second, so the tranny screamed as he accelerated, dropped her into third at sixty, the front-end shimmying some. And just as he made to pass, the very instant he pulled aside the long, sable trailer, the shadow semi was on him, in his lane, his passenger fender under the goddamn nose, a godawful sound.

Son of a bitch wanted him dead.

He skidded from eighty to a stop. Out there in front of him, the truck slowed, stopped.

She'd cut her lights, he couldn't really see it, the hole in the night. The growl was clear, steady, the stacks racking off.

"I'm sorry," he said out the window as he rolled it up. It was a hot night. The smell of rain, far off heat lightning, something else. A trace. Himself?

This time the son of a bitch Peterbilt jackknifed, so the whole highway was blocked, Edgar nearly flipped, slammed her in reverse, backed road side for a hundred solid yards. The fuck you say? What have I ever done to you?

But the truck, which Edgar now knew as a real-deal black hole, a swirling vortex of meanness on this earth, a representative from the other side come to rip his rompers, she straightened, sat astraddle the long white line, waited.

A strip of unearthly green shone between eastbound and westbound. He could make for it, head back home, crawl into his bed at Tri-County and be a grave digger again, sniff the panties folded in his top drawer Tina Casteen had left him the night before she was killed in a car wreck with the Shoates boy. He could go back. This truck meant to kill him.

He crossed the median, Edgar, his own lights off now, rattled up onto asphalt. The wrong way, he floored it, jammed gears, accelerated till the rods knocked, far off headlights flying his way.

Behind him, the Peterbilt flashed to life, came on an interstellar rush, but Edgar had the jump. Wrong way, he drove like a motherfucker, rods knock-knocking, so oncoming veered wildly to the side, gave him passage, their piddly horns blaring. And when he couldn't see the black hole of a truck anymore, Edgar cut back across the median. For one sick moment his rear tires spun. Glass broke. There came the thumpa-thump a flat tire makes. Here it was. Right here. But he made it onto the road. His tires were sound. He put pedal to metal, was in Texas soon. Flew through Amarillo and Tucumcari into the small hours, a hot dry wind blowing through the cab that dried him clean as leather. Thirsty, he eyed the rearview, the darkness from whence came the pursuit he'd feel in his heart for every one of the rest of his days on this earth.

Though he was running hell for leather from the rising sun, it lightened some, a fire and brimstone preacher all staticky on the dashboard radio, nodding, and for some reason he thought on the Harvell boy, how Ronnie Love'd chomped off his right index finger, swallowed it. "Gid me my fanger back," boy'd screamed. How they'd managed to sew the thing back on at St. Mary's was just too much, so he could move it and everything, finger pick that sweet Martin D-28, strum the sweet E for Mama.

It had pointed him to the broke down Indians, the finger, and then across Navajo land to Tuba City, named for the sound the wind made as it passed over the land, hard-ass desert, that bass note blowing while he pumped gas at the Flying J, pissed in the men's, a machine on the wall advertising *Rough Rider*s, this weasel-face moaning, giving him the look.

Somebody coughed from a bathroom stall. Edgar's piss is bright yellow—he needs to drink more water.

He paid for a case of little plastic water bottles with a fresh twenty, asked the clerk for one of those sausage and cheese biscuits behind the glass.

"Sure thing," the brown-eyed lady said. "You can have two if you like."

"I got somewhere to go," Edgar said.

"I can tell that," the woman said. "I don't doubt it."

"Okay, two," Edgar said.

"Can do," the woman said.

"Borrow your tire gauge?"

She passed it to him with the buttered biscuits wrapped in white paper. "You may. Be bringing it back when you're finished."

"I'm from Arkansas," Edgar said, the biscuits hot in his hand.

She said, "Sure you are, honey."

Outside in the heat, parked next to the free air, Edgar checked each tire, topped the driver's side rear off at thirty-six even. He kept an eye on the road coming and going. He'd see that Peterbilt again, Edgar knew it. She'd eyeballed his plates, the woman behind the counter, how she knew where he was from.

956 DMF, the thing said.

He'd never really looked at them, his license plates. Now, they halted him. His stomach sank. He understood for the first time that he's been hauling ass cross-country with Arky plates that announce him as *Dumb Mother Fucker* from the *Natural State*. The demon truck had known him as such, the broke down Indian, all the people parked behind him while the jaws of life did their thing. *Look at the DMF*, they'd laughed. *Ain't he a DMF*.

"I ain't no dumb mother fucker," he told the woman when he gave her back the gauge. "You don't know nothing about me."

She looked at him.

"Your gauge don't work, neither."

Back on the highway, he munched the biscuits, took a shortcut on Highway 23 where one sign said VISIT ECHO CLIFFS and another DINOSAUR TRACKS.

DMF.

Edgar said the words out loud, each one a sentence to itself.

2.

Yakov had blown an eye out while bomb-making in the Ukraine, so when he looked at you, the eyeless socket made him seem at once wise and old, of which he was neither. The sealed shut eye, the socket's indentation had the effect of staring through you, though, which made Joey Harvell queasy, with the endless rounds of vodka and pickled mushrooms had by the Russian's bonfire. Fine ash and sparks rose in a column above them, up and up to where the peaks shone with alpenglow at sunrise and sunset, and the high mountain air was brisk with the aroma of wild mushrooms from the day's picking, King Boletus and Slippery Jacks, a variety poisonous for some, not so for others.

The Ukrainian intern was dog drunk.

He chain-smoked hooter and slurred badly, sometimes breaking into Russian, his high voice marring the vowels, so neither Joey nor Renee had one idea in hell what they were saying, the Russians and the Ukrainian intern. Uphill, the Kukalov's RV might have been a flying saucer, or so it seemed to Joey, who had the vodka buzz, and the sillies from Misha's dope. It was Labor Day, Yelena's birthday weekend, and they'd joined them in the high Uintas for mushroom picking and drinking. A Saturday night, the Harvell's tent was pitched downhill in the dark. Above them the sky was afire, the Milky Way unfurling, the Hunter's shoulder showing, already.

"In Russia," Yakov said, the flap of skin sewn over the eye quivering just a little, "We never carry our shit around in bucket."

He motioned downhill at the Harvell's port-o-potty, a five-gallon bucket with a plastic toilet seat and lid. Yelena smiled, drank down her vodka. They hadn't brought a drop, the Kukalovs, but snapped to at Joey's half-gallon. Renee'd walked down to the tent already, pissed. She couldn't stand it when the Kukalovs spoke Russian to each other. She was sure they were talking about them, making fun of them, what dumb-fucks Americans were, which was probably what they *were* saying, Joey thought. Earlier, Yakov'd taught him to say I'll shit on you from the highest tree in Russian.

Yelena offered him more, the Slippery Jacks. "If it doesn't kill you," she said, "it's so good." She smiled that smile.

Misha, the drunk Ukrainian, laughed so hard he lost his breath. "If it doesn't kill you, is so good" he kept saying.

They'd talked their way through the story of how Yakov's father had fathered the Soviet Nuclear program, how he'd grown up in a house full of bugs and hidden cameras and had sworn at an early age he'd get out, swim the Bering Strait if he had to. He'd won the Lenin Prize, Yakov's father, and there was a framed picture of the old man standing beside a warhead in the RV.

A visiting intern was always at his side, Yakov's, speaking in that loud in-your-face way of people who know you can't understand what they're saying, who could look you in the face and say *enjoy the love of donkey*, and you'd never know it. His wife, Yelena, was a blonde beauty, who on a river trip had said to Joey, *I take off my clothes, all of them,* peeled off her shorts and shirt and dove into the river just like that. Now she sautéed the scarlet mushroom caps they'd picked that morning after the rain, while boiling a potful of Slippery Jacks, the fist-size caps they preferred for pickling, to be eaten with glassfuls of chilled vodka by the fire for Russian happy hour and fireworks. The Kukalovs were big on fireworks.

Now the conversation had turned to how the last intern had died, fallen off a cliff to save little Yelena, their youngest daughter. Yakov had had to accompany the body back to mother Russia, where the Stalingrad Heroic Prize for Bravery was awarded posthumously. The family had met him at the airport in Moscow, his hometown, to collect the casket, over which was cast a flag, and a lock of little Yelena's blonde hair, twisted with red ribbon, for all things red were holy to their people. The mother had wept, and wife had laughed, both at the same time, and they'd had drinks, gone to a beer barn. *In Russia we always go to beer barn*, Yakov said, that glint in his eye. Yelena translated, the warm liquory breath in Joey's face, leaving out some parts, he was sure. She'd many times hinted to him how they'd come to the states, the nature of their mission, how it had been necessary for them to marry beforehand and have children once settled, to assimilate, to become Americans.

"He was good man," Yakov said, held up a tall, skinny glass filled to the rim with Joey's Bartel, "a brother."

They toasted the hero intern, who'd slid down the face of a cliff near Mount Olympus, having secured the girl to a mountain mahogany. His first day in Utah, the day he died.

Yakov cursed. "He deserved better."

The fire popped and hissed, and there were the stars and Misha's wacky weed going around. The kids, all grown save little Yelena, who'd for some reason stayed the same size exactly as when she had the accident, were all grown, off at University, they studied physics and architecture and consumer studies. The Kukalov's oldest had managed a Fulbright. Their middle, the boy, was in Chicago, and only little Yelena remained, sacked out up in the RV with Lara, Joey's daughter who, at twenty, refused to sleep in the tent with her parents. Early in the day, while she napped in their tent, a cow had stuck its head through the screen door and mooed.

Yelena said, "You must roll me cigarette."

Joey rolled a cigarette.

"The air smells funny," she said.

Misha was talking, his every word running together. The first day of September, a chill had come on, change was coming, he could feel it, Joey. Him and Renee were knocking on the door of sixty, she'd talked about retirement, twenty-five years flown by now since they'd come west, arrived in Rawlings, Wyoming on the eve of Rodeo Weekend, cowboys in buckskin galloping down Main Street firing six-shooters, the Medicine Bow range spread behind them as backdrop.

"*Joey.*"

From the tent, she called him, Renee.

"We will make tribute," Yakov said, cold enough now for his breath to fog, firelight on his face, the eye.

Misha threw a hunk of wood on the fire so flames jumped head high. This was bear country, maybe there was a bear down there, a spirit bear dressed in white and Renee'd seen it. Lara was in the RV. The red mushrooms, sautéed in butter and garlic, had a bite to them.

"I wanted to be poet," Yelena said, puffing out a smoke ring, and then another. "But I am here. Tomorrow is my birthday. The real one."

"*Joey.*" Renee said it again.

"How about you?" She'd been to architecture school, Yelena, before having kids. Twenty years younger than Yakov, tomorrow she'd be forty.

"This I do for my brother," Yakov said, and there was a hissing sound, something like locusts buzzing in Arkansas summer, when the sound got under your teeth and made you crazy.

Joey was fifty-seven, thirty years married now, they'd made it, him and Renee. Lara was a college sophomore, their house was paid for, their cars. Last year they'd toured Prague and Vienna, Berlin and Paris. His retirement fund had hit a quarter million. So far from laying bricks in Lonoke County and that far-off field of Brown-eyed Susan where his mother and brother, Grandpa Stepwell and the rest lay buried, what more was there in this life. Toward what, the rest of his days?

"*There,*" Yelena said, and in her eyes he saw the explosion coming.

Like many who make up for what they've lost or miss by mastering some overly difficult task, Yakov had gone in for computers and surveillance, one of the big ski resorts used his hardware, and his devices had accompanied a non-manned flight to the moon. He drove like a maniac, if Renee's story about the drive to the float trip on Green be trusted—she said he used some sort of jamming device against speed guns and hauled a trailer full of gear upwards of ninety on Highway 80, the whole truck filled with the racket of their fighting, though they just might have been talking, she couldn't tell the difference, Renee claimed. They think we're stupid, Renee said, he kept asking me, "Why would you need to study English if you speak English?"

And she'd said, "Don't you study Russian in Russia?"

"In Russia, our teachers know their own language," he'd said, his good eye rolling, flat out flooring his SUV, so that by the time they made it to the river camp, Renee'd had all she could take, and little Yelena threw up a bellyful of pretzels, and the Russians screamed at each other in Russian.

His Ph.D. in Physics was from the Moscow Institute for Physics and Technology and he'd held the Chair for the General Physics Institute. Yakov engineered high speed resolution cameras and microprocessor embedded systems, what it said on his website's home page, where a headshot of him looks old and wise and not a little scary, the way the blank eye searched you out. His digital cameras might turn their gaze on a crater, a rock on the side of the moon where no light had ever shone, that's how it seemed to Joey, that unseeing eye that searched you out.

One of those cameras sat on top of a pole on the RV uphill, a little red light flashing every now and then, as if Yakov could train the lens by sheer thought, isn't that what he was working toward, what he'd confessed on the river after shish kabob, when Joey'd got him and Yelena drunk on vodka and Yakov had confessed to being a sleeper. It had been their night to cook, the Kukalovs, the fourth night on the Green just above Swallow Canyon where the tiny darting birds built mud nests on a cliff face under which lay brown trout fat with the fledgling swallows, so the tackle stores back in Dutch John sold a version of the fledgling swallow as a tied fly, along with the mouse and snake, and Joey'd fed them three nights running on fresh trout, but that night it was Yakov and Yelena's time at the fire.

Yelena'd marinated leg of lamb, cut chunks in red wine vinegar and fresh ground pepper, Yakov's homemade shish kabob skewers, aluminum and about three feet of furled red cloth for the occasion. Joey'd set up the grill pan on a fire blanket, loaded charcoal in a lighter chimney, ready to roll.

Only Yakov had looked at the charcoal and scowled. He shook his head. "Charcoal is poison. In Russia, we do not cook our food with poison."

"It's charcoal, Yakov," Joey'd said, and Renee'd given him the look. Her father

Rock was a Navy Captain, and she'd spent her formative years during the cold war, she'd suspected them from day one. "It's *made* for cooking."

Yakov just shook his head, summoned Yelena and little Yelena, and off they'd walked toward a far-off mesa, till they were little dots moving.

"See," Renee'd said. "*See?*"

The Kukalovs returned an hour later, dark coming, bearing little bundles of pinyon on their heads, so that Yelena and little Yelena looked like peasants from one of Lara's kids' books, and Joey'd laughed, because he was half plowed on vodka tonics by then.

But Yakov had lit the fire, fanned it with a newspaper, laid skewered meat over the shining coals so that it smelled like heaven there at sunset on the river, and Yelena boiled red potatoes and cabbage, and their first Russian shish kabob, the Harvells and the Kukalovs, on the Green River made a memory that bridged the families. They felt at home together, or that's how it seemed, both so far from home.

Later, the vodka hot in his belly, Yakov had confessed, though he'd remember none of it the next morning. Yelena, her blonde hair gleaming in the firelight, she'd moaned, "I have slept for fifteen years now. And who to wake me?"

When they awoke, it had snowed six inches, so the mound of dirt lifted and piled by Yakov's homemade bomb was now a sledding hill for little Yelena and Lara, who took turns sliding down on their butts while Yakov filmed the frolicking in the season's first snow, hungover Misha joining them, the sun out and fierce by then. They woke to a half foot of fresh powder, Joey and Renee, their flip flops covered, the tent sagging, the icy drip falling between them. It's cold out, hell yeah, steam rising, and the mountains through the screen are spectacular. On the heels of the eleventh hottest summer in history, the snow is miraculous, a gift, manna from heaven. Out there, twenty-year-old Lara yelped, Little Yelena almost seventeen now, blonde hair like her mother's shining, and Misha, lighting cigarettes, the wild light in his eyes. A patch of raw dirt showed through the bomb mound.

Renee's bag was zipped up over her head. In there she sighed, moaned, said, "I want to go home."

There was the smell of coffee. A fire was popping. He had to pee. Joey unzipped the screen door, stepped out into the snow in his underwear. He said, "Wake up and pee, the world's on fire," words his grandfather Si had once woke him with, forty years ago, on Lake Ouachita in Arkansas, about to hit the lake before first light and cast Devil's Toothpicks at schooling largemouth.

Renee said, "Is it bad?"

He'd seen what was coming last night in Yelena's eyes, Yakov punching both fist into the night sky, the Milky Way, the hiss of vacuum before ignition, and the suddenness of impact, the mist and then fine dust spray and the arc of light before the explosion. All there in her eye, the combo birthday present for her turning forty, and tribute to the Russian intern who'd sacrificed his life for little Yelena, who was nearly a woman now, who would one day give birth to twin sons and name the first one for him.

Joey said, "It's not so bad."

Uphill, they're shoeless, every last one of them. If there's anything Russians love more than explosives, it's snow, made them giddy, reminded them of home.

Someone was frying bacon.

He could smell it, sharp against the fresh snow. Thirty years ago, when they were first married, that first winter after their Christmas wedding, an unforecast snow had dusted their North Carolina yard, and Joey'd talked her into running barefoot, the way MaMa Stepwell used to in Solgohachia, what she'd learned from her own grandma Poteet, who'd learned it from the Cherokee who'd walked the Trail of Tears, and reenacted the snow dance for the joy and love of their people, the remembrance of a happy home. They'd been deep in love then, that winter in Greensboro, that season when people had called them Bonnie and Clyde.

Joey met his daughter's eyes. Uphill, she looked so like Mama, that same smile, the earth and good sun in her eyes. She'd run away from home last Thanksgiving, driven off to Tucson with a boy named Jack, where the dwarf Uncle had welcomed her as long lost prodigal daughter of the Washers returned. Something had happened down there, she'd come back different. *Geronimo*, she'd say when asked what happened. *Geronimo.*

"Look at this," Joey said.

It's to his calves, the snow, hot for some reason, burning.

The freight train of who we are, do we not drag it all our days, the sound dopplering between the place we come from and the place we go? Sometimes out of nowhere it comes to Joey Harvell who he is, what his right place is on this earth. How love had saved his life three times, and that maybe the fourth was coming, just down the road, on the periphery of his vision. And that morning of the new snow, the first of the season, holy to Cherokee who'd walked it to hell and back, and for the Stepwells, who'd learned the dance, from whom he'd learned it and taught it to his new love way back in Carolina, and then his daughter, Lara, how they'd rise to the first powder of winter and dance out the back door, hold hands up to the infinite sky and throw heads back, *good crazy* grandpa Si'd say, hopping on his one leg, the size eleven footprint marking the way of a one-legged man. Sometimes who he was would come on him when he least expected it, and now was a moment like that, when he'd learn again.

The tablet of snow glittered in front. of him, pure white and gleaming. It slid from the forks of trees and hung hovering in the air, pixie dust, they called it on Alta Mountain.

Full-bladdered, he waded to the right spot, hauled down his underwear and began to make the word. He wrote the five letters, carefully linked in cursive, just as he had in the snow thirty years before.

Lara'd once let it slip that he'd written her name that way. It was on Camino, when they'd ridden across the breadth of Spain and ended up at the ancient cathedral in Santiago de Compostela. The field of stars where headless Saint James was said to have been buried by the hand of God, and that he'd rise again when the world was in most need and slay the wicked. For no reason in particular, she'd just blurted it out to a fellow pilgrim on the steep ride down to the brickyard before the face of the time-stained cathedral where they'd wept for joy and it had come to her and she said it.

Behind him, the tent rustled. The nylon door zipped open and he heard the crunch of her foot on fresh snow. Their sandals were snow covered, the tent on the verge of collapse. It was heavy, this early season fall. The packing and slip-side driving on the dirt road out of these mountain woods was in front of them, the work days next week, the rest of their lives. If it didn't kill you, it was good. She joined him just as he spurted the last of it.

Bright yellow in front of them, her name, the crisp-edged letters a foot tall.

She put one arm around his neck, leaned into him, and lifted a foot, rested the bare sole against her left knee. He knew, could tell by the way her skin felt that she was smiling, that they were in love that they would make it through whatever was coming.

"He's crazy," she said, "that Yakov."

3.

The poetry of her childhood, those percussive bursts from the mouth of *mamochka*, the brick walls of the garden shining sweet enough to taste, these are not possible in English. Nor the light. When she'd count the floorboards left to right, from the dresser with its missing knob to the window that looked out onto a field where crows made a ruckus over what was left of the winter greens and she could see them out there raising all kinds of hell, and left to right, seventeen, eighteen, nineteen, to the corner where shadow lived, and the shafts of sunlight would dance and flicker—she could not think such thoughts in English. How her father would wake her at daylight on a snow day and they'd walk out, turn faces to it and he'd open his mouth and sing out the folk song he'd learned from his mother in the sweet beautiful by and by, I was once lost but now I'm found—where had that come from? There were twenty-four of them, the floorboards left to right in the bedroom where she'd come of age. At five inches each, that made ten feet—in English. In *makhovaya sazhen*, the distance between the tips of her arms stretched as far as she could reach the summer she met Yakov Kukalov, two and some, in *pyads*, the spread of her palm flattened beneath the weight of her body, nearly forty. So what was ten for some was forty for others, and that is to say twenty four, the numbers danced behind her eyes, their loops and curls and angles making faces, the way *mamochka's* goat did when it stared into the sun at breakfast time, curled its little goat lips back and made the face, sun aglow in its slit eyes. The floorboards were made of timber felled at the edge of a great dark wood, the trees old, so they had within them the air Peter the Great had breathed, Ivan, Catherine, the beasts of the southern wild. They creaked, the boards, when Yakov slipped through the window that summer night and the stars made a W in the sky, the dwarf moon flowers came blowing their medicine breath on her dream. Ten, twenty-four, forty, the wood knew her secrets, knew the oaths she'd sworn in her native tongue on the day she said *yes*, she would go with him to the city, to Moscow, she would sign the paper, study architecture, learn the numbers, and go with him to be his wife for Mother Russia. The poetry of her childhood is not possible in English, but that is all she has now, she'd sworn the other away.

But it came to her in dream, goat-lipped and shadow crows, the floor always creaked in Russian, the brick wall sweet enough, still, to taste.

The Americans had changed Labor Day to Yelena's birthday, the third of September, because they did not want it to coincide with May Day, day of revolution back home, but oddly enough, none of them had even the foggiest that that had happened. The moving of the day. It was true, they were stupid. Not all of them. But most. They knew no history, nor geography, that the properties of light were chemical, it was hard to talk about anything with them, really, well mostly. There was Nancy from Open Classroom, and her husband the mad scientist who studied flatworms—they had lived in Berlin and knew Schnitzel from Kentucky Fried Chicken, that beer was best from a glass, that for a mad dog, seven *versts* is not a long detour. Now that kids were out of O.C., she never saw them, Nancy and her mad scientist husband. To make real friends—and keep them, especially now when it was Russia this and Russia that—you had to bend over backwards.

Forget work where everyone was named Jensen or Larsen or Christiansen, or Hansen, Petersen, Rasmussen, and they all wanted you to join them for funeral potatoes with no tea nor vodka, because they were forbidden to anyone save gentiles. In Russia they drank tea three times a day and never a mention of funeral potatoes. But she tried, Yelena. The endless birthday parties and sleepovers and Thanksgivings and Christmas eves, she'd dragged Yakov by the nose and ears, and they'd done their part to fit in, to acclimate, to be American. She'd slept that way for fifteen years, twenty if you counted training in Moscow. Had she forgot who she was, Yelena?

Yakov was oblivious. He lived in his head. It was all about cameras and computer, Google and NASA and don't forget the phones are tapped. He'd grown up that way, with all the phones tapped.

"How can they tap a cell?" she'd asked him one night in bed, when baby was still nursing, so she stayed with them for some of the night, the wet sound of her sucking.

He'd just laughed. And then he was asleep, that slight snore. When he woke up next morning, he laughed again. It was so damn funny, all of it. Being a sleeper for fifteen years, twenty.

Two summers ago, they were awakened.

Two summers ago—*Trick or Treat,* the call had come. The message on Yakov's cell, on hers. *Trick or Treat.* In June, time for weddings. Their instructions followed, in code: *Beethoven's Fifth: 4 triumphant as the first and main.*

They awakened on a Sunday, little Yelena drawing out her map of the parallax measurements, how a star's position in the night sky is photographed at autumnal equinox and again on vernal equinox; if the star is close, Yelena said, its position will have greatly shifted, if far away, hardly at all.

Beethoven?

They lived in a placed called Magna in the foothills of the Ochers, not so far from largest open pit copper mine on earth, a mountain of stone inverted. It was peasant class, Magna, a place away from Salt Lake where the miners could afford, and there were bars—the place had a grain to it. People kept horses in their backyards and there were remnants of the original orchards Mormons had planted a hundred and fifty years ago. It was their house, they'd bought and owned it, a dump, really, it should be torn down, but it was theirs, they had papers. Yakov had a camera fixed on them from space, so his computers could zoom in on Misha huffing weed on the back deck that she had designed and built herself with Rudi. There was Yakov's brick pit for shish kabob, and a shed where tools were kept for garden, though Yelena had lost the knack and will in her years of sleeping. She did not have *mamochka's* gift for all that is green, and *Pirate*, their hooligan dog, had chewed up all her garlic so there was no *chesnok* to plant. She had a son, Yelena, who'd ice-skated with her on frozen lake last winter, but he'd gone off to University of Chicago, and stayed for summer, waiting tables and spending all his tips on weed and dumb ass American girl with her skinny legs and white teeth. She missed Rudi—it hurt her heart to have him gone. He threw her fifteen feet across ice and she'd landed on one foot, a pirouette, and said, *Mama*, and *I'm sorry*. English words.

"What are you sorry for?"

Rudi'd said, "Growing up."

An inversion had hung over the valley from the smelters and refineries and ten zillion cars the Mormons drove because they couldn't stand to bus or take train or car pool.

His hair was red, like her father's, her Papa, who'd awakened her with his booming voice and they had walked in snow on mornings before sun came and she came of age in room with its shadow in corner, always the murder of crows flap-flapping amongst the harvest, the sky a mirror, only in reverse, reflecting the cosmos back on itself. *We live as we dream*, Nietzsche said, *and that is alone. Stare into the abyss long enough and it will stare back into you. Life without music would be an error.*

Sorry for growing up, the silliest thing. She imagined Yakov looking down on them from the sky, the winter before they were awakened. How might they have looked, her and their son, when he threw her across frozen lake and said he was sorry for becoming a man?

In Chicago, fucking skinny America girl and huffing pot. *I'm sorry Mama?*

Of course, Beethoven's Fifth, the fourth movement, in which the triumphant trumpet, for so long relegated to the margins of symphonic ridicule, the rude blare she'd heard as a girl from back row of opera house in Stalingrad, their reason for awakening was to take the trumpet to triumph.

They must paint the world red.

The Americans were suckers for anything that had to do with queers fucking or sucking or getting married or adopting or using the bathrooms of gender opposite of their genitals. They went crazy over anything to do with guns—big guns, little guns, guns in their pockets, shotguns and rifles, especially assault rifles, the bigger the better, give her machine gun with five hundred rounds and she could make the American go crazy, Yelena told herself in dreams, Slim Pickens riding the bucking warhead home—*yee haw.* Say anything ever about taking guns away, about regulating the buying of weapons, anything at all, we're talking don't let a clinically identified psychopath purchase handgun after threatening to kill his mother, try to keep him from buying gun and these red state patriots would go apeshit crazy. Then there was the black man, the red man, the brown man, the anything but white man, but especially black man. If queers and guns didn't get them riled up enough to do your bidding, show them the black man with his big hard on bulging in his britches, eyeing the blonde walking down every street in America, swaying those hips, the juices running hot between her legs, and there's the dark man giving her the eye, maybe wolf whistling her, or if not, he was thinking about it, just sure as the world. Wasn't he. Give them the uppity one with his gloved right fist held ignorant against the sky— Tommy C. Smith with the gold medal swaying against his chest down in Mexico, Malcolm, Martin, and especially Cassius Clay who'd gone Muslim and changed his name to Ali, give them a black Ali, dance like a butterfly, sting like a bee, let him protest the draft, the red, white and blue and go *A-Rab*, you'd have them foaming at the mouth, these red-blooded Yankee boys. There were the Black Panthers who carried guns in both back pockets, oh the thoughts they must think about the white girls who showed up in droves to hear them rap about the hood, the dope, the do me daddy please say the ho ho hoes—feed them a little of this medicine and these American boys go wild, they march on Charlottesville, they shoot up Treyvon, they use the black boy's face for target practice, even police will do it, throw in the welfare queens laying on the couch watching *Dialing For Dollars*, the food stamp pork chops piled on plates from here to there and back again, laying on butts and taking our money—Jesus, God almighty, and they voted Democrat, every last one of them voted Dem, the black party, the party that gave us the Clintons, Slick Willy

who called himself the first black president, party who gave us crooked Hillary—
lock her up, lock her up, lock her up.

And if the queers and the guns and the Black Panthers and welfare queens didn't
do the trick, how about a dose of the big O, living up in the White House like his
shit didn't stink? His two little frizzy-haired girls curled on Lincoln's couch, and
wife, Michelle, digging up the back yard to grow her collards and watermelon. Put
his right hand on the Bible and swore to God, who did he think he was, who? Right
here in America. What had happened, what on earth had happened? Give them the
old Obama-rama, Obama-care, Obama take your guns, Obama, from Kenya, won't
show you his birth certificate, been to Harvard and thinks he's better than you. He'd
smoked crack. Mother was a white girl, his father from Kenya, shoot you straight.
Give them some Obama-rama, with Mexicans on the side, take your job, steal your
money, illegal, illegal, illegal. Kenya, Muslim, mongrel, queer going to take your gun
and make you pray to Allah, rename your kid Ali, the black gloved fist your new flag.
I pledge allegiance to the flag of collards and watermelon, and to the republic where
they take your guns, one nation, under Allah, with Kenya and Obama-rama for all.

Even stupid Misha got it. How pathetically easy it would be to bait these fat,
stupid, proud dolts. *Beethoven's Fifth*, the fourth movement, initiated and closed with
the triumphant trumpet, Trick or Treat. Hello? A piece of cake is what they say, the
Americans. She was American, Yelena, she bled red, white and blue. Didn't she. She
had her citizenship, her children in schools, Rudi in Chicago with skinny bitch, little
Yelena at Science Academy. She was registered to vote. Her bases were covered, her
and Yakov's. They had earned their stripes. They had walked a mile in another man's
shoes. They bled red. Were the real McCoy.

It would be fun, electing Ronald Trumpet.

The son of a bitch.

Yes, trick or treat.

Two years earlier, when she could take it no longer and Yakov was raking it in with
his camera this and camera that, camera to photograph book, to watch the house, to
see dark side of moon, when little *babushka* had forgot one night how to say I love
you in her mother tongue, Yelena had booked passage to Moscow where she met her
mother, and together they drove down to Black Sea. The world would see Sochi for
its Olympics and mountains that towered eighteen-

thousand feet above the sea, but for Yelena it had been a place her father had taken
the family when they needed to get away, when they needed to gather themselves
back to their selves.

Rudi had started smoking dope by then. He thought he hid it, always on his hair he'd grown to the middle of his back. Her mother was old for sixty-five, and Papa had been buried in the ground for six years by then, she'd never told him goodbye, Yelena hadn't. On the way to sea they'd stopped at the grave where his name, the one she'd given her only son, was carved in stone. She'd been there before, that cemetery, had a place marked out for herself, even, if, when her part was done, she didn't want her bones to lay in enemy soil.

Rudi'd thrown a rock. Surely he hadn't carried on the plane, through customs, surely he knew better. Little Yelena wore a blue ribbon in her hair. The breeze caught it, and her mother wished that big Rudi could see her that moment. She'd thrown her arms around the stone, went to her knees, and spoke to him through the walls of time.

She spoke the words. In Russian, she said that she was sorry. That she'd done what she'd done. That he had not known the birth and raising of his grandchildren, that she had taken all of the family he had on this earth, that she'd become American.

She said that she missed him. That she loved him. That she'd wakened her kids on the mornings of first snows and ran barefoot with them in the backyard and the neighbors had thought them crazy. Crazy Russians.

She'd brought flowers. She lay them on her father's grave, lit a candle and walked away from it burning.

They'd talked for four days straight, her and mother, at the lake house with its view and fire pit, clean sheets and blankets. They'd talked their ways through all they could remember, the time she'd gashed her knee in the ravine while smoking cigarettes with the Armenian boy, the Christmas the barn burned, the feather bed in her bedroom where the twenty-four floorboards stretched left to right, where the shadow lay. They remembered old *mamochka*, how she always said that Yelena was *seven pyad across the forehead,* which meant that she was very smart, and that that would be her ruin. How the slit-eyed goat would curl back its lips so its green scum teeth showed and stare at the sun till it fell down blind one day, *bah, bah, bahhing.* The way the garden wall shone before the field, the harvest of cabbage, the dumplings and borscht and good peasant bread buttered with the sweet cream from the family downhill where a girl the same age as Yelena milked in white gloves. How Papa's laugh would shake the table the way light looked through the kitchen window, always a murder of crows raising hell on the horizon.

"What will you do?" her mother asked on the last day before they drove back to Moscow and flew back to States, maybe the last time they'd ever see each other in world of living, one can ever know.

Kids were off doing who knows what. They'd taken to the water, this ancestral escape from the heat of summer with its fresh fish and caviar from nineteen-foot-long sturgeon that lived a hundred and fifty years. It was good for kids, being in homeland. Yakov had stayed behind, so much work to do, so many presentations and connections and hardware. Google had brought him to corporate headquarters, a town in northern California where there was once a Russian fort. It still stood, the abandoned arms and sardine tins. So much to do at home, for Yakov, in Utah, Magna, the house watched from the sky with someone listening on every phone.

She was combing and braiding her hair, mother was, the way *mamochka* had once done hers, and the way Yelena did her daughter's. The feel of her mother's fingers, pulling the strands together, bunching and knotting, the overlay and under, how it felt so good on her scalp. It was a feeling she had forgotten from before she'd come of age and crawled out the window with Yakov, gone to Moscow to study architecture, which was really espionage training with KGB, she'd had to learn both at once, one for cover, one for real. She'd learned English, the poetry of Wordsworth, Yeats, and once had a look at Ginsberg, who was considered queer and therefore degenerate. She learned to know what the other needs—not what they want, what they *need.* And so often, the other doesn't even *know* what it is they need. Desire lines, the trick was to braid desire to need.

They remembered how Papa would open his mouth and belt out folksong he'd learned from his mother, and that they'd forgot now, save snippets with words foreign as moons of Jupiter.

"But what will you do?" her mother asked a second time, when her hair was done and it was time to gather kids, pack, go home. Her eyes were the same way Yelena remembered, soft, a touch of blood in the left one, kind, something to hold in mind against whatever.

"Do?" Yelena heard herself say. "I don't have to do anything. I'm American now. I do anything I want."

4.

At Marble Canyon there are two bridges across the Colorado River, one you can walk and the other you can drive, both called Navajo Bridge, and they're twins, the two steel bridges. Edgar pulls into the parking lot of the walking bridge, eyeballs the thing, sun shining on a band of pale green river flowing way down there. There's something about it, the bridges, as if he's made of steel and it's a magnet, back at the Coon Club in the presence of the carriers who'd sworn eternal vengeance. Belonged to the godson of the fat man, brother Brigham, the very mouth give the word to slaughter the innocents, eighteen and fifty-seven. The 120 Arkansawyers that made the Fancher Party, the grand lead wagon emblazoned with silver oxen so that nobody who ever laid eyes on it forgot it, leather reins in the true hands of the captain himself, six-hundred head of beef cattle in tow, mothers and children and expectant, en route through Ute Territory to California, hope of the new home beating in their hearts. There's grease in the floorboard where the Indian'd sat his battery. Son of a bitch Indian. That's what they'd dressed up as, Indians, the Mormons who'd executed his kith and kin. The bridge hauls him forward, a sliver of gas station biscuit under his homemade filling.

Under a shade built of wilted tree branches, an Indian woman sat at a folding table, her eyes dark under black hair that hung down her back. She was twisting wire around a green rock. 8.18.18, what a day it had been. Edgar wondered where the black Peterbilt was now, the spirit truck that had chased him into Oklahoma, they'll cross paths again, Edgar knows it.

Spread out on the table, all kinds of mojos, little fans and trinkets, rings and necklaces, bracelets of a thousand colors, the odd pink from cliff rocks over yonder, the black and blue and grey, and water color in some, there's wooden flutes and arrowheads and feathered staffs, a whole lot of shit there on the Indian woman's table on the eastern side of the Grand Canyon near the foot of the two Navajo bridges that had drawn him cross-country to this moment.

"Name's Paris," Edgar said. "Edgar Paris."

The Indian woman didn't look him in the eyes, not exactly. She smiled, nodded, went on twisting silver around the green rock. He could smell her, the Indian woman, like some kind of bread, she smelled like.

"I driven here from Arkansas."

She nodded, smiled, the bread-smelling Indian woman. Of a sudden he was hit with the urge to see the river, throw something in it, pee, he'd had to pee since Bitter Springs, where a sign had said PROTECT OUR WATER, WE STAND WITH STANDING ROCK.

"You got a lot of stuff."

There was no one around anywhere, just Edgar and the Indian woman. Under a blue sky so huge it seemed like the earth had broken open and run away in all directions. It was big, this land, wide open, and there was the river, all his life Edgar'd been drawn to rivers. He'd been baptized in one, Illinois Bayou back in Dover, held under till his heart thud-thudded in his head, and when the preacher let him up the light flashed bright and the people who'd waded out with him all sang with the tongues of angels, and Edgar'd felt new and clean and right.

"Reckon I ought to buy something. You from around here?"

She smiled for the third time, nodded. A way off under the river bridge something caught Edgar's eye, he couldn't tell what.

"It's for my daughter," Edgar said, he didn't know why, he had no children, none he knew of.

The brown fingers flashed, held up the pink bracelet made from beads prayed over in a blue-doored hogan, but of course Edgar didn't know that, nor had he yet tasted frybread that had fragranced the woman's skin at lunch time, nor did he know that her name was Rita Begay, and her daughter Rose was teaching her first year of school over in Monument Valley where they'd buried the placenta she'd been born in and the medicine priest had prophesied that she'd one day return here to teach the new generation, so the language of the Diné would not perish, but have everlasting life.

Edgar said, "I need something for good luck. She does."

Rita held out the pink bracelet, and with her other brown hand, held up two fingers. Rose had been Miss University of Utah Native American before graduating, had studied history, conflict resolution. She liked ice water, Rose.

He peeled out his billfold, Edgar. It was sticky where the duct-tape had long ago peeled off. Held out a dog-eared five, and Rita Begay made change in a flash, went back to winding the silver wire around the green rock.

Edgar said, "Thank you." He slid the thing on his right wrist before setting foot on the bridge. It had been a day. She hadn't said a word to him, the Indian woman.

The stretch of river where he'd been baptized, it was a trash dump now, a place where people drank Black Label, fired off shotguns and set fire to their worn-out tires. A lot of things going on down there that shouldn't be. But the kicker, the real shit kicker was how old Gino Simms had gone off and buried the little Love girl on Edgar's stretch of bayou, so he'd had to dig her up, the sunflower jammies tattooed to his brain for all time. He'd been the one to dig her up, Edgar, all the cops and scent dogs and silver gurney that tail-end of August, not a rock's throw from where he'd gone under, the sweet voices coloring the air he breathed ever after. He remembered both days equally, as if they were the same holy and shimmering moment, but that makes no sense—how can one moment be the same as another?

They were twin bridges, side by side, one for driving and one for walking, how about them apples? East to west, he was walking, Edgar, in his fifty-seventh year to this earth, drawn for some reason that he did not know but was sure of, nonetheless, toward what was on the other side. He could hear his footfall, the breath in his lungs, the sound of a far-off diesel and the river below, green as new leaf. Behind him Rita Begay sat stone faced looking after him, she was thinking of Rose, that day they'd photographed her standing on red rock under shining sun and blue sky, Mitten Butte rising off her left shoulder, how the turquoise shone on her wrists and fingers, the blue-blue dress beaded at the waist, moccasins of new doe and white leggings, her hair night-black lifted by a breeze, she stood there smiling at them from the Class of 2014 as if she were queen of this good earth and all things on it.

She stared holes through his back, that Indian woman.

The bird appeared out of nowhere.

Edgar stopped walking. There on the rail in front of him it sat, big as a buffalo. Looked him straight in the eyes, the bird, making a sound that was ugly and rude and seemed to be asking Edgar for something. It took him aback. His feet itched. Why was he here in this godawful place? Why'd he gone off and driven away from a job and a bed? What was wrong with him? Maybe he was DMF, no accident, him getting that plate.

The bird spread black wings, ten feet tip to tip, shook them off, trembling.

Goddamn, Edgar said.

It looked at him like he was supper, made the ugly sound. Showed the inside of its terrible wings. Edgar saw the inlaid white stripe, the width of a hand, eight feet long if an inch, so it looked like a skeleton standing there on Navajo Bridge, begging Edgar for flesh, for blood, for his soul.

"*Get,*" Edgar said.

He took off the pink mojo and hurled it at the bird, who snatched it clean from the air, swallowed it down. Maybe a minute had passed by the clock. He felt the Indian woman watching his back, the black Peterbilt out there somewhere cruising, on the lookout, sniffing out his ass.

The condor lowered its wings, turned gaze up river. A white 4 was spray-painted on the ugly bird's shoulder. Number four. How Rangers knew one from the other. Edgar'd learn that the head was bald pink and featherless so none of the rotted flesh it fed on would stick there, that the ancient species had scavenged the continent during the Pleistocene, hog-gobbling the giant camels and sloth, a kind of house-size flying pig. They shit on themselves, Condors, to lower body temperatures, and lacked a syrinx, so their only language was to grunt and hiss and turn their bald necks red. People mistook them for planes. They had no sense of smell. The Grand Canyon was the number one suicide destination in the whole U. S. of A., and the rangers followed the comings and goings of condors to seek and find the dead.

The pink mojo bracelet he'd bought for the daughter he'd never known bulged in the rat-black bird's throat. As if to contest the hideousness he faced, Edgar pictured an Indian princess gazing down from on high, blue stones at her neck and throat, white-winged and holy, and so the two images twined for a second, then came undone.

"I said GET." Edgar said it, stomped his foot.

The bird flap-flapped over to a shit-splattered stone, regarded him. The mojo'd disappeared into its craw.

"Fine by me," he said. "You'll need all the goddamn good luck you can get. Ugly bird."

He commenced to walking the span of silver bridge, the urge on him and his heart beating some from the encounter. It was still looking at him, old ugly, scanning the expanse for corpses.

On the other side was a bathroom, its door padlocked shut with a silver chain. He smells what's on the other side. Just as well. Where he's from there's no rule says a man can't just pull down and go when he has to. Edgar followed the rock wall into an otherwise invisible alcove.

Then he sees it, why he's come.

The granite panel is dark brown, the carved letters white:

LEE'S FERRY

NORTHERN GATEWAY TO ARIZONA
FOR 54 YEARS—FROM 1873 TO
1927—IS LOCATED SIX MILES
UPSTREAM FROM THIS BRIDGE.

THIS MONUMENT ERECTED
TO THE FOUNDER

JOHN DOYLE LEE

WHO WITH SUPERHUMAN EFFORT
AND IN THE FACE OF ALMOST
INSURMOUNTABLE OBSTACLES,
MAINTAINED THIS FERRY
WHICH MADE POSSIBLE THE
COLONIZATION OF ARIZONA.

FRONTIERSMAN, TRAIL BLAZER,
BUILDER, A MAN OF GREAT
FAITH, SOUND JUDGEMENT, AND
INDOMITABLE COURAGE.

AUTHORITY FOR ERECTION OF THIS MONUMENT
GRANTED BY THE STATE OF ARIZONA
1960

Edgar spits. A way off across the ridge a car door shuts, echoes in the canyon where evening's first shadows grow. He hears the footsteps coming for him, Edgar Paris, who knows the name that glares from the almost hidden alcove. He knows and knows and knows. When he was younger, Edgar had a temper. He hurt a cat once, pretty bad. He'd broke a Cherokee's nose one fall at the hog killing boxing match, then punched the boy again in the same spot because his blood was up, and he couldn't help it. Him and his old man had had it out in the kitchen one night and he'd knocked one of the old man's teeth out, buried it under the persimmon tree where raccoons shat out the golden fruit's seed in piles that were poisonous to touch the witch lady said. He'd lost his temper with the Casteen girl, but just the one time and hadn't he paid a hunk of his own flesh for that. In the old days, things could get his blood up. But this? *This?*

Take 9-11, wind it back 144 years, 120 of Arkansas folk bound for California, toward hope and life and love, what we all want. They had money and cattle, a fine carriage emblazoned with a silver stag. Men, women, and children, they were massacred in cold blood at a place called Mountain Meadows, even the littlest skulls shot through with a revolver bullet.

By Mormons.

The adopted son of Brigham Young bearing the white flag that tricked anyone in the Fancher party who wasn't already shot to shit into handing over their weapons, the promise of transport to Cedar City, and continued journey west. All they had to do was lay down their weapons, these Arkies. And the siege had gone on four days by then. They were fucked up pretty bad.

Guns collected, he walked uphill and played a game of horseshoes, Brigham's adopted son, a grown man with kids of his own, about a half-dozen wives. He played horseshoes while the slaughter took place—three points for a ringer, two for a leaner.

The son of a bitch played horseshoes, the white flag trembling ever so slightly with a breeze that carried their screams.

Folded in his pocket, the letter from Salt Lake, the wax seal of the prophet, sent for the Bishop's eyes only. No one old enough to tell the tale should live.

And no one did.

Footsteps on the bridge of time.

Edgar spat again. This time a blue lugie aimed at the name. The name that the U.S. of A. had found guilty and executed for the single most brutal mass murder of all the manifest destiny west.

Women's' hair, locks and tresses, hanging from the blue sage.

Who'd run off here to hide. From the law. From the eyes of angry God.

Who'd got away with it for a time. Who'd lived fifteen more years.

Goddamn son of a bitch.

Edgar unzipped his pants. He pulled out and let fly, the arced piss splattering the carved, white letters, staining for a while the words *superhuman, great, faith, sound judgement.* Darkening till daylight *Indomitable Courage.*

"*Just who do you think you are?*" the last words Edgar heard before he hit the ground.

He did not hear the next thing Officer Stoner said, nor the thing after that. He was out cold, the egg-shaped lump on the back of his skull already purpling, concussion dilating his pupils.

While his hands were being cuffed behind his back, Edgar hallucinated the Navajo girl, the Indian princess of this western world, wearing her wealth of turquoise and blue-eyed porcupine quill, her turtle amulet whipping in the wind, borne up on the wings of the mutant angel-bird, the fierce white cross zigzagged on its underside. She beckoned for him to follow, did Rose Marie Begay. The great speckled bird lifted them to the place, whatever they chose to name it in the human tongue. No words, finally, for that eternal home, that way of being, where the future is judged by the past.

There they leave him lay, Edgar.

5.

All that fall Joey Harvell'd been haunted by the grave he'd found at sunrise on the morning of his grandfather Si's 100th birthday, how it was a sign, had to be, but of what? It appeared in his dreams—he saw it the way he saw it that morning, when he'd bought tickets and planned the trip out to the T, his first return to Arkansas in the ten years since his grandmother Floradee died, and so ended the blood entanglement he had with the Natural State. But he had to go back. It was Si's 100th. He needed to see Lake Ouachita again, wade off into the water by the sunken bridge where one-legged Si'd once stood on an invisible piling and appeared to walk on water after happy hour on a Sunday when the light shafts poured through the water, and whatever soul Joey had then. He'd escaped to Mount Ida, crystal capital of the world, at times when O.W. and Mama were at each other's' throats, and it was there he'd learned to pick okra and fry fish and run barefoot in a freak snow during a hand of five card draw. Si'd saved his ass, shown him something in himself to believe in. That's how it seemed now, when the old man would be a hundred. Who to pour a glass of bourbon on his grave? A fistful of tobacco, flathead fillet?

A tornado of the class that had blown his town away when he was fifteen had diverted the flight from Dallas, where they were supposed to land, to Oklahoma City, so by the time they finally touched down in Little Rock it was after midnight. The last remaining rental was an eight-passenger minivan, a Mormon assault vehicle, they called it back in Salt Lake—and so they set off for Hot Springs and the Arlington, where an ancient valet met them in the garage outside the back entrance. Joey waved him off, unloaded their suitcases and let Renee work the check-in. He maneuvered the hulking vehicle to the third level, grazed a concrete piling and tried to polish the scratch way with an airplane napkin. Lara was waiting for him in the lobby, and together they rode the elevator up to the decrepit fourth floor, where a rollaway was shoved up against one of the double beds. When brushing his teeth, Joey'd noticed and extracted a wad of hair from the sink drain. Then they all fell in bed and slept past breakfast.

Hot Springs, Arkansas was built on top of forty-seven springs where enemy tribes historically laid down arms to take the healing waters. From vast underground caves of pure clear quartzite poured waters that had fallen as rain and percolated into the earth on the distant afternoons before the first human ever drew breath or said I love you or I am afraid. Trace minerals in the water were said to heal, and at an average temperature of 147 degrees Fahrenheit and seemingly eternal at 700,000 gallons a day from the fault line leading up the West slope of Hot Springs Mountain, Crystal City was deemed holy ground. The Quapaw, Caddo, Akansi, Choctaw, Cherokee, Seminole, Anasazi and Mescalero, tribes who'd fashioned the Clovis Point to hunt wooly mammoth, who'd walked across the Siberian land bridge down into the new world fecund with life, they'd found the trail through the ancient mountains, laid down spear and shaft, tomahawk and atlatl, bow, point and bone, the fine obsidian blade that sharpened keener than a razor. Surrounded by the protective Ouachitas, the ancestral enemies soaked in the medicine water and put off their quarrels for another day, another life.

Later, the Gambino family soaked next to the Bonannos, the Decavalcantes next to the Luccheses—Al Capone kept a whole suite in the Arlington overlooking Zig Zag Mountain to the east. Pretty Boy Floyd was said to enjoy the wildflowers at Goat Rock Overlook. Like those who'd walked this way before them, they lay their instruments of killing down. If only for a while, they made peace.

From the mountainside pool the next morning, bathed in godawful seventies music, they could see the luxurious rooftop tower for which the Arlington was known, how the loose tiles had been weighted down with old tires like trailer trash back in Lonoke County. They'd wandered out one at a time—Renee, Joey, Lara, finally, and now the entirety of the National Forest lay out in a panorama of green, a giant magnolia blooming fiercely at the mouth of Bathhouse Row. Later, they'd walk together there, tour the Fordyce with its steam cabinets and sitz baths, polished brass and stained glass, a mansion outfitted to hydrotherapy rich Yankees and world travelers who ailed and sought out the valley of steam, the place of peace. The heat would come on them and they'd visit a knife store on Main Street, outside of which was a glass encased fortune teller named Zoltar the Great who Joey'd consulted as a boy, a bearded mannequin whose mouth had opened when the quarter hit bottom, and said *the angels of this world sometimes go as devils.*

"There were bedbugs, Dad."

The cooling pool beneath the hot pool was twelve feet deep, and someone had left a face mask that Joey retrieved from the bottom. He passed it to his daughter who dangled legs into the chill water.

"How do you know?"

Renee'd gone in to dress and pack. The heat was on. Check in at the vacation rental was noon—they had the hour to drive to Lake Ouachita in front of them.

She pointed. "Look."

One whole calf was covered with furious-red welts. "Play That Funky Music" gave way to "Nights in White Satin."

"Jesus," Joey said.

He'd one time stayed in the Arlington as a college student, a history conference, and a woman he'd waved to at a red light had followed him to the hotel, and then up to his room, and paid him twenty dollars to take his pants off in front of her. It had happened, the thought colors his cheeks.

"Chiggers," he said.

"What's that?"

A black family'd walked through the rusty gate, a couple with two boys, and a teenage girl whose hair was gathered in a colorful ribbon. They smiled, lowered eyes, walked to the other pool.

Lara said, "Good morning," and one of the little boys turned back and waved and his dad said, "Morning."

"We used to live here. In Arkansas. You've been in this exact pool before."

She'd be twenty-one that year, old enough to drink. Already she'd voted, and the first great catastrophe of her life as a citizen of the United States had gone down—the sleaze ball president whose name was not allowed to be spoken in the Harvell household.

One of the amphibious duck vehicles that was always sinking in Lake Hamilton and drowning all the lard-assed tourists aboard drove by, beeped its shrill horn.

She said, "I don't remember."

Up in the hot pool, someone squealed. Uncle Earl had made Joey wipe down chigger bites with pee from a coke bottle. It had burned like hell.

Goggle-eyed, Lara's splash was sudden. He watched his daughter take strong strokes for the length of the pool and back—she had Rockerson in her, her mother's blood. Eighteen years since they'd moved away, and a decade since they'd visited Mom Dee at the nursing home, where Lara'd played "*Fur Elyse*," and the elderly had shut their eyes and danced in place.

She had Joey's sister call him when she was breathing her last, Floradee, beyond speech already, but all Joey'd heard was his own breath in the receiver. Hello?" he'd said. "Hello?"

On the patio outside the black double doors, Renee was making the sign to eat, that breakfast closed in ten. Lara held one thumb up—yes, we understand.

The road to the lake held a ghost on every corner.

They'd hit the liquor store, big as a barn with not a real good wine selection, Renee complained, and walked out to sit in the heat with Lara, the minivan's door thrown open to the swelter, and Joey'd paid, $140 goddamn dollars, what were they going to do, drink themselves into comas, though Si would've loved it, yelled *Humphrey the Camel*, his name for afternoon highballs, at 2:10, his head thrown back like that at this rolling goddamn thunder bar of a vehicle. Joey in the big ole driver's seat and Renee the passenger, Lara tucked back in one of the ten cargo seats, as they rolled on down 270, past the Alligator Farm and Petting Zoo, with its swamp gators scaring the bejesus out of spectators gathered the hell around the cement pond, where a live chicken was strung up by its feet, squawking to beat the band, doing the funky chicken, wings flapping and shitting itself, and up jumped big Arky, a ten-footer who'd crawled up out of the *Fourche LaFave*, where old Si'd trotlined a ninety-pound flathead, just waddled on out one October and got himself hogtied, taken to the Farm, where every day save Sunday he had to jump his ole alligator ass up out of the dirty water and chomp Jesus out of a shitass chicken, what kind of life? just tell me, all the little kiddoes begging Mama for the two dollars required to buy baby Arkie and a ziplock full of Crunchy Crickets, little son of a bitches scritch-scratching inside the cardboard box, about to get loose in the backseat on the way home, bite sister on the butt, cruise on out, the Hamilton Bridge to Royal and that long green fall toward the Ouachita River, when of a sudden things would get familiar, like some magic focus knob on time was somehow being fiddled with, and there's Crystal City just as it ever was, the same goddamn tick-bit dog laying under the shade of a Chinaberry tree—hadn't Mama once crammed them up her nose so she'd had to go to the emergency room where doc had gouged them out with a silver teaspoon?—and all the tables heavy with head-size hunks of quartz crystal, the points jutting this way and that and catching light, turning all the colors Joey'd ever dreamed of as a ten-year-old goofball whose mama and step daddy tried to kill each other back home, burning each other's clothes and breaking sheetrock walls with their heads, and Si'd drive him here in one of the new Chevrolets he traded for every two years, and it would be summer, the bats chasing mosquitos into ecliptic shade, his 2:10 Humphrey hot on his breath, giving it the gas with his good foot. Joplin Bait, Worm and Video, Tompkins Bend where the snooty ass Mountain Harbor folk ate their ribeyes rare overlooking the marina, Hickory Nut Mountain past Shangri-La's giant bass sign still waving you in, so Joey'd turned there, and again on sunken bridge road, drove right up to where the road ran into water, little white lines down there glowing, said this is it. All three got out and stripped to their scivvies, waded in just like Si had fifty years earlier, late of the afternoon, with a bar of soap that floated white-bellied as a fish. They washed off the day's grime in the chill of the lake that shone blue and real, and Si'd swum out to a submerged piling, stood on the one leg, held his arms out for balance so he looked for all the world to Joey like some burly man-angel, flown down to save him from the world that chomped its jaws down on you. Si, flapping his shadow wings on the piling, leapt off with a hoarse holler, swam to Joey a moving maze. A hundred years old tomorrow, Simon Marion Stepwell, a Poteet on his mama's side. Joey let himself sink to the mud, light shafts pouring through like they always had, and there was Lara, wading in behind him, looking for the world like his mother, like Si, like his own ghost self that once turned eyes on blue water, and knew this place as shelter, a protector there, no one coming behind his back.

The rental's on the dark side, one whole shelf in the kitchen stuffed with new-agey books. A sign outside said to take your shoes off, which Joey obeyed, then stepped on a carpet tack first thing just inside the front door. His little toe dripped blood. *A peaceful, forested vacation home,* the advertisement said, young apple, cherry and persimmon trees, established asparagus and muscadine, a clean wading stream that flowed all year long. Inside were shadows, no north facing windows, the air-conditioner unit in the living room humming. Lara walked off past the New Age bookshelf—titles about Indians and teepees, roundhouses, finding your spirit totem animal, *How To Learn the Magic of Crop Circles*, and all about transferring energy into money. He'd paid $170 a night for the place, a three bedroom, two bath, with an old wing and a new. It had a feel, the place. Joey unloaded the food they'd bought for supper into the empty refrigerator, humped in the shitload of wine and whiskey and vodka, felt eyes on him, a dog barking off down the gravel road. On a seven-acre wooded lot, sure enough a creek on the west side, a smaller house, a cottage hidden behind trees next door with a colorful teepee rising up from the space somewhere behind it, east, Joey'd learn, where whoever was watching them watched them.

Lara staked out the back bedrooms, one with sunshine pouring through the windows, and the other dark, nothing save a door that opened to a full view of a teepee built at the mouth of a deep dark wood. All tooled out with handmade cabinetry and a gun rack, a big ass closet full of toilet paper. Dark, dark, dark.

"Are you sure," Joey'd asked. She'd claimed the dark room for sleeping, the light one for reading.

There was a smell, a thing he remembered.

"It's me," Lara'd said. "Mine."

She shut herself in the dark room whose humidifier was plugged in a socket sawzalled into the lacquered gun cabinet. He could hear it in there, the wheeze and cough. There were rules: please leave the stream side of the circular driveway open—a friend who has maintained the property for years may sometimes come while guests are present; this is a no-smoking, no shoes home; do not trespass on our neighbor's property; the dirt is red clay and stains everything it touches—keep ALL dirt out of the vacation home and DO NOT bring crystals into the house. You will be charged EXTRA if you bring any dirt into the vacation house; do not open doors or windows; do not leave shoes or valuables on front porch because the neighbors let their dogs run loose, things disappear; you will be charged from your insurance/damage deposit it you do not follow these instructions.

That first night at Holly Ridge, after they'd washed their dishes and poured an after dinner whiskey neat, while Renee wrestled with the TV system and ended up playing a cd of a Bob Dylan concert because that's all that would work, while Lara lay in bed in the dark room poking on her phone and receiving whatever messages came from the satellites floating in the dark beyond the world, Joey sat outside on the front porch at a table with three chairs, west-facing, where he smoked and sipped whiskey and remembered the evenings he'd spent within a mile of this spot, how he'd sleep on the pull out couch at the head of Si's silver Airstream, how the night would go violent with the sound of cicadas that got under your teeth, so he'd bury fingers in his ears, and in the morning, hours before light, Si'd wake him saying, *get up and piss, boy, the world's on fire.*

Now the sound was urgent, demanded action, witness. He knocked on Lara's door, retrieved Renee who'd gone into the new bedroom wing to read already. He walked them out onto the circle of lawn under the gaudy spray of sky. "Wow," Lara said, "Wow." She took her phone and recorded a full minute's worth, and back inside she played it again and again, each time saying, "I just can't believe it Dad. No one would."

He bolt-locked the door, brushed his teeth in the bath that adjoined the new wing. In bed, Renee kissed him, said *goodnight*, and "I don't miss that sound for a second."

He switched on his headlight and read from the book on roundhouses. The room had its own air unit, hung on the south wall between twin windows where a gardenia bloomed above a birdhouse on a stilt gone crooked.

She said, "You?"

That night he'd got out of bed and walked to the back of the old part of the house where a doggy door in the original bathroom was nose-stained from the openings of a long-dead pet. He opened the door to the dark room. She was okay. He could hear her breathing.

Back in bed he opened his eyes and she was standing there, Lara.

"That scared me," she said.

First light fell on the colorful dome of the teepee, visible above the roof from the bathroom window where Joey Harvell washed his face and realized that today was the twelfth of July, the reason they'd come here, at great expense, from Utah and summer vacation, to Mount Ida and Crystal City, Holly Ridge, not a mile by the way the crow flew from the old man's trailer on the hickory lot where the garden grew and he'd learned to wear a long sleeve shirt while picking okra stems on an afternoon when they'd batter and fry it with fillets cut from fish that had swum that very morning, ham-spiked purple hulls on the side, two-fister Big Boys cut finger-thick with banana pepper that might be hot as fire because sometimes things just got mixed up in this life, didn't they, Joey boy? When all the red-headed humming birds would swoop high, then low, then high, gladiator fighting over the feeders filled with red-dyed sugar water, and the compost pile would steam and burp gas from coffee, skinned out tomatoes and fish guts, and they'd go to town with tartar sauce, hushpuppies and home fries, those summer days when he came of age on Ouachita.

Outside was fresh, the way he remembered.

There was the smell of morning, the horns of the new moon goring hell out of Mercury on the horizon. Heavy dew, no rain today. The cicadas had shut up, sweet Jesus. On the way out, he'd checked Lara one more time there in the dark room with its door opening to the shed, and beyond that the teepee. He walked out across the circle drive, where gravel crunched beneath his river sandals, right down the path to the silver creek that oohed and awed and shushed over milk quartz, a hunk over there the size of a hand, glowing in the low light. The waters forked right there—he smelled it, a hole under the tree trunk on the right fork, the one that drew him into the wood, the shadow where bluegill lay, spawn, a hole over there for bathing, red wigglers under the dead leaf, kick a bushel basket back and they'd writhe, on the bare bank of memory.

Knee deep, he saw the cottage, a silver car parked in the garage. Not yet six, the light low, a woodpecker—Pileated?—went off high in a hickory, and it feels like home, how he'd wander off from Si's some afternoons, beyond the periphery of wood to a creek bottom that flowed all the way to the lake, maybe the very same vein, follow it into the deep dark wood and what lay beyond. Once, he'd had to go, squatted down over a rotten log and cleared his bowel, the smell of his own shit, reached for a handful of dry leaves to wipe, only when he opened his hand a flaked obsidian point so dark it seemed to suck in light. *Spear point? Knife?* He knew that it had taken life, and it was holy to him, was wrapped in blue sage and red cloth back in Utah on the medicine bundle with eagle feather and bone.

He drew the sweet water to his face, washed, tasted the mineral in it, same as Si's well water, the sump pump thumping as they readied to fish before light. *Happy Birthday*, he said it out loud. No one watched him, no one was coming from behind.

Up the stone stairs past the bench to the gravel, he walked a hundred yards north to the fence line where the wood sprung up, followed it east to a gate, wide enough for a truck to pass, opened it, walked right on hell in, just like that. The teepee rose up and shone through the clearing, the first of the eastern sun shining on the pine boughs that forked above its smoke hole.

The trail was clean, led right up to a waist high lean-to, under which was stacked split wood for the ceremony that was clearly still happening, he felt that much, the ceremony, the sun rising, new day.

Now he stood within the circle, the sun full on the immaculately set roundhouse, painted with the holy symbols he'd learned from Uwipi Medicine Keepers, the wheels nearest the ground all painted the sacred colors—black, red, yellow, and white for the four directions, west, north, east and south, only they were rendered backward here, white, yellow, red, then black, which meant *heyoka*, the backward forward being, the holy clown who'd bare his ass to *wakinyantanka*, the thunder beings. This all registered for Joey Harvell the second the sun fell on the grave.

Time went wavy-gravy.

Bass were schooling that second on Ouachita, out on Sow's Tittie, Lucky Rebel. The door was pinned shut with willow sticks, the sharpened ends all pointing south.

The grave was fierce, red dirt piled three feet high, encircled by burnt crystals—swear to God. It was piled and ragged, hand printed and tobacco strewn. The body lay on its back, east-facing, the way of blue doors in Navajo land.

The sun shone on it. Joey thought to sing, the high aching death song Evangeline, the Mandan woman, had sung to him in his death plot, his hamblecheya, vision of hummingbirds thrumming in his head.

Hoy ye tenea kenaje pelo hey.

Now he could see all, shining and golden and new.

The teepee with the sun on its face. The cottage with its back window ablaze. Over there, behind that door, the dark room where his daughter slept. And beyond that, up the hall, his wife—all he had on this earth, all the love in the world. A hammock slung between two trees. Close enough to talk to the man. And he was *sure* it was a man, a *heyoka*, addressed from the hammock where the woman lay and sang to him his holy death song.

Tunkasila, tiwan kunecha la na chi chu yelo hey.

Go home, spirit, go home.

Light fell on a cedar sapling, living, grown crooked out of the head. Hanging from its highest point, light flashed on a fragment of skull, hair still on it, a scrap of red cloth binding it to the bough.

Sun and moon, the circlet of skull.

6.

Twice he'd return.

The first time with Renee who'd later say that she felt unspeakable peace radiating from the sunlit grave, that it might be a place she'd like to go on afternoons when it rained and the air was chill on her face, lay in the hammock and let life go by in a good way. They'd walked around the teepee, Joey and his wife of thirty years. He'd brought her for Si's 100th—he'd brought them, the last of his full blood people on this earth, to say to Arkansas where his people lay buried *goodbye forever.* But of course they did not know that, Joey and Renee, walking the circumference of the teepee, touching the fabric lightly with the palms of their hands, laughing some, their backs to the cottage window where a curtain fluttered then held. An extension cord, yellow, coiled under the bottom fringe. Joey nudged it with his foot, had just enough time to think: *they run lights out here.*

The third time, when the sun had grown hard and the heat was coming on, he brought his daughter, Lara, who looked in face and manner like his mother, Si's daughter, so the four of them walked together, in a way, through the wide gate and down the oft-trod path that all must walk one day or another. She had no idea what they walked toward, Lara, had in fact just awakened in the dark room where the window unit hummed, and the world outside had not yet impeded on her. So, half asleep, really, Joey walked her out, come on, I've got something to show you.

Past the wood shelter, where he noticed that the pile had shaken down, as if ready for fire, light from west to east, the fastened shut mouth of the teepee, they walked. Later, when they talked about this moment, they'd agree about how everything went silent, and the blast furnace heat from the eyes in the window, the sheer hatred, the nakedness and fear and knowing that this gaze wished them great harm, and he'd turned around and she was gone, *poof,* disappeared. And for a second, the length of time that was allowed for him to get his ass out, he knew for a third time in his life the rage the dead feel when the living trespass their boundary, bringing nothing but their sorry breath and heartbeat and belly-full of fecal shit—how dare they? Who did they think they were, these two?

From unspeakable peace, to white-hot rage, three times walking to the backyard grave. It would haunt him, Joey, because he knew that it was a sign of something, and that Lara disappearing in a finger snap, that was a sign, too, the extension cord, and the slice of skull with hair growing on it, reddish, a shade in his beard before it went white. On Si's 100th, not a mile as the crow flies from the old man's place, the silver airstream near the banks of Ouachita where Joey'd lived as a boy some summers when O.W. and Mama's fights got bad, when Si'd show up with a sack full of tomatoes and whiskey on his breath, have him pack a few things and drive the back roads back to Mount Ida, Crystal City, and wild turkeys would cross the road and Si'd gobble at them. Before new-agers like *Sharonogoti*, who owned the rental, Joey'd learn, an Iowa nurse who night lighted as a self-help Shaman, whose specialty was coaxing the newly dead to depart their earthly bodies, so you could pull up goddamn YouTube videos of her, backlit, shaking a rattle around a human body, unlocking the nine chakras, and all the umbilical cords that held flesh to life. With her own hand she'd buried the dead man behind her vacation rental, concealed it behind a teepee at the mouth of the wood, burnt crystals marking the circle where the body lay beneath the sliver of skull that spun on its string so slightly in the blast furnace heat of the moment when Joey Harvell and his twenty-year-old daughter were allowed to get out with their lives.

The only boat available for rental was a thirty-foot party barge at $450 for the day, *a pretty incredible deal*, the Mountain Harbor Marina cashier woman told them on birthday afternoon. "Pick up's at 8 a.m., and you can keep her till 6. She holds fourteen. You only live oncet."

Hillbilly Hootenanny regalia still decorated the place, leftover from Fourth of July, when well-to-do Arkansawyers had hit the water *en masse*, craft of every imaginable shape and size, tanks full to the brim with boat dock unleaded, who'd lit the starry sky with every firework conceivable for three nights running.

Joey and Renee'd once rented a flat-bottom and got caught in a thunderstorm, so they'd hit a cove and got under some bushes with a six-pack and Fritos. Now, it was important to show Lara her roots, make the place hers, because a time was coming when Joey and Renee would be gone, and she needed to know her roots, didn't she, that was the important thing, to know where you come from.

Of course, the boat wouldn't start.

Friday the 13th of July, 8 a.m. sharp, with a styro cooler full of good sandwich meat and pickles, frosty Budweisers and NuGrapes for Lara, two thirty-dollar fishing licenses, rods, reels, and a tackle box replete with three Devil's Toothpicks from the antique tackle box Joey'd inherited from his mother's father, and the goddamn five-hundred-dollar-a-day boat wouldn't start. "No way. Not going to happen," the boat dock girl who'd retrieved three life jackets from the shed said. "You'll have to switch."

Two sixteen-year-old boys who acted like they knew their shit, walked up, asked if she'd primed, gave her another try and still, no go. "You'll have to switch," they said.

By the time they got on the lake—motoring the dock's brand ass new thirty-six-footer—the heat was on, and Lara'd cannon balled off the metal roof in a hundred feet of water, the original river channel underneath clear blue water.

He could see her down there, his daughter's face, taking big strokes.

Renee lay out long on the padded cushions, the sunshine good on her skin. A captain's daughter, she'd grown up on water like this. She was a horse, this boat. Ouachita had a thousand miles of shoreline, a flooded river at the foot of mountains where diamonds once formed, the six-sided crystals glinting on the serene banks of every cove, shining from the one where Si and him once tied a trotline, hooks every six feet, and bream fished the afternoon with red wigglers, filled a bucket with blue gill and shoulder hooked them on heavy-shanked hooks, weighted with stones, let the line sink into the deep in between. Later, under the full Flower Moon, they'd motor out over still water and find the marker, heave up the bright white line, and he'd see the monsters from forty feet, big son of a bitch flatheads that fought like devils. Si'd told the story of a man who, lining alone, let a hook get him through his palm so he was hauled down where no light went. He'd whomp the shit out of each catfish head with the boat paddle, and later they'd nail them to the skinning tree.

They passed islands, thirty foot cliffs shining where he'd once jumped, the lake clear and cold and real. Lara and her mother took the sun. They'd made it. Here, now.

In time, he found the place he was looking for, the wedge of water and shade and stone that spoke to him. One more time he'd made it to the lake, his fortress, his refuge. A shoulder of pink quartz ran up out of the water through the trees, six-feet wide, you could see it from the deep to the light, to timber and sky. It ran all night and all day. Surely this was it.

He eased off starboard, rope in one hand, tied off.

"Are we here?" Lara asked.

He'd parked the party barge right on top of it—God's own vein. There in Arkansas, where he'd grown up, where he was raised and came of age, where he met Renee, where his people lay buried in a field of Brown-eyed Susan overlooking a lightning struck tree, and Si is a hundred now, *here*.

Now time.

Everything forward and everything behind—it all comes from here. He doesn't know it, exactly, none of them do for sure. But he suspects, they suspect.

"Yeah," Joey said. "We're here."

She said, "Good," hopped in the water wearing the face mask from the Arlington pool when the cracked speakers belted "Play That Funky Music White Boy."

She said, "I kept it," smiled.

Renee leaned on an elbow. She said, "Lunch? Or beer?"

Joey said, "Both."

Si called them "field hippies," the New Agers who'd descended on the Ouachitas from back east, from Boston where he'd been sent for rehab and prosthesis fitting after he'd cut his leg off by accident and got hooked on morphine, so his whole family fell apart, Floradee and the kids, Josephine and Earl. He was a Poteet, Si, named for Marion Francis, who'd survived the Mountain Meadows Massacre of Arkies who'd walked their trail of tears clear to Utah Territory, south from Cedar City to the cold water spring where they died. They, the field hippies, held that clear quartz crystal was the master healer, that it amplified energy and thought. It aided concentration and unlocked memory, harmonized and aligned. Ancients believed the stone to be alive, the incarnation of the divine. It intensified prayer, quartz crystal, was a channel of communication, a goddamn telephone across space and time. In your iPhone, your Smart Phone, your radio and your watch, quartz crystal. Solidified light, dispeller of evil, transformer, transmitter, memory chip. Bridge between all that has ever been and all that will ever be, earth mother, matter, life force, light.

Through the face mask, Lara's eyes were hazel—the color of fall, of persimmon ripe at the Mayfields' where Mountain Spring leaked the good tasting water they washed their faces with on the afternoon Joey'd been taken there to live while Mama was in the hospital, and the dogs all barked on Four Mile Creek, they could see Little Rock from the mountain, the river bridge. It was hog killing day, first frost, the smell of pine needles burning.

Before that, a hard snow, on Christmas, all of them outside running barefoot with MaMa Stepwell, eighty years old, and it was Morrilton, the banty chickens *bock-bocking* in the lean-to barn. Joey'd needed a haircut, Si said. O.W. skidded on a boot heel outside the back door.

In the deep wood was a *boom-boom*, Ajax they called it, the inner sanctum, Renee's mother had said when the turkey was taking forever. "You hurt me," Mama'd said, a snake hanging in the V of a dogwood, full wolf moon turning to blood, then stone, a rock hanging hairless in the sky, dead, nothing.

More.

He was faintly aware of his wife, Joey. There was Lara in the water, fish swimming circles around her. The sky was far off and so were the clouds, big cumuli that shone on the water, sailing by. He was in the driver's seat, the forward and reverse lever at his right hand, the silver steering wheel. There was beer and food, fishing rods, the Devil's Toothpick.

The barge lay on rose quartz that sank ten miles deep, where the earth remained hot with magnetic pulse secret in the veins of pure white light emboldened by the dream of Tao, of Jesus, Tunkasila, Father God, Mohammad, Krishna, Wakan Tanka, Allah, of Zeus and Ra and the ones whose names had been forgotten from the minds of men, and for the ones, feathered with beak, whose images were bowed down to before there were words for name making, to the first she-apes who'd wrapped their dead infants foreheads with wild rose garland, to the stone people, the stone world, the first. And *mini-wakan*, first medicine, *ska-ska*, all that is holy.

The afternoon rolled on by, his fish daughter flouncing in the shallows, where sun shafts shone clear to the bottom. The quartz vein thrummed. Somewhere, Renee, love of his life, hadn't he found the arrowhead, the night-black point, the April they met? and then Jimmy died, six-feet tall and sawdust bronze, his one brother, hadn't he stuck his hand wrist-deep in blood, the floorboard of the wrecked car, come up clutching the senior ring, a green stone, hadn't Mama cried and worn it every day for the rest of her life?

The rest of her life?

Her hair floats in the hot tub, and the whales swim close enough to hit with a goddamn plug. The blue doors of kivas shine from there, that place, he lets himself go down and down, opens the blue door and goes inside, and there are his people, the air of his breath shows, he sees their hazel eyes, the fierce women who bookend his life, and there is peace, healing.

The vision comes on hard then, from the abyss, and he would not ever wish this on an enemy, not on the man who walked down to the sacred spring carrying a white flag, the breeze just rustling it, a tiny stone in the sock of his right foot, lay down weapons, we will let ye go in peace. He touched a blond girl's bangs, said "In the name of God, I beg you."

While twenty-six and gutful of himself, he was summoned to raise his grandfather from the Dead. The only time the old man ever cried, Mama swore, was when granny Poteet died. He was named Marion, for the survivor.

When Joey was born in Tucson, it had rained like a motherfucker for a whole year and snow-covered Mount Lemon shone out the window when Josephine asked the nurse, "Have you castrated my son yet?"

Frosty castrado.

A dwarf was always hopping out the screen door, grabbing the water hose and spurting off the hood of the over-heated car. They ate roast goat for dinner. All the dogs in Tucson were named goat. It wasn't entirely a lie.

Fish flashed in the lips of breakers. On the day Mama drowned, he was knee-deep in a blue run. The son of a bitches would lay you open, take a finger or a hand. It had happened.

It throbbed, the old wound, where Doc had reattached the finger.

Be careful what you wish.

How now brown cow, Mama'd said it in bed on the night of a thunderstorm, when a wind had scared him to her bed, or was it a man who reached for him through the open window. All the trees in Lonoke County looked like men walking.

I did it, Joe. Okay? Is that what you wanted?

The very last time he saw O.W. on this earth, the old man didn't know him, had called him *Bud*, the name of the blood father he'd never meet. His last words: *I've enjoyed every minute of it, Bud.*

Every barbed wire fence at Adams Cemetery in Solgohachia on the Trail of Tears was blown over with honeysuckle, and somebody'd run down the gate, it lay all smashed up, and far below the chicken houses light up at night, and it's a real quiet place to sleep, the stars fanning out like that, whippoorwill, moonlight in the grooves of carved letters.

Lara carried her a glass of ice water, mama, what she loved in life. Poured it right down so it splashed her face over yonder, good cold water with ice in it from her granddaughter in the world of the living. *Thank you, sweetie. You know I loved you best.*

The backside of her stone said, *I Believe*. Something between her and daddy. Lara doesn't know how she knows this. He had a funny look on his face, sitting there in the captain's seat, that glint in his eye.

He'd walked off downhill to the part of the cemetery where sons were buried at the feet of their fathers for four generations of Stepwells, all the way back to where they'd walked down from Henry County, Tennessee, and then to California, though some never made it, but that was Daddy's story, him against the Mormons. All of that. She could see him down at the tomb, a tall glass of whiskey, a fistful of tobacco, he laid them on the silver stone, and she could see his lips moving, talking to the old man, making the magic, the old medicine.

What did you do with a man like your father?

The minivan was hot inside. The place was always hot. It was hot the day they buried Josephine, the white casket—*is MaMa hungry in there*, Lara'd asked. What is he doing, pouring out good liquor for the dead? Cigarettes? The chapstick in her purse had melted. How far was it to Dover? Moreland? Remember the Love woman, how she'd answered the door that day with a black eye and flour up to her elbows? Baking bread, a frame holding the photograph of her murdered daughter. How it caught light.

The telescope shop? Name day? The unspeakable stench and Lara holding up a box cutter blade? *Mines*, she said, *mines*. How Renee'd frozen?

What happened to the curtains? The ones she'd stolen from her own house that last day, before the long haul to Utah, back to that ratty-ass house with one bathroom on party street, close enough to hit the stadium parking lot with a rock. That's what Joe always said. *Close enough to hit with a rock*. Crazy man. She'd seen him do it. Hit it with a rock. What would become of them?

Don't ask: be careful. Love.

Mama's gone home. She drowned of a heart attack.

What to ask of all truth?

Geronimo is there, Dragon's Back. Mama'd made her peace and gone home. O.W., Jimmy, the whole lot. Those who'd walked west though truth and time. Field hippies, Si'd called the new agers, who believed in the master healer.

What else was there?

You've had your say.

The last of it, before Renee made Lara get in and push the boat back, off the rose quartz and into the lake where she'd wake Joey and say it was time to go home, back to Mountain Harbor. It was getting late, they had to turn the thing in. It's that way, write it in the sunrise sky, this morning, today, right by god now.

Two things which were maybe one: an Indian girl in a turquoise blouse shimmering on a bridge at sunrise. It was always coldest then, at sunrise. On the last day there was a chill, and when the sliver of sun shone above the cliff line an angel shimmied its wings, painted on them the black cross, Bible black, where he kept the picture of his dwarf uncle, or had it disappeared? A black semi lowballs up the mountain, and *yes*, its sound is pure heartbreak. Flowing beneath, the blue-green river, and there ravens caw-caw on the cliff face where scarlet gilia bloomed, fell, and floated on the water's face, through eddy lines and riffle. Thrown there, shadow wings, stone Shilohs, the blue doors of hogans repeating and repeated. How it ends, how it begins.

And on the last day before leaving the Natural State forever, they find the last grave, north of Little Rock toward Bauxite, too close to the road, hard to find, much walking and reading of wrong names. The directions were all mixed up, the mausoleum in the wrong place, the trees. The three of them wandered the wilderness together, how it should be, how it is. Father, mother, and daughter, straining eyes for the last tie before home. Lara walked up on her grave first, just like the time before, and the time before that.

"Here," she said. "Here."

The words of her name jolt, no preparing, ever.

No moonlit grooves, just hard sun. An old truck, a jalopy, whirred around the curve, not forty yards away. It hit Joey that his grandmother had weighed the place, had worked the figures over with pencil and paper, the auditor in her kicking in behind those guileless green eyes. Whose hand Joey'd held in Mena, in Paragould and Dumas, this good ooking white woman in a foreign car checking into hotels, ordering in their restaurants—darling, won't you have a piece of pie—and praying in their sanctuaries, come to audit their high school, weed out the graft, send some to the pokey, likely, and Joey'd go with her some days, get to lay out and swim at the pools, or go with her to the offices that smelled like Xerox and whiteout, sharpened pencils and perfume, a magnolia bloom sometimes floating in a bowl. And one time when he was four or something, he'd crawled naked into the shower with her, and she'd laughed and let him stay, his grandmother.

She'd played the numbers against each other. Thought about it. Prayed. Visited the exact spot and watched that same truck pass, backfire. Not a soul here that belonged to her or her people. Hadn't Si's sister embedded a granite slab the size of a shoe box with her initials on it, set it at her ex's feet. Their plan—bury her beside the bastard, grind Jewell's name off the stone, carve hers on. Well, we'll see about that.

She'd rather spit.

This was what she'd come up with, Floradee, what was good enough in the end, and what on earth did it matter, really? To shed earthly skin at a curve in the road where the dead were every bit as good—and dead—as those at Chapel Glen or Holy Oak. Pleasant Valley.

Weren't they.

7.

For a long time she missed the world of things: *chesnok, zira, petruska—garlic, cumin, parsley.* Take *chesnok,* not the puny shit they sold at Smith's, but the real stuff mamochka would smash with the broad side of a butcher knife on a board Papa'd sanded so the grain showed, and the air would go radiant with that smell when it hit the sizzling butter. They'd share a bulb, chew it raw, so the taste would get under her tongue and make her words magical. *Muzyka,* she called *chesnok,* so that it flavored their talks on afternoons when the sun shone down on the cackling crows, and they'd sauté Slippery Jacks in a skillet of butter and garlic, *maslo and chesnok.* Music, the old lady'd called her garlic, the fat bulbs they'd separate and plant in October when the light turned to gold and glowed on the gate, sprout up green in spring time, so Mama'd braid the long stems the way she had her hair, and they'd hang from nails Papa'd hammered into the rafter joists in the cool of the dark basement, the music.

Now the basement was strung up with Yakov's hard drives, what she'd traded her music for. She could hear them down there hissing and blinking and sending out a million billion messages to everyone with half a brain that Beethoven's Fifth concludes with the triumphant trumpet. He'd flooded the web, Yakov, made it so no one can ever trace it to them in Magna, one of Yakov's cameras circling in a satellite above, clickety-clacking its pictures of their house, the back deck she and Rudi built before he moved to Chicago to smoke dope and sleep with skinny American bitch who wanted not one thing in the world to do with being free. *Svobodnaya,* the last thing anybody here wanted, really, to have to choose for themselves, to decide what to do and when to do it and who to do it with. What they wanted most of all was to be told what to do, to be swayed, to have their choices limited.

So it was a lie that Americans could do anything they wanted. She thought to confess this to mama, next time she saw her, when their words make magic again, and she'd call her *Lyuba,* braid her hair like *chesnok.*

When she would be allowed again to rejoin the world of things.

Things.

They live not far from the deepest open pit copper mine on earth, on the whole fucking earth, where a whole mountain has been dug up so the hole is like the mountain upside down. Not ten miles from her back door, the Kennecott Copper Mine, where trucks the size of houses with tires ten feet tall drive this zig-zagged track down into the earth so deep the air gets hot and they have to pipe in fresh from a hundred stories above. She'd seen it first, the earth's biggest hole, from the sky, the dirt shining and little yellow trucks like Rudi's toys, but of course Rudi wasn't born yet, nor little Yelena, and she did not know she'd be sleeping forever in Mormon Utah, where miners from Magna—it was their high school mascot for God's sake— had dug to the earth's heart and back for gold and silver, aluminum and magnesium, nickel and platinum, iron, *zhelezo*—tin, *olovo*, zinc, *tsink*, and copper, of course, *med*, they'd plated whole buildings with it up at the University that was not good enough for Rudi, the roofline shining like some enormous version of Yakov's RV, from the hole in the earth where she lived now, so far from home, trying with her whole heart to be American, to do something she wanted at any time, and now to steal their election, to elect Vladmir's man, to start the revolution in a good way, Yakov snored beside her in bed, little Yelena's room just beyond there, in the kitchen her jars of pickled mushrooms and *baranina* marinating in vinegar, red potatoes and of course bread for the party, because today is the day. They had their marching orders. Their ducks are in a row. They've had a hard row to hoe. Be careful because our karma will come back to bite you on the butt. Do unto others as you would have them do unto you. Do not covet neighbor's ass. I have come to pit father against son, husband against wife. In my father's house are many mansions; if it wasn't true, I would have told you so. If you can't beat them join them. Concrete finishers stay harder longer. Dip him in the river who loves water. Sooner murder an infant in its cradle than nurse unacted upon desires.

All of that.

Yakov snored beside her. How long since they were married? Hadn't she worn a blue dress that smelled like licorice? Had Papa been there? *Mamochka?* In her dream, the crows rip up the cabbage, and the garden gate is overgrown with garlic, music everywhere. They chew it raw, it's on the tip of their tongues.

She breathed, remembered counting the floorboards of her room, the shadow always in *that* corner, the window, the field beyond, and beyond that to here, the pit, the everlasting hole in the earth's heart.

She didn't have to do a thing, they couldn't touch her here, how could they, so far from mother? They'd acclimated, acculturated, migrated, emigrated, immigrated, saturated, transubstantiated, the words fly through, leave trails of light through the room, there was no way, really, to know yourself and name yourself and be yourself in a language that killed the world, that dug out its heart and made you eat it. And yes, whoever said it was bitter, they were right.

Right Rudi?

Right.

She had to pee. That was real. Might as well get out of bed and let the new day dawn. Hear the wakeup call. The early bird gets the worm.

Good morning, America. They were always saying that. Good morning, America. As if. Outside the moon is waxing, one week from the snow moon, a supermoon that would shine over Black Sea and light the bellies of sturgeon whose eggs were deep purple and succulent.

November 8, 2016. Election Day, they're invited to the party, what a surprise, a great good thrill, being awake, feeling the cold floor beneath her feet, the little blips of light coming through from Yakov's computers spinning their lies below, the news of the world.

Yes. Good morning America. The fourth movement begins.

They are not to speak Russian. Not one word. Should seem neither overly happy nor sad at any point of the evening. Fit in. Smile. Say you don't know and have never heard the word *kompromat*, it simply is not used. Stand, do not sit. Do not go to the bathroom in backyard. No pictures, put away camera. Tell Yakov. Tell him again. Do not over-drink, nor smoke Turkish cigarettes. The lamb should not be too rare, they don't like it that way, nor potatoes too mushy. Do not for life take cabbage, nor breathe the word *borsht*. Laugh at their jokes. More smiling. A lot. Nod if you don't understand what they're saying. Do not say, *In Russia we always elect our mad men*. Or, *In Russia we have most beautiful prostitutes*. Or, I will shit on you from highest tree. Say yes when offered food. Do not wear see-through blouse. Be careful with rouge. Not too much red. Lipstick. Do not talk on telephone in house bathroom. Do not stay late. Do not leave early. Be surprised. Show that you care. Nod head. Thank them for invitation. Smile when they say *privet*.

Do not suffer the word "comrade."

Do not know Beethoven's Fifth nor anything at all about trumpets or triumph or triumph of the will or any history, not even for the history guy who will try to talk to you about Stalin, tell you his code name was Uncle Joe, that he'd asked Winston Churchill for his autograph the last time they met, outside of Paris, at peace accord, or was it Berlin, Potsdam. Do not discuss what happened to the Polish officers, nor anything regarding Poland at all. It is not on map. Smile at history professor and let him pour you wine. Don't let him see you spit it out. No, you have not heard of *Petticoat Junction*. Laugh at funny joke. Be careful what you think. Thought is energy. They're not *absolute* dolts.

Pay attention to Eric. Burgin. He is scientist, has contact in Berlin.

And Harvell man. He had somehow worked with Clinton, had photograph of his mother arm and arm with the man hanging in study, but of course you have never seen his study, nor do you know about photograph of mother with president. He will be interested in explosives—Harvell man. Humor him. Tell him about Ukraine incident. He rolls his own cigarettes. You may accept one of these. Step outside. Let him see how your hair shines. Say you'd love to go on river trip, your family and his. Be very interested in his southernness, let him quote the poetry of his childhood. Show him skin and teeth.

A black man will be there, a Dr. Charley. He'd talk of Coltrane's later years, that Jazz from space, the movement, Sun Ra, heroin, you can play along, you have nothing against black men. Obama was black man, don't dare say that name.

Know their dumb-fuck rules, who absolutely will not vote for Vladmir's man, who he had *kompromat* on, deep, deep, deep shit, and in Russia we never carry shit with us, do we?

Who will not vote for Trumpet. *Know.*

People with passports.

Anyone speaking foreign language.

Vegans.

Those who have listened to Beethoven's Fifth.

Who drive Volvos.

Who have ever attended ballet, double for anyone who has seen *Madam Butterfly* as ballet and opera in same year. Triple for anyone who says they saw *Moby Dick* when it came through as an opera, and quadruple for anyone who can name Raskolnikov as killer.

That you just said, "I will shit on you from the highest tree."

Whose disdain for biscuits and gravy has limited their growth of an all-American double chin. Who will not hit the drive thru at McDonald's. Who've never nibbled the nuggets. Who knows the fries have meat juice in them. Who know about the meat juice court case. Whose sister never-ever stayed at Ronald McDonald house. Not a chance, they will not covert to red.

Who live at 6000 feet or above—the higher reasoners.

Who know difference between the cabernet you are sipping and their glass of pinot grigio. Who've ever bought a case of wine. Who know of Rioja as place. Who recognize Iago as James. Who quote the sons of thunder. Who have kept an *Año de la Fe.*

Who have ever made béchamel and not spread it on chicken fried steak and called it white gravy.

Who've read *Pravda.*

Who marry foreigners.

Who love water.

Who doubt their knowledge of truth.

That part of the city near the University was a mix of students and professors, so outside Burgin's nice house, clearly visible above their six-foot cedar fence, was a balcony of scantily dressed coeds and big-chested boys who in turns pissed and puked projectile vomit into their wealthy neighbors' backyard, loud bass thumpa-thumping from apartment windows. Nancy met them at the door of the three-car garage they had transformed into an election night party room. They took their bottle of red to a table where it joined a shitload of others, took care to situate the lamb the on table with red potatoes and coarse bread joining the overflowing buffet on the night to celebrate the election of the first woman who had been first lady and Secretary of State to U.S. President.

A dog named Jupiter chewed a pig's ear.

Over the fence, Yelena watched a blonde girl vomit chunks of watermelon— it looked like watermelon, pink and glowing just inside the Burgin's fence line. A badminton net stretched across the backyard, two or three shuttlecocks caught up in the net. The first corners of Orion, Betelgeuse and Bellatrix, the Bull's red eye. Little Yelena had stayed home sketching polar bears, *polyarniy medved*, for her science project. Yakov chose a blue shirt, she red. High up on the hill, the red rock stadium glows, a silver U on either tower.

Inside the decorated garage, the mood is party-hearty, a wide-screen TV lit up in the corner, flashing numbers that show Madam Secretary rolling through her home stage of New York, a wide-smiling tape of her and ex-president waving to cheering crowd at the polls.

The screen flashed to Trumpett, his prissy lips pursed, his little right hand held in front of his face, the index finger and thumb touching—did he know what was up? What was about to happen?

Surely he knew, Vladmir's golden boy, dog-faced Slovenian Helena at his side, about to bawl her head off because she'd have to give up Manhattan penthouse and move into the White House dump, everyone find out from newspapers that she'd been a high-dollar whore when she'd met who'd be the Prez.

"Are you familiar with Dunning-Kruger?" He switched his wine to his left hand, the bright-eyed fat man who'd spoken to her, held out his right to shake.

Two water balloons smack the wide-screen and the channels flash to Obama and Michelle, their two daughters, a shot of Washington Monument and reflecting pool.

"Forgive me?" Yelena shakes the man's hand.

He said, "Eric Burgin. We met last Christmas at the Simmons'. You wore a see-through blouse."

Wild applause grips the room, numbers pouring from idiot TV. Rhode Island had come in for Madam Secretary, Connecticut about to call it with Massachusetts set to go any minute. Well, *duh*. The crowd is apeshit, somebody's dancing on the dining table which is really a ping pong table with a checkered tablecloth thrown over it.

"Yes," Yelena said and laughed, but not too much. "Thank you."

Yakov's one eye finds her. Be careful tonight.

"Kunning-Druger?"

The host still held her hand. "You're so funny," he said. "I remember you being so funny."

His wife joins them, pretty Nancy, their little circle. "What a night," she said.

"This is very nice," Yelena said. "Thank you for inviting us." He wouldn't let go of her hand, Eric Burgin.

"Did you hear about Vermont?" the wife asked. Nancy. She was left-handed. Their house was once owned by a couple who divorced and the son became a film maker, wrote a whole script that took place at the house, so they—the Burgins—had to move out one whole summer so they could film. They'd gone to Berlin—Yakov had kept up with them somehow, where they dined, the little nude beach on the river, the holocaust museum.

Someone in front of TV moaned. The fourth movement had begun.

"Your son, Rudi?"

"Thank you for asking."

"He's in school where now?"

The wife had straight, white teeth. Everyone loved her. Her smile was real and she meant everything she said with her whole heart. In Munich there are men who look like weasels. Keep thinking it. Outside, a boy pees off the balcony. What is this husband with his hand fetish?

The Harvell man was watching them. He'd found Yakov. They were talking about Wisconsin. Michigan. The bottom falling out.

"Chicago," Yelena said. "Our Rudi is in Chicago."

White teeth and smiling, the wife wanders, and finally the bright-eyed little host turned her lose. What happened to Michigan? *Oh no.* Someone sobbed. *Oh no no no* they went. *Don't let it happen.*

"I know a place to eat there. The Russian Tea Room. In Chicago."

Where was food? Why was no one eating here?

He said, "Illinois," Eric Burgin.

Two couches were formed into an L beneath the ceiling rafters where a florescent light hung alongside a disco ball which flashed deep purple—a black light.

Yakov had stepped outside with Harvell man. He was professor. History. They had met at Simmons party when she'd worn see-through dress. All night long, men and women looking at her chest, her ass. What is this Russian woman? they asked. Go figure. People were crying inside, on the couch.

They were smoking, Yakov and Harvell.

She joined.

He rolled her cigarette, remembered.

"I never smoke," Yelena said. "Thank you."

Yakov nodded his head, inhaled. He'd grown up with tapped phone lines, KGB listening through the drain pipes, seeing his mother shower. Up on the balcony, a skinny bitch in a short skirt *blurps* over the railing, her puke bright yellow.

The three of them stand like that, smoking.

"In Russia we always elect our mad men," Yakov said, his English perfecto. "Why I came here. To get away from mad men."

The light from his cigarette shone in his eyes, Harvell. He was not a talker. She liked that, not talking. Too much talk. Everywhere. On TV that second, the shocked sad-faced commentators commentating. Better to just breathe the smoke out, let idiot kids vomit off balcony.

Back inside the three-car garage, everyone sat on couches with glow on faces. Numbers flashed on the screen: Texas, Arkansas, Tennessee.

They made plates, her and Yakov, the good lamb not too rare, the red potatoes not too mush. Eric was opening bottles, walking around the room and filling glasses. Madam Secretary's headquarters was no longer party central, people standing with that look like King Kong had just whipped it out and peed on them. Worse. Mascara running.

She made call, Madam Secretary. Now the speech.

The Statue of Liberty—erected in 1886, symbol of refuge and democracy.

The Mayflower—pilgrims who'd sailed to Plymouth, Massachusetts. Squanto fed them squash and wild turkey, the first Thanksgiving.

Lobster fishing fuels Maine's economy. Shells turn red when cooked.

Empire State Building: Architect designed it to look like pencil.

Woodstock. Hippy-dippy. Canned Heat.

Baseball is national sport.

Go Chicago, go Cubs. 8-7 in the tenth. Rudi'd watched it with his skinny American girl. He'd called and she'd heard the girl's voice in the background, beer-breathed, singing the "Star Spangled Banner."

On screen, the last images of Trumpett triumphant before they said thank you and goodbye and yes, let's do it again. Helena, that whore, now first lady, bawled her fool Slav head off on live TV.

In car, they rode in silence, toward the great hole in earth.

Above them, Yakov's cameras seeing all, tonight and tomorrow, the next day and the next. Seeing inside of them, where their hearts were.

8.

Coconino's county seat was in Flagstaff, and it was there that Edgar hallucinated the Indian princess—the knock to his head?—in jail, where the sink was also the urinal and shitter—and it was princess this and princess that, the goddamn ugly-ass dino bird flying them up and up to who knows where, and it was all about her, Rose Marie Begay, though he didn't know that yet, and the Harvell boy, a carrier, who'd come to break him aloose, and it hit him like a brick thrown from nowhere, where's my goddamn truck? His ears popped. And *whoa*, his head. Where on earth was he? Why? The bird had stayed with him, of course, and that White Buffalo Calf woman—what was she about? There was a river bridge, he'd had to pee. The faint recollection of pissing in public. It was a jail he was in, on a mattress-less bed, his clothes sour. That killer's plaque, ten feet tall if an inch, hiding in the alcove, a *man of great courage*, piss on him. That's why he was here, for peeing on Lee.

Edgar's seen the inside of a jail before, the sound the electric locks make and how the lights never go out, and they make you unlace your shoes and take off your belt. Somebody's talking in a foreign language, *Mexican?* Sounds like a church service, a whole lot of *dios*, *padre* and *Jesus Cristo.*

So it was Sunday, his third day west.

His wrists are rubbed raw from the cuffs. There had been an officer. "Just who do you think you are?" the last words he heard before the billy stick smacked up aside his head.

He'd mostly stayed out from Marble Canyon to Flag—it'd been a long day, a haul from Arkansas to Arizona. His head hurt. Terribly. There was no blanket, no pillow, nothing. Just this voice out there praying to God in Mexican.

Edgar sat up in his steel bed. He said, "Hello?"

Across the hall, somebody said, "Hale-oh?"

It was the bucky-bubba accent people used to make fun of Arkies and Okies and anybody come from the stars and bars. Tina'd talked that way sometimes. After college messed her mind up. Why'd he have to go and think of her?

Salvaçion, somebody down there said.

Edgar knew what it meant, he'd been under the water. And it hit him that he could pray, ask God and Jesus and Holy Ghost to help his sorry ass out of the sling he'd got himself into. Whatever that was. He'd once been part of the flock—did you ever get run out entirely? Wasn't there something about it sticking? About neither death nor life, nor angels nor any other such shit being able to separate us from the love of Almighty God?

He opened his eyes and there was a fake light falling from the fluorescents up and down the hall. Sunday morning. The black Peterbilt that had tried to run him down blew through somewhere outside, all eyes. Edgar felt it, somebody walking over his grave.

Edgar prayed.

Not out loud like the Sadducees and Pharisees, but to himself on the metal bunk on top of what he did not know but would one day learn was a mountain island in the desert, an archipelago, they called it, where, before they let him walk free after serving his sixty days, the snow would fly and would so shine as an obelisk amidst oblivion. Help me Jesus.

Amen.

Stoner, the arresting officer, was a Lee on his mother's side. Son of a bitch had had nineteen wives and he must have gone at them right much because there were more Lees than you could shake a stick at in south Utah and north Arizona. You couldn't throw a rock without hitting a Lee. They were senators and congressmen and supreme court justices, the goddamn secretary of the interior under Kennedy and Johnson. And Stoner, who had accompanied Edgar to court that first time, and whose voice it was through Edgar learned that he was found guilty of indecent exposure and vandalism on federal land, urinating in public and defamation of distinguished persons as manifest in heritage sites, not to mention slander and assault on an officer of the peace.

The last one got Edgar's goat. Assault on a peace officer. He'd blasphemed the Prophet, Stoner claimed with that self-righteous smirk. Said, "And is my right hand not consecrated to avenge the blood of the prophet?" or some silly shit.

Officer Stoner'd looked him in the eye, right in front of the high judge who'd whomped his desk a few times with a wooden gavel. "You're lucky," he said. I hope you *understand* that."

Edgar understood.

He knew full-well what Stoner-Lee meant.

After sentencing, the officer'd escorted him to county, where he was issued a ziplock with a toothbrush and bar of soap. "Where's my truck?" Edgar'd asked while Stoner signed him onto the list of jailees. Blue ink—he watched his name in cursive come from the man's hand.

"Belongings?" the clerk asked.

Stoner said, "None."

And that was that. He was led to a cell where a metal bunk like the one before had a Book of Mormon on it, the only sanctioned reading Edgar'd be allowed during his sixty days in. He should be prepared to produce a legal adult with picture ID, and proof of good standing in the State of Arizona upon his release, and subsequent probationary time.

He settled into county on 24 August, his 52nd birthday.

In Harrison, there's a sign says THIS STRETCH OF HIGHWAY KEPT BY THE ROYAL KNIGHTS OF THE KU KLUX KLAN. Not far out of town, on the slight rise of a hill toward Booger Holler where they had Blue Grass on Sundays after Bible service while the barbecue smoked in a fifty-five-gallon barrel split in half, loaded with charcoal and hickory, throw old Snorkey in there, yessir. He didn't know what the Klan would have to say about Mormons—truth was he didn't really know anybody in the Klan, like they were some kind of ghost riders with special signals so they'd know each other, like the Mormons, if Chief Joseph could be trusted far as you could throw him. There's a big library right downtown where Edgar once witnessed the Harvell boy—who he hopes will remember him and save his ass—read from his account of the Mountain Meadows Massacre, a discourse so fiery and inspired that it got him invited to speak at the Lupercalia Fish Fry over to Tri-County Coon Club where Edgar was caretaker, and that's where Ronnie Love, stoked on meth, had bit the boy's finger off, swallowed it, then run off into the woods so they had to turn the dogs on him, run him like a deer in November, till they found him naked in the trunk of a tree, and got it back, the finger.

All that seemed like a hundred miles ago to Edgar, sliding into September, being the ninth month, Labor Day, the new moon, breakfast—a piece of bread and apple sauce, lunch—two pieces of bread with a piece of baloney in between, dinner—mystery meat on a piece of bread with gravy over it, mashed potatoes on the side onest, sweet peas on their way to being defrosted, for some reason they didn't believe in coffee here. I'm not a coffee drinker, Chief Joseph had said, as if Edgar'd asked for heroin or bootleg whiskey. So it was bread and water, more or less, a walk in the yard onest a day, then back to his room, where the Mormon Bible lay on one side, Edgar on the other, the black book eyeing him, taking his measure, sniffing out the gentile in him.

He could do things to that book, Edgar.

"I can get you out of here," Chief Joseph said on a Tuesday during their yard walk, which amounted to one lap around a dirt path at the foot of a chain link fence topped off with razor wire.

Chief Joseph was some kind of free Indian who got to walk the halls and keep his own cat which he called Rudolph the Red because that was a name in some book he was reading. After you finished the Book of Mormon and passed the test, they let you visit the Coconino County Jail Library where you earned a reading pizza every time you finished a book, and after ten you could sign up for a community college creative writing class where you got to write your own story.

Stoner'd not darkened the door since delivering Edgar, thanks be. That fellow cast a shadow both ways. Somebody said you just keep on meeting the same three or four people your whole life—they just keep repeating. If that was true, who would Stoner be? The man had seemed to know him, and hate him to his core, Edgar. "Who the hell do you think you are?" he'd asked. He gave Edgar the willies. He did not doubt for a second that Stoner would drive him out to the boondocks, put a bullet in his head and leave him in a ditch for the pigs and vultures. "How?" Edgar asked.

Chief Joseph pointed to the center of the yard where a tall stake was driven with a scrap of red cloth flapping off the tip end. Smoke hung in the air above. California was on fire, half of Nevada.

Chief said, "Inipi."

What he'd give for some sausage and eggs. Edgar said, "I don't speak injun." His stomach His stomach rumbled and rolled. Somebody out there in the free world was frying sausage. Edgar smelt it.

"Sign up for lodge. On Equinox. You know what that means?"

Edgar had the whitest skin in the whole jail. Behind him all the other men blended in. "You said two things. Which'n?"

A door in the wall opened and a hand waved them back—the walk was done. Back in the room, Edgar gave the book a dirty look. He stared a hole through to the words inside.

Down the hall, Rudolph the Red meowed.

Edgar wanted out. Like a man whose head's on fire wants a bucket of water, he wanted out of this place, and as many miles between hisself and Stoner as Edgar could make.

A darker piece of dark, the book when the lights that never went out went out.

Equinox Inipi was a sweat lodge ceremony granted to all Indians by federal law as part of their religion and civil rights, just like they could carry eagle feathers and eat peyote, Chief Joseph explained, and if Edgar had as much as a thimble full of Indian blood then he too could attend, and they'd all escape the confines of the county jail for the duration. They'd sing these prayer songs, pour water on the grandfather stones and their spirits would float out with the steam, join up with the clouds and roll down the river. Edgar's mama'd onest taken him to a Pentecost revival where this preacher kept a boxful of copperheads up by the altar. He'd get to preaching so hard, spittle flying, and sometimes he'd just rear back and shitkick the cardboard box to punctuate a sentence, and you could hear the little fuckers in there going at it. Once the box flew across the floor and dumped snakes all up the middle aisle, and one old geezer picked one up and danced the herkey-jerk, singing angel words.

Water, rocks, steam. Why not?

Edgar signed up as part Cherokee on his mama's side—some Mayfields lay way back in the family thickets, Indians who'd walked the Trail of Tears, clean down from North Carolina to Arkansas on the way to Oklahoma.

Chief Joseph drew a diagram of what the lodge was to look like, the eight-sided star of its structure that mirrored the Navajo universe. "Take it to heart," he said, passed it through the bars to Edgar—an envelope to him with Dinnehotso writ on the left-hand corner for return address. Inside, in that kind of pencil that writes in four different colors, Arkansas DMF 668 and then a whole lot of mess Chief Joseph interpreted as code talk for *I have your Chevy, ridiculous talk to bird peeing man. RB.*

That's sister Begay," Chief said. "Everyone's in love with her daughter Rose."

"How'd she know it was me. Only talked to her the one time."

Getting a letter from Rita Begay made Edgar sort of famous at county, where mail day was almost big as Equinox Sweat Lodge or Thanksgiving, when the Flagstaff Aztecs delivered turkey and dressing and the cheerleaders wore their skirts and did "Funky Monkey" and "Satisfied"—*well it's a two steps forward, um um, and a one step back.*

That Chief, he loved to talk, sit outside the bars with ole Rudolph the Red curled around his feet. His eyes sparkled and the cat purred, and one time he produced a piece of smoked salmon out of his tee-shirt, and the three of them split it right there.

"Everyone arrested comes here," Chief said. "You don't need the big medicine to know that do you."

"How'd she know my name?"

Chief pointed at the letter with his pinky. "DMF," he said. Everyone knows."

They'd given him orange clothes to wear, but he still had on the same skivvies he'd been washing in the sink with bar soap, hang them up to dry at night while he slept on the metal bunk, fifteen different kinds of snores going off like hootennannies.

"I ain't no DMF, Chief."

Rudolph curled his long tail in the air, made a helicopter sound. Chief Joseph picked him up and walked away whistling, code for the man is coming, best watch your ass. And sure enough there came Stoner, dark sunglasses on, the badge shining on his chest. He stood outside Edgar's cell for thirty seconds by the clock, the dark sunglasses like the sharpshooter chain gang warden in *Cool Hand Luke*, Edgar's favorite movie because of when Luke ate fifty eggs in an hour.

"Hey pisser," Stoner said. "Long way to Arkansas."

Edgar looked at the floor where sat the evil black book. "Reckon," he said.

The underwear never completely dried—he could feel them that second, the cold spot. In front of him, the man sucked his teeth. Five minutes after he was gone Edgar still had the chill. Then a guard came and told him to get the goddamn gospel off the floor.

He rat-tat-tatted his billy stick against Edgar's bars.

"Yessir," he said.

From then on he'd had to sleep with it, the black book. He took care not to let it touch him, not even through the sheet.

The building of a sweat lodge is an all-day affair that involved the locating of thirty-three willows on a creek bank that were prayed to and offered tobacco before being lopped down, tied in a heavy bundle and hauled to the site of the ceremony, where Chief Joseph had overseen the digging of the fire pit, in the center of which Edgar'd taken a sharpshooter shovel and dug a deeper hole, and into this was placed a stiff golden eagle, head and beak facing west, so the lodge became *medicine eagle inipi,* a space with the power to heal. Only Indians were allowed to kill an eagle, but the truth was somebody'd found it hit on the side of the road, and a half-blood deputy had rolled it up in the Sunday Aztec and brought it for ceremony.Sage and tobacco and cedar were sprinkled over the dead eagle, and Chief Joseph prayed for a good thirty minutes before asking Edgar to shovel dirt over it. Part of Chief's prayer had been asking that what they were about to do would not bring harm to any being, living or dead, which the old gravedigger had to chew on for a while: how could the living bring harm upon the dead? It stayed with him, the question, while he shoveled the pit that would be the inipi's center and arranged the dirt into an altar outside. It puzzled him while he made the sixteen holes Chief sifted tobacco into and prayed over, before hip-bending the first of the willow people. He wondered as the Indian tied the medicine hoop into the eight-pointed star roof, called for the blankets to be tied on in a clockwise way because the other direction was *heyoka,* the backward-forward way of holy clowns, the *wakinyan tanka,* and it troubled Edgar as the *cannupas* were filled with *chinchasha,* and the first of the holy songs were sung—*kola lecel ecun, kola lecel ecun.*

The pipes were fitted together, their male parts into the female parts. The tang of white sage hung in the air, and there was the smell of cedar burning, sweet and pungent like Christmas when his mama'd light the angel candles that dinged, the little bells she'd heard on the morning he was to be born, Edgar, after hard labor, and the doctor'd come out and say the baby won't make it, and then the mama won't make it, and they both won't make it, but of course they did, on Christmas, he was a Christmas baby, Edgar, or was that someone else?

Another of the Indians played a drum that boom-boomed off the walls of the county pen and could be heard by the pizza delivery boy across town who opened a box and swiped a round of pepperoni, popped it into his mouth, and beat out the rhythm of the pipe song on the pizza box, *whop, whop, whop,* and so joined ceremony without ever even knowing it.

Once inside, the fire popping through the open door, seven grandfathers were carried on a pitchfork and slid through the open door, little coals glowing on them like eyes. Fireman shut the door. Chief Joseph sang the Four Directions Song, poured the first of the water, hot steam instantly filling the pitch-black void so that the hair on his head got so hot it burned his fingers, Edgar's.

And still the question gnawed at him. It was his business, goddamnit, he ought to know. He ought to.

And when the prayer round came, there he was, babbling like an idiot, asking *Tunkasila, Wakan Tanka* to right his broke heart, his crooked soul, to take from him the hurt and pain and sorry-ass loathing he had in this life, to forgive him the boatload of wrongs he'd perpetrated on his fellow man and woman, all his mean-spirited petty bullshit. He thanked Rita Begay and the Navajo Nation for saving his truck from that devil Stoner, and, come to think of it, maybe Officer Stoner could use some blessings, too, if *Tunkasila* found him deserving. And by the time he said *Metakuye Oyasin*, all my relations, and lapsed into the quiet place that would be with him for the rest of his days, he was free, he soared. By god, he did.

Edgar T. Paris was no longer captive in an Arizona jail.

9.

All day long he'd traced their path, along the Jordan River to Provo, where Mount Olympus reared twelve-thousand feet, breathtaking in its beauty, and oblivious. 24 October, the full Hunter's Moon, aspen quaking and golden up on the mountain where new snow shined already, two-powdery feet from the monsoon storm come blowing in from the Sea of Cortez last week. Him and Lara'd driven up the canyon, strapped on back country skis and trekked over moose tracks, then eaten big bowlfuls of chili at Hell's Gate, named by Mormons for the mining town where there had been bars, and they once strung a dead man up on a flagpole as their flag. Now this land just rolls out forever in all directions from the Wasatch Range which blocks any friend or foe that might venture from the east, a wall of granite and stone upthrust from the ancestral ocean bed, so the striations in the heat-compressed stone run straight up and down sometimes seven thousand feet from valley floor to peak —the great fence line against manifest destiny. And there's something about being able to see seventy miles off your front porch, clear to Nevada, Joey was convinced, that opened a human being up, so with all that space, possibility flowed into the vacuum, and there was hope. Anything at all might come your way. Sweet clean air with a tang of sage on it, October gold in the light, it felt good to turn south and west and let fly, no one out gave two shits about the speed limit—just gear that fucker up and go. *Go.*

They would have by now that they were being followed. That they were up shit creek. Word is, the Fancher party'd been scouted from the word go, and heading out on the heels of Parley Pratt's killing by the hand of Hector McLean over a woman Hector was legally married to that ole Parley'd decided to claim as his nineteenth wife. No shit, it was true, the old son of a bitch, as if eighteen wasn't enough. Pratt had made the long-ass haul to Arkansas in spring 1857, and Arkansas's not Missouri, where Hiram and Joseph Smith had lost their lives—which they probably deserved for that skull crushing episode—and no one with a lick of sense would just ride in like they owned the place, especially when they were already wanted for homicide one state over, as Parley was. But that's what happened, and the boy—beloved amongst Mormons—took a knife in the chest and bled out somewhere close to Fort Smith. And Fort Smith is a long goddamn way from Harrison from whence the Fanchers departed, and so none of their 120 some would have known Parley Pratt if he'd walked up and bit them on the butt. Nor would they have any idea what celestial marriage was, nor sealing, nor Quorum of the Twelve, nor the Doctrine of Blood Atonement. All this would have been as foreign to those Ozark folk as their own ways—their mountain witchcraft and superstition—would have been to the Mormons. But the fat man in Salt Lake saw it different. They'd sworn the blood oath to avenge their prophets, and here come the Fanchers over the mountain, forty some men among them. Folk who'd fought in the War Between the States, and the rest women and children, set out for the walk to sunny California, a new life in the sun.

Highway 15 rolled on out through sweet little towns, each one with the spattering of white steeples and the roads diametrically constructed to make them ground zero. Santaquin and Nephi and Scipio, the cones of extinct volcanos and mesas and buttes, a sea of sage spilling into the Great Basin where Buffalo once wintered by the hundred thousands. Where the Utes, Wakara and his forefathers, lived off the fat of the land and sweet water from rivers ran down from the central spine of mountains, south to the Paria and what would be Lee's Ferry east of Jacob's Pool. Away from Salt Lake, the place had a feel to it, that much hadn't changed. A big- ass Suburban flew by with a bumper sticker that said SIX COW WIFE, a reference to a Mormon story about a man who traded six cows for a wife. They still eyed you at gas stations and grocery checkouts, and if you asked them where the liquor store was, they'd claim they'd never heard of such a thing—the liquor store, what was that? There was some sort of secret sign they gave each other that Joey'd never figured out, though he knew it was real. It was how they'd taught the Paiute Indians to differentiate Mormons from *Mericats*, which stood for *Americans,* which the Mormons, according to their Prophet, were damn sure not.

After twenty-five years, Joey was used to their wackiness. But the sense of not belonging, of being an outsider, of telling everybody that you ever met that you lived in Utah but you were not *from* there, that never went away. And the feeling in your gut that you were in danger sometimes, that here was a people who when married had their right arms consecrated to avenge the blood of their prophets, that 120-some of your very own people had been murdered, stripped naked, and left to lay on the ground for more than half a century before they were even buried. Their possessions disappeared, and no one ever said sorry for dressing up as Indians and perpetrating the single worst mass murder of the entire migration west, that grated on him, on Joey Harvell, it did.

You never forgot.

And when people like Congressman Butters made fun of Arkansans on the floor of the Capitol Building, when he slandered them as illiterate and stupid in a public forum, Joey was of a mind to show him an Arkansas Toothpick, descendant of the one that had found its way so deep into brother Parley's chest.

In Beaver, they sold *I Love Beaver* bumper stickers at the truck stop where Joey stopped to piss and fill up, check the Pathfinder's oil and squeegee the windshield. A *Rough Rider* condom machine was strung up in the men's room. Somebody'd had a shit fit in one of the stalls. He checked the air in all four tires with the gauge daddy'd given him before he left home, topped the left rear off to 36 even, lay on his back and kicked the spare. Afternoon, he bought a bag of Fritos and a can of bean dip, refilled his water bottle. In the back compartment a cooler with ground beef and whiskey, two buns and a squeeze bottle of mustard. A half-gallon of apple juice and whole lemon chill on ice. Renee'd packed a hunk of cheddar and Tupperware of apple crisps, and Lara'd folded an *I Love You Be Careful* note around a bar of sea salt chocolate. He wished for a pistol, that he'd brought Jimmy's pistol. The silver-plated .38 in its leather holster with bronze snap, the one that had been in the center console of the red Toyota Supra on the night of his brother's one car crash. The one Joey'd retrieved along with his senior ring from the floorboard wrist deep in head blood.

Cedar City: He had a colleague, Joey did, who got on at Dixie State, where coffee was not allowed at faculty meetings, which this colleague had complained about, though he himself was Mormon, Joey suspected, because he'd written a review of one of Joey's Mountain Meadows papers that called it, "just another instance of Mormon bashing," which Joey'd thought odd—definitely the wrong phrase—all those skulls down to New Harmony, they were all bashed in. This was known because somebody from Brigham Young University, some archeologist on a field trip, had dug up twenty or so and took them back to school, where they were examined on tables in a science building named after Lee, and each one showed blunt force trauma, they'd been bashed, so Joey's paper'd noted. Word from the fat man to kill everyone in the Fancher party old enough to tell the tale had not come sewn in the lining of a coat as was customary, but on the lips of one George Smith, cousin to the prophet, who'd stirred the shit, preached sermons summoning fire and brimstone on the heads of the gentiles, blood atonement, as did Young from the pulpit in Salt Lake, the very week, the very day the Fanchers emerged from Emigration Canyon, not two miles from Joey's front door—he could have seen them, smelled their mules, listened to the trill of the younger Baker twins, Sarah and Margaret, how their voices rang out from the camp at the foot of the canyon.

Here was where Haight and Higbee and Colonel Dame formalized what was to happen, to call out the Nauvoo troop, summoning all those whose right arms had been consecrated to avenge the blood of the prophets. *Coming apart man,* the Paiutes had called him, George Smith, the man who'd carried Brigham's command, with his eye glasses and wig and false teeth. He'd have no truck with Cedar goddamn City, Joey Harvell. He took a long slug from the coffee thermos, black, it burned his throat. A whole slew of them had confessed to the deed, given lurid details down to the pulling of teeth filled with precious metal, the fine hair of the girls, one asked to dance naked in a grassy glade before her throat was cut. Mama'd been shocked to read the story— no one had ever heard of it. *Surely this isn't true, Joe, it just couldn't happen that way,* she'd written in her fine blue cursive. *Joey, what do you mean by this,* she'd written.

Yes, it did, Mama.

Herself married in the big heart of Texas by a sleepy justice on her way West, where she'd learn it was all a lie, everything his blood father had ever said, a dwarf come jumping out the trailer's screen door, spurting off the overheating car's radiator with a cut off piece of water hose. Pregnant already, surely it couldn't happen that way. What do you mean by this?

Fuck Cedar City. The hard faces that eyed him at three red lights, the big climb out of town where the Fanchers had felt cold breath down their necks and started to bear down, to make time and a half. Close now, close.

It's called Legacy Loop Highway, up Leach Canyon to Iron Mountain and Iron Town, Little Pinto and Pinto, and the fall into the vast meadow itself, not thirty miles from Nevada and safe passage to California where new life would take root and flourish, maybe.

Maybe no.

They'd camped near here once, the three of them, Joey, Renee, Lara. A National Park dotted with scenic venues for hikers: Towers of the Virgin, South Guardian Angel, Tabernacle Dome, The Pulpit, and the most popular where ropes and crampons were needed in winter, Angel's Landing. It had snowed that spring, and their skunk-sprayed dog was crying. He'd zipped her into the mummy bag with him till daylight, so the smell never went away.

The Old Spanish Trail, slaves run behind pack mules from Santa Fe and Los Angeles, the northern outposts of Mexico, which had only just gained independence from Spain, Joey fell south and west past Hamblin's Ranch—that old liar—to Abe's Spring and the empty parking lot. His right knee cracked when he got out the door. He brought the water bottle. Sage. A fistful of tobacco. Places like this—him and Renee'd once visited a concentration camp outside Prague, Terezin, it was named, after the King's mother, who he loved. Hitler turned it into a stopping point on the way to Auschwitz, and there's a trove of children's drawings there, one of a sleigh ride in the snow, a boy with a bright red scarf.

The smell of fear.

The monument connected to the parking lot, a black slab encased in gravel, engraved *Mountain Meadows, 1990, Historic Sites View Finder*. Dead flowers have blown off to the side. View Number One traces the gravel road to the piece of earth where the Fanchers understood that the time was at hand, where they'd circled and lashed together their wagons and dug the inner trench against the onslaught. Historic View Number Two has an A and a B part: A—The Place Where the Women and Children Were Killed, B—The Place Where the Men Were Killed.

Open ground for miles, no cover save sage, rabbit bush.

Today was full Hunter's Moon—it would light Mountain Meadow, so that the faces of white men painted as Indians would be visible targets. They were good shots, the Fanchers. They had long guns, forty men to tie to. And they could by god shoot.

Joey breathed, took water from the bottle, swished and spit. It could get under your teeth. He turned west, walked—the half mile into the sun. The siege lasted five days. September 7 through 11, in the year 18 and 57, 144 years to the goddamn day from the Mountain Meadows Massacre to 9-11, and wasn't 144 a Biblical number, the square of 12, natural, the tribes of Israel, disciples, months of that year when the Mormons and their prophet chose to avenge the blood of their prophet here, on this ground, where John D. Lee, the prophet's adopted son, bodyguard to Joseph Smith, was appointed to be the right hand of their angry God, to spare none old enough to tell the tale.

First frost came in September, the desert night cold. Hot in the daytime. And water? What about water? When the Mandan woman put Joey on the mountain, made around him the burial plot he was not to trespass until the vision came, the sun had parched him so after twenty-four hours without a drink, he would have given a finger for a mouthful of clean, cool water. After thirty-six hours, the finger became a hand. And after the second day, hallucinating ancestors manifest in earth, air, fire and water, he would have given his life in a finger snap for a sip.

Sometimes a place will open itself up to you.

There were no trees save willows growing from a dry creek bed. A cairn, ten feet tall, rough stone to the hands, torn down then rebuilt, then torn down then rebuilt.

He took it in. The quiet. It opened to him. There beneath the blue sky of an afternoon that would brighten into Hunger's Moon, he took the moment into his heart.

His right heel was cracked from a summer in sandals, from Arkansas, three times walking to the bright teepee with wood stacked for the fire, the heyoka sign's painted medicine. The carpet tack had cut him. This is a no shoes house.

They'd circled their wagons, lashed the wheels with the harness reins from turned loose doomed oxen. In the morning before first light, sixty Mormons dressed as Indians and some real Indians who'd painted the white's faces, attacked. It was a hell of a fight. The Arkies could shoot, forty men with long guns. They fought like lions. By ten that first dance was done. What real Indians there were deserted. It was a lie—that the Mormon's god would protect them. They attacked again in the afternoon, no go. The Mormons had not counted on the Arkies fighting back. The siege lasted five days.

He'd slept beside his brother's grave once. A night in summer, the bricklaying tools he'd used to put down stone and mortar as the Stepwell men ever had for their loved dead, soaking in the wheelbarrow where he'd poured a five-gallon bucket of pond water from downhill. He'd unrolled his sleeping bag beside Jimmy's silver stone, saw how it glittered under starlight, the whippoorwill off in the bottoms and fireflies going off all around. Peaceful as Jesus, there beside Jimmy in Arkansas August at night.

The sunset would be tangerine orange, a sage-fragrant breeze that tasted of dust and bitterweed, he could feel it under his tongue, on the roof of his mouth.

Sometimes a place opens itself up to you. Sometimes it does.

He lit the medicine bundle with a kitchen match struck on the cardboard box that said *keep away from children* in bright red letters.

Up in the parking lot a car pulled in beside the Historic Sites View Finder. Its door slammed and the echo slammed again. He fought the fear, sudden in his gut, felt like he'd shit himself that second.

At his feet shone a trinket, a thing that had been missed. It had not been seen by Prophet Gordon B. Hinckley when he dedicated the monument; passed over by the ones who'd pilfered the clothes of the dead, of the blonde girl in her only clean dress who'd held the white flag, who was thirsty, who'd said *bring your leader*, and *can I have some water?*

And he'd come, Lee. Said, *Lay down your weapons and we'll tell the Indians to let you walk free.*

And that's what they did. Five days of siege, the men had whooped when they saw the Nauvoo Legion in the soldier outfits. Walked willingly away from their women, from their daughters and sons, mothers and wives to The Place Where the Men Were Killed.

Smoke from the sage cleansed it—a hairpin?—so some of the green came through, the green of life, he put it in his front jeans pocket, turned to meet the two of them come walking, they always come at you in twos.

Elders, they called themselves, gifted with the magic to call down fire, to consecrate or curse.

He'd seen their faces a thousand times, in the meat aisle at Smith's and at the gun store, once when he'd taken the broken Yamaha cd player for repair and he'd thought the man behind the counter would kill him—*due diligence*, the guy'd growled when Joey'd questioned the ungodly price, *due diligence*. There was a color to their eyelashes, a shape of the face, something just out of kilter that made Joey think of the country folk back in Dover who fucked their first cousins, so their offspring grew up touched.

"Good afternoon, sir," the missionary on the right said.

"Good afternoon," went the one on the left.

Joey spit in his left hand, touched the sage bundle to his palm and put it out. He'd yet to offer tobacco.

They had on name tags, the Mormons.

Joey said, "Hey," nodded.

"We are representatives of the Church of Jesus Christ of Latter Day Saints," the one on the right said, who was taller, had rolled his creased white shirt sleeves up on his forearms.

Joey said, "I know who you are."

"Whatcha doing?"

Abe's Spring was a good half mile north and east. They'd had to suffer fire from the rim of the basin to fill their buckets.

"Paying respects," Joey said.

"I can tell you're not from around here."

Joey said, "You?"

They were red-eyed, the missionaries. High. One of his students had written an essay in which two teens drive a car to the end of a road and smoke dope till they're fucked out of their skulls, then drive to the temple where they get baptized for dead strangers over and over all night long and they cannot tell under penalty of death.

"Cedar City," the boy said. "Toquerville," said the other, and smiled.

It was after five, happy hour now.

"Seen you pick something up. Historic site, can't take nothing."

"Didn't," Joey said. His finger hurt, where it was sewn back on, the jagged scar.

The missionaries looked at each other for a second, then back at Joey, in his face, as if seeing something he was not aware of showing. Traces of the girl's DNA laced the emerald hairpin, strands of yellow hair tangled in the clasp. It told the tale, even still.

"We could smell your sage from the parking lot. We come here sometimes. We're off duty now."

Joey said, "Right."

"I mean no one knows we're here."

"Me neither."

Elder says, "Good. Go on and pay your respects. But don't take nothing. Hear?" He looked Joey straight in the face, the last word hung between them.

"*Hear.*"

"Good," tall elder said.

"Evenin'," said the other.

Every adult male in all of south Utah, then called Deseret, had partaken in the massacre. Their great grandfathers, the stoned Mormons. Pitched horseshoes, ringers clanging.

They left him be, the low sun throwing their shadows in front of their feet. He dug out the handful of tobacco from his pocket, sifted it onto the rock cairn. Much later, Renee would find what he'd missed in the dryer, tobacco, all mixed up with their underwear and t-shirts, bits of tissue and an ink pen.

They were gone when he got back to the parking lot. Sixteen orphans had been recovered after, too young to tell the tale. Word was the seventeenth had had her throat slit when she observed out loud that Emma Lee was wearing her mama's dress, her earrings, her hat. He'd heard her, John Lee, walked over just pretty as you please, reached down and took her hair in a hand, cut her throat from ear to ear. *This I saw with my own eye*, the nineteenth wife said.

He'd thrown her in a well over to New Harmony, named for the township on the Susquehanna where the Prophet Joseph Smith, Jr., who'd never studied a language, much less ancient Egyptian—which the golden plates were for some reason written in—translated the Book of Mormon, a history of Native Americans on the American Continent. The lost tribe of Israel. The whole shebang rooted in a lie. Figs ripened black over the grave of the girl, it was said.

Maybe it wasn't true, the neck slitting and well.

But that was all a long time ago, their prophet had said at the dedication of this place. *Nor can it be explained. No tongue can tell what happened.*

Let the Book of the Past be closed.

10.

Mary Elizabeth Baker

Our memories are in our teeth. Somebody said that. Teeth grow back, sometimes they do. I would not have known her name then, Saint Apollonia, my patron saint draped in the emerald cape clasped in front by a jeweled brooch. A circlet of desert flowers around her head—gilia, paintbrush, penstemon, fire chalice. How she came to me that winter bathed in light, in one hand the extraction forceps clamped around a single white tooth, and in the other a peacock feather, golden, as if to write my story, ours. And what are we but our stories? *Her* tormentors, they pulled out all her teeth. Every one. But sometimes teeth grow back. Sometimes they do.

Mine did.

The season of life both starts and ends at a spring. Vina, my sister, she had the long black hair shining down her back. Snakes sipped water below the flat rock where she taught me to pound laundry with a rock, rub fine sand in, then wade to our knees, wash out Mama's sky-blue sun dress and Papa's white shirt, brother's socks, the horses all making that sound they make when the time is at hand, the trip on, and it was April, the redbud in bloom. Dogwood laced with the wounds of our savior, white petals, that was our sign, *Sweet Jesus* Daddy said when he prayed, honeysuckle scenting the air. And it was a done deal, already. We didn't know that. Who could? Somebody named Parley done got himself killed chasing a woman, another man's wife, said she was sealed to him in the sky. Man killed him in our same district. In Arkansas, where I was born, and it was my birthday, FIVE on the cake Grandma made, gave me a sunbonnet made with her own hands, the only way she'd recognize me later, the stitch she'd learned from her mother and her from her mother, since the days they'd walked downhill from Henry County, Tennessee. Parley-Smarley, we didn't know shit, forgive my French. And those people called themselves the Danites, they'd got word of it. Avenging angels, I've since learned. They knew we were coming, salted our path with spies. So it was a done deal, our *ass was grass* the young-folk say.

Caravan Spring, that water was called afterward. Maybe I should go down there and make sure they put the marker at the right spring, the one where elms lined the creek bank, snakes sipped the silver water and Vina's hair grew past her waist. Black as night without stars.

Call me Betty, I'm not Martha anymore. Nor Mary. I'm especially not Mary. And never in a million years will I answer to Mary Beth, what Vina called me, the last two words Daddy ever said to me, only as a question, the last word rising, him walking off beside those fake soldiers who'd run off the fake Indians, so our men let out a whoop like the cavalry'd come to save the day or something like that, which was of course the furthest thing from the truth, not a real Indian in the mix for they went to the creek and washed off their fake war paint when it was done, washed off our blood.

The girl, Mary Beth, she had green eyes and hair like yellow corn silk held out of her face by the jade hair clasp Daddy'd traded for on the Oregon Trail where they camped so long it became home for her, the constant movement and going potty behind bushes, one front tooth growing in and then the other, waking up with the bright green piece of grown up jewelry under her pillow with the sky already turned to dust by the herd. Always the smell of wood smoke, they cooked with it in their hair, and then it was summer time, and what else was there to do but be Levina's baby doll, let her do my hair up in a French braid, the world flattening out and starting to rise, seemed to me, the career of my childhood spread over Oklahoma and Kansas, Nebraska where we followed this river for about ten years it seemed and saw our first live Indian, a Sioux on horseback who stole some of our cows, and taught me to say *mini wakan*, holy water, when we had him to our three wagons for supper. He wanted to touch my hair, I don't reckon he'd ever seen a towhead. *Mini wakan*, he said, pointed to the river and then west, *holy water*.

Daddy kept them in a leather pouch, my teeth. His name was George, Daddy. *Georgie Porgy puddin and pie, kissed the girls and made them cry*, Vina taught me to sing. She had this way of looking at you that made time go fast or slow, whichever she wanted. Are we almost there, are we?

Almost, Vina said. *Almost.*

Captain Fancher was a fiddler. He played some nights and I'd lay with my back to the ground in a land where wild Indians rode spotted ponies and feel that music thrum through the night air and once in August the sky got gaudy with shooting stars, so even the fiddle went quiet like church, little baby Jesus in the manger.

I lost six in all, one for each month? Where he kept them was a mystery to me then, the leathern pouch, but each time I'd wake with something under my pillow, which was no pillow at all, just a rolled up dress. And the last something under my pillow that was not a pillow was the emerald green hair pin, a piece for a grown up, the color of life and living. If I ever lost it, I knew, that would be it. The moment I lost my hair pin, that's the exact second Mary Beth ceased to be.

Maybe I should go out there and point to the right place?

Betty Terry, who I am now.

Newspaper man come up from Little Rock to take my story. He'd never been hungry a day in his life, can see it in his eyes, right there. Nope, never had his stomach roll over and then roll over again. Take a pot of chili, just for hell of it. For the hell of it. How you remember it. First thing, you and Vina get out the tripod and Dutch oven, set it up yonder in the spot where Georgie Porgy's to build a fire, he and brother get back with the wood. No fighting or pulling hair or saying *double-dog-dare.* Birds watch you go in the bushes—you can see their little birdie eyes, crickets making that crikety sound. Mama's name is Minerva, which Vina says is a name for a goddess. Mama's a goddess who teaches us to make chili on a night we've left town so fast because they don't like us, won't sell us no wheat for flour, *not one goddamn kernel,* one of them said.

So Georgie Porgy's got the fire going and we let it burn down some, just a little, the black cast iron's hot and Mama—Minerva—does some goddess stuff that renders oil into the pot, throws in onion dice grown from the soil where I was born, bell pepper and jalapeño, a bright red pimento for color and garlic to keep the vampires away, she swears on the Bible, Vina.

Georgie'd killed a deer, dressed it from a tree limb so the neck meat was cubed and sizzles when it hits the oil, the aroma already thick from the saute, and Mama takes out her wooden box with hinges Georgie'd made, inside little tins full of salt and red pepper flakes, cayenne, cumin, which Minerva called *zira,* sassafras leaf and bay, she throws in this and that and the dry wood cackles, old knotty knot. Red beans from last night, ladled into the cast iron and beefsteak tomato canned from last summer's garden. She let me drink the juice, mama. Vina peeled them with the sharp-sharp blue handled knife, quartered them, dumped in with both hands, and I get to stir with a wooden spoon size of a boat paddle. One of the horses screams from the meadow, you can hear the mules munching sweet grass while we make supper, and don't know what's coming, me and Vina and Georgie and Minerva, brother—I can't see their faces any more now, toothless old me.

Maybe there was cheese and cornbread and vinegar pepper and butter, even, so that each of our bowls set steaming on the board while Daddy prayed: *Sweet Jesus, dear God, thank you for this day, thank you for my family who I love, give us safe passage, Lord, help us this day to do things in a good way. Thank you for this food, bless those who do without.* Something like that, he prayed. I remember him looking down at the ground across from Mama, Vina to my right, my faceless brother.

Amen.

Amen, we said.

I taste that chili. It was a Sunday. The Lord's Day. We'd taken a rest. Mr. Fancher, he'd preached a sermon out of the book, forty days and forty nights in the wilderness, the devil tempting Jesus, *I can give all of this to you*, Satan said.

We'd taken the Lord's Supper. *Eat this in my name, for it is my body. Drink this in my name, for it is my blood.* Sung the songs. Mama'd played her dulcimer.

Sage as far as the eye could see, adrift on a sea of it. Daddy cut me a sliver of cornbread, topped it with molasses mashed with butter—poor man's jelly. Later, with my next family, I'd learn they eat it for dessert out here, cornbread. I'm from a place where cornbread isn't dessert, and a desert where it is.

"Here's for the pretty one," he said.

It was still hot, the bread. I crumbled some in my chili, brought the spoon to my mouth, and it was good. I fancy how we must have looked from afar, from the bluff and stone where they were hiding already, watching us, waiting for daylight, for the Lord's Day to pass.

Could they smell our food?

Were they hungry?

As they painted each other's faces, did they want to join our meal, clasp hands, pray to Jesus, break bread into chili? All the young men who missed their wives, their sisters.

Because we'd have shared, I know we would have, we'd have given all we had, more. And tomorrow might have never come.

Their men might have refused their orders, and that sunrise when the bullets waked us would undo itself, and Vina would yawn and call me sleepy head. We'd have washed our faces in the cold spring water, and Georgie Porgy would fry bacon in a cast iron over the re-stoked fire. The mules would bray and the cattle bawl, and I'd sit beside Minerva on the buckboard of the wagon pulled by six oxen, little silver bells jingling from their giddy up. Deseret would have grown small behind us, and the day when we'd top the hill, and before us all who'd walked from Arkansas would be the sea, spread out blue across the horizon from one end of the world to the other, and we'd know that this was the place, that we'd done the right thing, that for the rest of our lives we could do anything we set our minds to because we'd made it home.

And tomorrow might never have come.

11.

He's listening to Mohammed's radio. Driving Geronimo's Cadillac. Moonlight on his dashboard, the green-green hair clasp in his right front pocket chill against his thigh, he cruises, he flies through the space between places, towns named Toquerville and La Verkin and Hurricane, the Vermillion Cliffs, bumfuck, it might as well be the moon. Hard faces before and behind, Joey Harvell passes from Hilldale, Utah into Colorado City, Arizona—sister cities bound by polygamy, where the multitude is solemnized by celestial marriage. He wished for a second time he'd thought to bring Jimmy's silver-plated .38 with its leather holster and bronze snap. Arizona, where he was born, Joey, on Christmas Day, fifty-seven years ago, headed south, maybe he'd drive all goddamn night.

There's a town in Arizona named Surprise. He reads it by moonlight on the atlas O.W.'d given him along with Mama's blue and white Cougar after they'd buried Jimmy and he was headed back to Washington D.C. where Renee was pregnant, only he didn't know that yet. No shit, *Surprise.*

Had Mama noticed? Ever looked at a map? Seen that Arizona was on the left-hand side and Arkansas on the right, highway 10 bleeding up into 30, Bowie into Texarkana, she'd made the trip in a Greyhound bus when Joey was a toddler, some balls, taking a man's son away from him.

The last time he'd seen O.W., his adoptive father, when they'd driven from Mount Ida and Lake Ouachita, hit all the family cemeteries along the way, one great reckoning with the dead so Lara'd be able to find the way to her roots, the old man had looked him in the eye, maybe recognized him for a second, and called him *Bud.* Said, "I've enjoyed every minute of it, Bud," as they were leaving, after Trace had taken what would surely be the last, last photograph of them together in this living world. Bud, the name of his blood father, who was dead now, who he'd never meet. O.W. had called him Bud, sweet old man with his blue eyes losing his mind. Did he remember Mama, seeing the last look on her face? "She's pretty," he'd said on a bench outside the funeral home. Cigarette butts spilled out the front porch ashtray.

There'd been a woodpecker hammering up high in a hickory. Lonoke is beyond his being now. He would never go there again. He'd said the last words.

Surprise, Arizona. Goddamn.

He climbed the Kaibab Plateau, reverse of the time they'd driven out in a snowstorm, followed the plow whose blade threw sparks. The road one drove to Lee's Ferry, the launching point for the Grand, when fear of the big water was already in your gut and you ran House Rock left in a dream, hit the Ledge Hole at Lava.

At a rest stop overlook, the Milky Way spinning like a son of a bitch above, and the great gorge splicing a dark wedge below, he set up the cook stove at a picnic table where the Navajo lady sometimes sold her mojos, fried the burgers in Worcestershire, salted and peppered them, and squirted out mustard on two buns. He unfolded the Buck knife from his hip, sliced a tomato on the cooler lid, poured whiskey into his coffee mug, gave it a squeeze of lemon, a jolt of water. The moon threw his shadow sideways onto the rock wall and its interpretive guide for the mind boggling geography below.

He covered the pan and let the cheddar melt, munched a handful of Fritos from the Beaver gas station where he'd felt the eyes in the hard faces on him, where he'd kicked his tires and checked the oil before driving down to Mountain Meadows where his people lay buried.

Tomorrow was Thursday. Thoroughly Thursday, Renee'd say. Her back in Salt Lake, *I love you, be careful the note says*. Lara's gift of sea-salted chocolate.

The burger was good, the first one and the second. He wished for pickles, drink the juice to ward off cramps. He got them sometimes, hard in the thighs like his grandfather.

A satellite flew overhead—could it see him?

They were songs he'd heard a long time ago, "Mohammed's Radio," "Geronimo's Cadillac," hard to forget, like breaking your nose, it just wouldn't go away. O.W. loved Fritos. Kept a bag always in his eighteen-wheeler, the one they'd driven west that first time, Joey on the passenger side, look out on the middle of nowhere and see the flick of an ear, and of a sudden a hundred antelope appeared. Oddly enough, it had been O.W. that brought him west. Taking him back where he belonged?

On the hill outside Rawlins where they'd followed a truck hauling a Tilt-O-Whirl through a freak snow storm, and men walked in blaze orange shirts behind razor wire in the prison at the city limits.

He poured water in the pan, left it to soak. Zipped up in the mummy bag, be with me, Tunkasila, Renee and Lara. Keep us safe. Let us do things in a good way.

And Paris? Edgar? How on earth had the man tracked him down? Like Arkies had some kind of radar for each other. In jail. Arizona. They'd only release him to an adult who'd be responsible for him during the six weeks' probation.

For peeing. How could you get arrested for peeing?

Dumb mother fucker.

Flagstaff is an archipelago, a sky island that rears up in the very heart of Arizona, transitioning from dry grassland to desert to stands of spruce, which in turn gives way to the dwarf species and then Alpine, the shimmering aspen naked that morning when Joey drove into town, ears popping and hungry for breakfast, coffee, get this job over he'd dreaded since the first word. Brisk air streams through the cracked windows, October 25, a week before midterm elections, though Joey knows nothing about it, he's cut off all news since July 12, Si's 100th, when he'd stumbled on the grave at the edge of the cedars behind the teepee. What the hell could a Vacation Rental by Owner be thinking, up and burying people behind the rental. Who was it down there? A hammock swinging in the breeze just off to the south, somebody looking through the window glass, all those spirits. And then the party barge and driving home, stopping at all the cemeteries along the way, Si, Mama, Floradee, dragging all the dead behind them, and O.W.'d called him Bud, name of the blood father he'd never met but talked to on the phone sometimes before he died. And now here he was in Arizona where he was born on a Sunday morning, Christmas Day, in the year it had rained like a mother fucker for eight whole months, and the desert bloomed unbelievably, Mama'd said.

He drove past signs for Sunset Crater and Snow Bowl, Highway 89 turning into Old Route 66, past Industrial Drive to the Fourth Street Overpass, where he hangs a Louie on East Butler, and another on Old Sawmill, and there he is, a little shy of nine, at the Coconino County Detention Center, presided over by Sheriff James Lester Clark.

To provide safe and humane housing for perpetrators of both misdemeanor and felony offense, the Coconino County Sheriff's Office takes great pride in itself for the respect with which our employees treat our incarcerated family and their Significant Others, the website says. Commander of Detention is Mathia Figuro and the Lieutenant of Intake, Thomas Maxwell. Lieutenant for the Page Facility is Officer R. Stoner, the man he's been instructed to ask for upon arrival, so that Paris might be processed over to Joey's custody for six weeks until he's clear. He's to hook up with a nonprofit in Salt Lake, do the two hundred hours of community service. He can only be released to an acquaintance who agrees to be responsible for him, Paris. The call had come out of nowhere. What do you do? Edgar Paris was kith, if not kin. *Fuck it*, Joey'd said, made ready the place in the basement, across the concrete floor from the room their dog had slept in before they had to put her down. Renee wasn't happy. Lara was off at school.

Inside smells like jail.

The sounds are the same, buzzes and clicks, the smell of hidden cigarettes and bad food and toilet stink masked by Pine Sol. For the second time in twenty-four hours, Joey's stomach did a backflip, it all came back to him, his time in, that one time in Washington County when he'd walked home from the Library Club where the Cate Brothers had sung "Hey Mr. Union Man," and a cop had driven up on him, rolled down the window, said get in. Before Joey knew it, he was in county, mistaken for a felon from California who was 5'2" and had blond hair to Joey's 5'10" and brown. The arresting officer had had his foot run over in the field. He was pissed. It was in a silver brace, the foot. Three days, no blanket, metal bunk. In the heatless basement of the Washington County Jail. It had occurred to him then, at twenty-four, that he might not ever get out, that they'd find out about the other, send him down the river and he'd never come back.

It could have gone that way. It could have. The scar on the index finger of his right hand sears to the bone where the separation occurred. Twenty years ago, when he was Assistant Prof of History at the College in the Cow Pasture, Renee called it, Paris had helped him out then. He owed it to him, Joey did.

Was it possible to recover, from being locked down?

Officer Stoner hadn't arrived from Page yet, a pretty Indian clerk behind glass said, so Joey took a seat in waiting and waited. The television was on. Joey hated more than hardly anything daytime TV, especially the mind-numbing schlock on in the morning, *Good Morning America*, *Let's Make a Deal*. The magazines were all *People* or *Field and Stream*, "Will you trade for what's behind curtain number two on the screen," the big-cleavage brunette half-whispers, aside a jackass they've taught to bray on cue.

Outside the one window is the yard, a worn ribbon of dirt around the perimeter where prisoners clearly walk. A sweat lodge frame of bent willows curved above the ground west-facing, Uwipi colors tied into its branches. Grandfather stones were piled off to one side, twenty-eight of them, Joey knows, seven for each round.

A Mr. Coffee maker reeked of scorched coffee beside the TV. Joey poured a styro-cup, dumped in some powdered creamer, considered going out to his truck to gnaw on the cheese block. Knock back some cold apple juice. And it was at that moment, just as he was deciding, that he first met Officer Roger Stoner.

Had Chief Joseph the power of telecommunication, that hot-wired connection to animal and sky and spirit world so often assumed of the red man by whites who'd peed their pants when they found out you were a real Indian, who want to touch the twin Sundance scars above your nipples, see your scalps and buffalo skin, smoke your peace pipe, your peyote, go in your teepee, see your barefoot squaw, had he that mainline to *Wakan Tanka* and *Tunkasila* and *ska-ska*, he would have smoke-signaled Joey Harvell not to open his mouth nor look the man in the eye, bad shit happened when you sassed Stoner, when you met his gaze, Medusoid, son of a bitch turn you to stone. Worse. Chief knows.

Commander of Detention Figuro had taken an interest in Chief because of him being Lakota, which is different from the Navajo he was used to arresting, putting behind bars, all that blue door facing east hogan shit. That Chief was Lakota meant he was kin to the ancient race of horse raiders from the east, that he shared blood with Chief Arvel Lookinghorse up to Green Grass who was said to keep in his possession the original White Buffalo Calf Woman pipe, brought down to the people in person during this real bad time, and it was used for healing, bringing back the buffalo and creepy crawlers, the birds and deer and antelope and rabbit. She'd taught them to grind *chinchasha* from willow bark and mullein, to make prayer song in the *inipi*. Figuro knew all this because he'd once been a white Indian himself, walked the red road up in Salt Lake as a boy, a whole goddamn tribe of Jack Mormons up their shredding their Jesus Jammies and taking on the way of the pipe, going in lodge, Sundance in summer, offering flesh, the boom-boom of drums at daylight as elders donned their eagle feathers, danced their way in the eastern gate before first light. He'd seen all that as a young man, Figuro had, so when he got word that he had himself a real-deal Lakota on the premises, that the man knew the Bringing in the Stones song, and The Four Directions, Sending Home the Spirits, and Filling the Canupa, when he found out it became a matter of the 1978 Indian Religious Freedom Act. Cut and dried, and Chief Joseph—Figuro's call for him, but his real name was Fred Black, only sometimes he went as Fred Stone, what they called him at Cut Off Bar and Grill where he got caught the last time for taking the register one Sunday morning, when all he'd broke in for was a glass of cold tap beer, that's all, wasn't it?—he was given the task of gathering willow people from Wild Donkey Creek, grandfather stones from the UFO Crater, bundles of red, yellow, black and white cloth for tie ins, a twenty-pound bag of tobacco and tanned elk hide for the drums. Galvanized three-gallon bucket with a gourd strung to it for inside, two five-gallon sheetrock buckets for out. They'd prayed over the space, someone brought an eagle. Chief built a real sweat lodge in the yard of Coconino County Jail. Only rule was, no one but Indians could go inside.

No one but Indians.

And they had to plan lodges a month in advance—get approval for each man in. Which meant that Equinox Lodge, the one in September, the one he'd let that sad-faced Arky climb into so he could get free for a while, that was a violation of the deal, not to mention Federal Law. And Stoner, he had some kind of beef with the Arky. Who knows what. And when he found out from one of the rats about ceremony, how Arky'd gone off had had hisself a vision, he'd called Chief into the very same room where he just took Joey Harvell who—if Edgar be trusted—was also an Arky, only emigrated to Utah now. Not a Mormon. For sure not.

Problem was, Chief had started to believe in his own shit, like maybe the canupa and prayer songs were really working, that he maybe *did* have a radio channel straight to the great mystery. His cravings had left him. Everyone noticed a difference. Even his cat, Rudolph the Red, knew the difference. He purred, looked him in the eye, and came to understand human talk. Maybe he *was* hot-wired to the animals and sky, Chief, maybe he was.

Because after Stoner questioned him in the little white room with no windows, when Chief had looked him in the eye and said that the Indian did not own *Tunkasila*, that ceremony was what the heart understood, Stoner'd nodded, the two's eyes locked. He felt it then, Chief, the original black dog.

And after it was done, when he returned to the cell and Rudolph had gone missing, the engine caught and started out in the lot for the drive to Page which was Stoner's jurisdiction, Chief could read the scared animal's telegraphed thoughts.

I'm sorry Rudolph.

I know you are, Fred. I know.

Had he the power, he'd of told this new Arky to keep his head down, just say yes and no, take the other Arky, drive away in a good way.

But that Indian shit was all a load, wasn't it? When he got out, Fred would get himself a barrel of beer, jump in and never come out. The hell with them all. Especially Stoner. May he drop dead.

May he.

Tunkasila.

12.

But tomorrow did come, didn't it.

And that's what they want, those newspaper boys who suffer themselves to drive up from Little Rock, who've never been hungry a day in their lives and so do not fathom the part about the chili, how we'd live off it the five days, eat it and be sustained until the siege ended and they herded us that last mile, loaded the youngest into a wagon with little harness bells and from a distance we heard what the newspaper folk want to know, the tale no one should live to tell. To hell with all that. Let be.

Star man sees me though. November now, it's always November. Hanging up there bright enough to throw shadow, just to the left of the Hunter, lifts his club to whomp the bull, the one J.W. called Dog Star, Sirius, the brightest in the sky, he's there, I'm looking at him right now. Blood in my veins, breath in my throat, very real this moment to be alive.

He spreads his arms, feet wide, the Milky Way gauzy for his hair, he's my Star Man, and he's promised to look over me, to see me through, and hasn't he? No? Stars are made up of the same stuff as us, that's what J.W. said. On this very porch, star-lit with his hair combed back. See it on his teeth when he smiled.

My man.

The story I alone can tell.

At the center of our galaxy, the Dog Star, and isn't Boone County home? Where I married J.W. in a church by a preacher named Calvin. I was twenty-two and he was too, and he bought this land with sawmill money, ripped the timber hisself and built this house a stone's throw from Crooked Creek, right of Shake Rag Hollow, how about them apples. Fitted all the joints, the ceiling joist and rafters, the shake roof, tongue and groove floor, bright window panes puttied just so, glazed into the sash. We lived in a lean-to while he worked. I'd boil him potatoes, drizzle on butter from the neighbors, a little turnip mashed in for look, sass-greens. Some days he'd let me wear his nail apron with its frame hammer and square, plumb-bob, shiny nails with silver points, a knife with a curved blade and the thick pencil he'd scribed my name with, a heart with an arrow through it. At night, we'd lay under the quilt. I'd smell the sawdust in his hair, hear Crooked Creek running. There, right there, on our backs with nothing but the whole universe in front of our faces. And it was always November. We'd wake with frost in our hair.

But before sleep he'd tell me about my Star Man, how his head and face was nine light years from us that second, and that light travels at a hundred-and-eighty-six thousand miles-per-second, so that what we were seeing then from under the quilt where he smelled like creek water and sawdust, it was fossil light, didn't in fact even exist anymore except that we could still see it, what did I think about that?

The air was like before a snow. He'd not cut his hair—it tickled my shoulder. Star Man lifted his hands over us to pray, and I knew then, I knew. I breathed him in and he's still there, right here, this moment, he'll never leave me.

Not ever.

I tried to hate them. I did.

That first All Hallows with the Lees.

Well a Mormon loves Halloween, let me tell you. This was at the Fort, the one called New Harmony, I don't know why. And his other kids, they mamas'd made them all costumes out of old rags and ripped up sheets and such, one of them wore a wig and another feathers. "What are you going to be?" a girl who talked to me asked.

I said, "Nothing."

It was day before. Some of the wives were pumpkin carving, cooking the seeds over wood fire, row of jack-o-lanterns with their guts all spilling out, the women up to their elbows in the gore, the white seeds smeared with it.

She, the girl who sometimes talked to me, she said, "You can't be nothing. I'll be your sister."

"My sister is Vina," I said.

"Well I'll be Vina now."

The sun on her raven hair, how when they led her away the harness bells jingled. I said, "I hate you."

The girl, my new sister, she said, "No you don't." Put her arms around me, held me tight and I let her. And she was right, I didn't hate her. I didn't know how. They'd never taught me how to do that, Georgie and Minerva.

And what do you know, it *did* snow. Not flakes big as two hands joined together like it did in the desert, but silver dollars, six white inches by the time we woke, V-ed in the limbs of hickories, and still coming down, the day we moved into our house, laid a fire in its hearth. I dressed in his clothes that day, his warm flannel against my chest, wore his socks for gloves, his big ugly boots. And when he called me I came to him, in the front yard, what would be the front yard, right out there, you see. And together we tromped the outline of where the barn would be, the chicken coop, the pig's pen. A cellar where I'd stock blackberry jam in silver mason jars, fermented muscadine juice for the hollerdays, persimmons, country ham for Easter. Then we stood up on the tongue and groove front porch, right here on this spot where my chair rocks, and the sun came out, so it was bright as crystal in the desert. We surveyed what would become of our lives, me and J.W. Terry. I held his big carpenter's hand and he held mine, and I was Betty Terry then, Mary Beth Baker was dead with the rest of them, buried in a hole, covered with rocks.

One of the wives dressed up in an outfit that another of us—the ones who'd been carted away from our wagons near the spring in the meadow—recognized straight away as her mother's. I was with my new Vina, we'd switched clothes for the Trick or Treat, she was me and I was her. They'd cooked this kind of soup. The pumpkins were glowing, you could smell the candles scorching the insides. And Mormons love Halloween, all around there were devils and vampires and ghosts, demons and walking dead, werewolves devouring little girls while goat-headed boys danced the hoochie coo. Somebody, one of the women, had fake blood dripping from her mouth. A boy was Grim Reaper, a sharpened scythe gripped in his hands.

"That's Mama's," the girl who was one of us said. "You got on mama's dress."

The whole party got quiet. My sister hugged me and I hugged her back.

John D., who everyone called Father, he stood up. Drew the knife from inside his boot, so the light caught it, the jack-o-lantern glow. He crossed the room. Had to walk around people. They were demons.

With his left hand, he took the girl's hair. Leaned her back. Cut her throat from one ear to the other. Carried her out the front door.

No one else of us ever said a word.

The night of the November snow we made snow cream, me and J.W. I gathered a bowlful and he said to make sure it wasn't yellow. We didn't have a dog then, not yet. I filled a bowl, stayed away from the yellow. The house was not all closed in. There was vanilla, sugar, eggs maybe, I don't remember. Our first night in our house, and we were married. I was Betty Terry. The snow cream was sweet, it hurt my teeth. *Look*, J.W. said, *here*. Out the window that was not a window, a deer nibbling branches, chewing the bark off, the wind ruffling its fur.

"Supper," he said.

I said, "Don't."

He said, "We need the meat."

"Mama wore vanilla on her wrists. Just here." I lifted both mine to his face, so the moon thrown a shadow across the tongue and groove. "It's our first night."

A coyote sing-songed down off the branch.

He said, "Is this our dinner then? snow cream?"

"You like it?"

He said, "I like it fine."

Sixty-five years ago, right here on this place. We lay our pallet on the new laid floor, and the moon shone on the snow through the window that was not a window. Coyote yip-yap, and that quiet sound when all's covered with a layer of white, some yellow, my name shining out off the front porch I'd see in the morning. Skin on skin, I breathed him into me. He said *I love you*. And I said it back. That night I dreamed of Apollonia whose tormentors pulled out her teeth, and our teeth are where our memories are storied, somebody said that. I'd forgot about the snow cream, the first fire, the deer, what came after. Tomorrow I'll walk down to the creek, make sure they get the marker to the right spot, where me and first Vina washed clothes and snakes sipped water at our feet.

And tomorrow came, for me and J.W., deer tracks all over where we'd tromped our barn, our chicken coop, and those places we didn't have names for yet. Over there, the well, artesian at first, water chestnut grew on the water. Yonder, the roses where the Blue Racer lived. The turtle with the painted shell. Where we danced naked in a thunderstorm when I was pregnant with Willy. The new moon smiling even now. The place where I'd bury him, in November with his nail apron on, so it would always be November, hammer it into my heart. Made this house with his own hand, so I could be Betty Terry.

Snow cream, it was cold, hurt my teeth, but it was good. Wasn't it?

A man in a wagon come and hauled us home, took forever. That's how long it took to get home, forever. All downhill, where the rivers change directions and you fall for a mile and keep on falling so the air grows thick in your lungs, and the sounds you grew up with come again, cicada, whippoorwill, wind broken by new leaf. I was seven by then, I'm guessing. The new sister, she waved me bye, put her hand over her heart. Springtime in that place where storms blew in off the desert, so you could see the bruised band of wicked cold air coming forty miles off, snow in its teeth, and sometime dust devils, they'd whirl into the house, slamming all the doors so the wives would lay down with one another, and sister'd hold my hand, and the woman who'd dressed in the slit-necked girl's mama's clothes, she'd call my name, and the one we called Father, he'd not blink an eye, sit out front and watch it with that cold eye of his, the one he looked at me with sometimes, like he was trying see inside me. My heart?

The desert bloomed that spring the wagon come. He knew our names, the man with the beard. He called for us by name. *Martha Elizabeth Baker*, he said. *Mary Beth?*

They didn't want to let us go, the wives. Nor our new sisters and brothers, they cried. *Don't take them,* they said.

Sister wouldn't turn me loose. She said, "Don't go. Tell him you want to stay on here. Tell him."

We wore each other's clothes, me and sister. We were twins.

Father said, "Let the girl speak."

And they turned their faces to me, that desert light once seen, never forgot. I had not yet reached the age of accountability, when you took the vow and your soul was made clean and you were sealed to sainthood forever and ever. But some of the rest of us were.

Father was out under the sun. The bearded man had come for us and there had been words. He wore a gun on his hip, Captain did. Men on horseback accompanied the wagon. They were soldiers, bright eyes flashing. Some of Father's older boys had gone inside for long guns. I could see them looking out the windows, my big brothers. One of them had given me a rock for my birthday, with the print of an animal on it that had lived a thousand million years ago—that's what he said, a thousand million.

It got so quiet, thunder-quiet. Like during the wordless prayer that was so quiet no one knew when it was over. So it could go on forever, if Father didn't amen it done.

The horses knew.

They held their breaths, the bright-eyed soldiers frozen in their saddles.

Let the girl speak, Father'd said. I'd ate their food, wore their clothes, said their prayers, had taken their doctoring, their medicine, sang their songs, laughed their laughs, our time had blended, the desert had got into me. The wife who'd become my mother, I looked her in the eye. She did not look away, and I could see it in her face. She loved me.

I tried to hate them. With all my heart, I tried to hate them. But they were just people. Like us, Georgie Porgy and Minerva, my faceless brother, Vina with her shining black hair eating chili in September, our last supper before the other thing started, the one the newspaper boys suffer themselves to drive up to the sticks, what they want to hear about, shout it from the rooftop, paint it in the sky.

Bearded Captain man, he said, "Get your stuff. All of you, get your stuff."

"Give us some time?" Father said.

Shadow flashed over the bearded man's face. He was afraid Father'd hurt us. That he'd do what had been done to the others, the rest of us who'd walked from Arkansas. That's what he was thinking, that Father might hurt us. Part of me knew. Say it was May, June, maybe. Not hot yet. They let us eat lunch together, and the new mama, I never knew her name, she wrapped some food for me in burlap, an apple, cheese, a piece of sugar candy. "And you'll be wanting this," she said.

In her hand, a woven hat, the design of which my grandmother would recognize in Boone county when forever passed and I was home again, but did we ever really get there, home? Do we ever?

So we broke bread and ate soup together. Bearded Captain joined us, and one of the bright-eyed cowboy soldiers, he had a bowl of soup, buttered bread. And then we said our goodbyes, each to each.

Sister gave me a comb with a silver clasp on it something like the one I'd lost at the siege, where bullets had flown through the wagon roof and hit a bag of flour, and we'd got down low to do everything, except at night time when it was safe, and then it wasn't. I dreamed the flour was snowing in our hair. I gave her the rock brother'd give me with the thousand-million-year-old animal inside.

She said, "I'll always be your sister."

"I know," I said.

The new mama hugged me bye. She said, "Don't forget me."

I said, "I won't."

We loaded up. There were more of us up the road, and more even further. We'd be picking up Mountain Meadow orphans clean to Salt Lake City it seemed. We all looked back at that wind-swept desert of sage and juniper, red rock in the distance, big country with room to grow, where you could see forty miles off the front porch and know a storm was coming two hours before it got there. They've shown me pictures of the monument, the one with Father's name on it, how it was named for the town where the prophet discovered golden tablets, and how the Indians who'd attacked us that far-off September were the lost tribe of Israel, the Lamanites whose reunion with the lost white brother and sister would signal the end of the old world and the beginning of the new.

We all looked back, we all did. They stood in the front yard waving, and we waved back. They cried, and so did we. I'd tried to hate them. Lord, God, I tried with every ounce that is me. But I couldn't.

Sister stood out alone from the rest. I held up my hand. I made the sign that meant *I love you.* The harness jingle-jingled.

And this is how I lost my second family.

13.

The days leading up to his release from jail were the very worst for Edgar, something would go wrong—the Harvell boy'd get cold feet, Stoner'd root out some dirt on him, they'd somehow translate his pissing on John D. Lee from state to federal because it was the Grand Fucking Canyon and all, a National Park, DMF, who'd he think he was, pulling his dick out in a national park? Something'd go squirrely on him and he'd be stuck in the pokey forever, walking the thin bare line around the perimeter of the yard, hearing dogs bark over in the subdivision off Butler Road, the click-clack of his cell locking and unlocking, twelve cinder blocks one way, twelve the other, 144, a devil number if he recalls right, those days back home on Illinois Bayou, where his mama'd take him of a Sunday to the Full Gospel where preacher Roy Dale Shoates shitkicked the cardboard box full of copperheads, little fuckers in there rattling around, sticking out they forked tongues, striking, so poison leaked through. Then Sister Yvonne would strap on her pink Flying V, belt out "I'm in the Gloryland Way," and somebody'd go into a shit fit, start speaking in tongues, and another'd interpret, *Gog rises in the east against Magog,* and then they'd pass the serpents, set to anointing the heads of sinners with oil, the healings would begin. Somebody'd scream something about the twelve tribes and another the twelve apostles, and a third, "lo, a lamb stood on a mount, and with him a hundred and forty-four with their Father's name writ on they foreheads," and had that prophecy not chased his ass here to this very place, twelve one way and twelve the other. 144. DMF. Something would go wrong. Edgar knew it.

That last Wednesday night was a full moon, and he woke to Chief Joseph standing outside his cell, washed in moonlight, in one hand a white eagle feather, the holiest of all, and in the other the very book from whence he'd found the name Rudolph the Red, what he had called the calico cat that could commune with him in a language no tongue could speak.

"Hello Chief."

"Ain't my name."

The moon threw him shadow wings. Across the floor outside the bars, they trembled and glowed.

Edgar had a cousin named Beaver, changed his name to Bob.

"Name's Fred. Fred Black or Fred Stone. Sometimes just Red Fred."

Whoever got used to sleeping on a metal bunk? What on earth were they thinking, making a man sleep on a metal cot. Nothing to read but the Book of MoMo, lay over there burning a hole through the bed. He dare not look at a word, Edgar.

"I like that. Red Fred."

"You never told me what you did." His moonshadow quivered. "You kill a man?"

Edgar said, "Pissed. Peed on one. And he weren't even real."

Chief laughed, just one syllable, *huh.*

"You?"

"Stole a beer. I'm here for stealing beer."

"That's the shits."

"Is, idn't it."

Who knew what time it was, something going wrong already, he could feet it. Harvell'd run into trouble, changed his mind, who knew what all could happen. Bad moon a'rising, trouble on the way, his stomach scrunched up like a fist.

"Thanks for pouring water. In that sweat."

The Indian's eyes were darker than the rest, icepick holes in the dark that lead to a darker dark.

"It's a load. All that."

Stoner'd taken his cat, thrown it out of his truck at ninety, word was. "Sorry about Rudolph."

"Here," he said. "Brung you this."

Edgar climbed down once more from the metal bunk, the concrete chill beneath his feet. What he'd give for a pair of wool socks. Maybe the Harvell boy'd bring him some socks.

"Your book."

Chief said, "My book. It's about real people. I met one."

Inside the cover, on the first page, in blue ink, somebody'd written:

Fred—

       Resist much. Obey little.
       Now. Or Never.

           Ken Sleight

"He a real person? Ken Sleight?"

"Seldom Seen Smith. Bought me a beer once at the Cut Off. You'd like him. He's one of us."

To be honest, Edgar wasn't big on book reading. Used to be, he'd read the Bible just to keep awake in church, the endless drone of whatever square-necked preacher was going at it from the pulpit. X-rated Song of Solomon, Revelations, the Devil and God Almighty making bets on Job, the book of Revelations.

"Is he the author? Ken?"

"Sort of. He did the things in the book."

A door out there somewhere opened, shut, the lock clicking. Tomorrow, he'd walk out of here, put this place behind him, never come back. Six weeks' mandatory custody with the Harvell kid, then Katy bar the door, he'd take his ass back to Arkansas, better believe it.

"You giving it to me?"

"Going away gift. I don't need it no more. *Rudolph lives*."

"What's 'at mean?"

Someone was coming. The white feather disappeared, the shadow wings. Chief reached a brown hand through the bars and Edgar shook it, and for all the rest of his last moonlit night in the Coconino County Detention Center, his back to the metal bunk, Edgar poured over the words that turned into a story that got into his blood some, so that he imagined answers to his future and his past, the feathery seam of the present.

He waited that way, hope sour in his stomach.

Stoner'd had him cold, Joey.

A little side office with a desk and two chairs, nothing on the walls, a manila folder with papers paper-clipped together inside, a pen on top of the folder. One man sat on one side, the other on the other. He wore a gun, Stoner. A badge on his chest, heart side. It was a Thursday, can anything good ever come from a Thursday. A calendar lay in front of him, the officer. Paris was in here somewhere, who he really didn't know much except he'd helped him out once—he'd of lost the finger if it hadn't been for Edgar there at the Tri-County Coon Club. Where he'd been invited to give the Mardi Gras Lupercalia Catfish Supper talk on his dissertation: the history of strife between Mormons and Southerners. There'd been a man there named Love, who'd lost a daughter to this crazy lived up in the hills south of Long Pool, a Fundamental Latter Day Saint, turned out, who ran sort of a commune out in the sticks with six wives or whatever. The Love girl'd been invited to a Christmas party which turned out to be an execution. He'd killed them all, this crazy FLDS Bishop, arranged them at a big long table and had Christmas dinner with them, each in their spot. It had been big news, the R'Ville killings, how they'd uncovered the Love girl down off Illinois Bayou. She'd been wearing sunflower pajamas—for some reason he remembered the sunflower pajamas.

So, when he got to the Mountain Meadows part of the talk, where all those bodies got thrown into a shallow grave, each one with a bullet hole or blunt force trauma in back of its skull, the father—who sat straight across the table from him, just like Stoner—lost his shit. He made a sound, stood up and screamed. He'd just got to the part about the white flag treachery, how the Fancher party'd been sworn freedom if they lay down their weapons, how they'd sent Captain Fancher's daughter out with a white flag.

And Love exploded.

Joey'd pointed an index finger at him, his right hand, said *Is he talking to me?* or *Is he alright?* or something like that, and the man had leaned over the table and bit his finger off, just below the top knuckle, swallowed it, run out the front door and into the wood. They'd set dogs on him. Found him naked in the fork of a tree, somehow coaxed the finger from him—Joey'd never really understood this part, hadn't he *swallowed* it?—put it on ice. And Edgar Paris had driven it to the surgeon at St. Mary's who'd sewn it back on, predicting he'd get some mobility back, not all. That was the story, how it had come down. How he'd come to be sitting across a desk from Roger D. Stoner, a Lee on his mother's side, the *D* of his middle name standing for Doyle, as in John *Doyle* Lee, thus tying him to the incident at Mountain Meadows just as surely as Joey's *M* for *Marion* ties him to the same. On either side of the table, the two men stared.

He was hungry, Joey, should've eaten breakfast before coming here to the Coconino County Jail, where that emptiness in his stomach—ever since he'd hit fifty—was liable to make him queasy and weak, and he knew within an instant of setting eyes on Stoner that this was not a man to be weak in front of.

Dr. Harvell," Stoner'd said, "welcome to our jail."

Joey said, "Thank you. My privilege."

The calendar under his elbows was from Paxton Garage in Salt Lake City, had a glossy photograph of Yosemite for the month of October, where today's date was circled in red.

He smelled scorched coffee from the waiting room pot, caught just a snippet of TV which was now into the soaps, *One Life to Live, Days of Our Lives*.

"Says here you're from Salt Lake."

"I am," Joey said, his hands flat on the table.

Stoner nodded. Then he nodded some more. "Thing is, you don't sound like you're from Salt Lake. Do you?"

Then Joey said the thing they always said, him and Renee, wherever they ever went, Vienna, Paris, Berlin, Madrid, Mount Ida, Lonoke, or San Francisco, didn't matter a shit. "I *live* there, but I'm not *from* there."

Stoner's face did not give away that he'd gotten the code for every last thing that stood between them all the way back to the Poteets and Lees, and before, even, New York to Missouri to the Carthage, Illinois jail where who would be the prophet and see of the Lord was done in by bullets and bayonets.

He took the ink pen in his right hand, opened the file and made a note. And then he made another. "Driver's license. Proof of residence," Stoner said. He laid out three sheets of yellow paper and one pink, swiveled them for Joey to read.

The photo on Joey's license is old—his hair's long. From when his students said he looked like Eric Clapton. Stoner turns it over in his hands, sniffs it, rubs it with a thumb and forefinger.

"Not an organ donor," he said. "Why not?"

Joey said, "I don't know," passed over the title to his house from his own folder full of paper.

"*I-own-know*," Stoner said.

Let me tell you something about people who fake a Southern accent in front of a Southerner: they better by god be sure they're on the right side of the table and the door, and that the Southerner they mock doesn't get the draw on them. No road rage where I'm from, Joey tells his students, every one of them with a twelve-gauge shotgun behind the seat. Goofy fucking Mormons with their *Oh my heck*, tater tot casserole. He had the knife on his hip, Joey, but he hadn't brought Jimmy's silver .38, snapped in its leather case, the one he'd pulled from under the driver's seat after the car wreck, wrist deep in head blood.

The scar on his right index finger seared up his arm, and with a force of will that most often escaped him, he bit back the words about to come out of his mouth.

"You were seen at New Harmony yesterday. What for?"

Joey said, "Paying my respects."

"Took something."

He shook his head, Joey.

"No?"

Joey said, "No."

He wrote another note in the manila file, three words. "What's in your pockets?"

"I don't have to tell you that."

"Nope," Stoner said, "you don't."

He smiled. Just a little. He could have him searched. Look where the sun don't shine. They regarded each other.

Time passed. How breeze ruffles the fur of a run over dog, or a flipped bicycle tire keeps spinning after the wreck, a glint in the eye of certain snow men.

And that was that.

Joey filled out the paperwork, signed his name in blue ink on the pink form which was triplicate, and the yellow ones. He agreed to oversee the accused and convicted inmate, Edgar T. Paris from Arkansas, for a period of six (6) weeks, and report back prior to final release. If said inmate were to engage in any of the following, his rights to release were immediately revoked and the undersigned Joey Marion Harvell should return him immediately to the Coconino County Detention Center or become Accessory to the Crime After the Fact.

So help you, God.

So help me, God.

Edgar was released to Joey's custody. He was given back his wallet and street clothes. A beat-up pair of Redwings. The folding knife's gone. His truck is impounded back at the Page facility. He can pick it up during regular office hours with the proper paperwork. Were there any questions?

Stoner followed them out the front glass double-door. "I'm traveling same way as you'uns. Escort you if you like." That smile again.

Joey said, "No thank you, sir."

"Suit yourself."

He had those glasses on, mirrored like the sharpshooter in *Cool Hand Luke*, smiling that poisonous smile like he knew them through space and time back to some primordial level when one had fundamentally slighted the other.

"Be seeing you," Officer Stoner said.

Right there at the end, just as the two Arkansawyers climbed into the Pathfinder with its cracked side view, Joey made sure to use his blinker and not speed on the way out to the freeway and south toward home. But he knew that what the man had said was true, that they'd be seeing each other. All too soon.

He'd dreamed the last night, finally able to sleep through the last hours with Chief's magical book on his chest, moonlight getting in from somewhere, of the black semi-truck that had chased him across Oklahoma, somehow able to stay in front, cut him off at every pass. Whatever was inside had wanted Edgar dead, he was sure of it, hated him to the core. They'd been alone on the highway west. He'd never seen the face of who would kill him. And in the dream, lo, it was Edgar driving the truck, hauling ass, and when he tried the air brakes, no go, she sped up instead of slowing down. The Casteen girl, long-legged Tina who'd once carried his child, she was back behind in the refrigerated trailer, Elvis, the Shoates boy she'd died with, and all the rest, the poor souls in the caskets on aluminum racks designed to be invisible on fake grass beside the holes he'd dug from Dover to Lanty to Danville and the Hector cemetery where his daddy lay buried, a stake through his heart to keep the son of a bitch dead, even little Shiloh Love in her sunflower jammies, they were all back there clamoring like the snakes in the cardboard box the preacher'd shit-kick, all the naked dead from here to high water, after him, Edgar Paris, and why?

What had he ever done to them?

On this earth?

The good book lay on his chest in the moonlight, he could feel his heartbeat against it, through his chest, through his dream the answer in there somehow, the black marks that swirled together to make meaning. Crazed dreamer, Edgar dragged death down the road—toward what? What could hurt them now?

Before he knew it there was a whole goddamn caravan of black semis, of which he was only one, the walls of the trailers trembling and translucent, so he could see through to the passengers' anguish, their desire, what they wanted most in this world. And there was this one truck, so dark it sucked whatever light was left from the dashboards, the foglights, the blinking stars marking refrigerant checks, it sucked the moonlight from the room so the chill came, and even the book on his chest yielded to the cold.

What do you want from me?

They were from Arkansas, the women and boys and girls with their hideous grins and bone fingers. They'd been left unburied too long. A couple got away, let them be. The hollow sockets where their eyes should be, they questioned him, Edgar, begged him, *please.*

Please what, goddamnit?

And Chief Joseph's prayer came back to him then, *let what we're about to do bring no harm to any being, living or dead,* what he'd had to chew on between then and now: how could the living bring harm upon the dead? It was his business, death. Covering it up, making sure every shovelful settled down in a good way, tamping it with the metal bar, letting it settle, growing green grass over so the blades shone with dew drops of the morning, and ain't nobody going to claw their way out. No way, done deal. He'd buried for keeps, Edgar, hadn't he?

Behind him the wails of the dead, and before him, he could tell now, the cliff he'd driven toward his whole life. Now. Or never.

14.

Edgar unzipped and pulled it out, the book, slid between the empty cover of the Book of Mormon, the only words he'd been allowed to see, so they thought. The real pages he'd weighted with the smallest grandfather stone he could ferret from the pile, right down in the bottom of the toilet tank. Clever Edgar, he'd salvaged Chief's gift, and so the answer, in there somewhere. With his peripheral vision, Harvell watched. Shook his head and gave a dirty look when he touched his zipper. The new cover had no words, just a man emblazoned in gold with a trumpet to his lips, standing on a ball, blowing.

Harvell raised his eyebrows, spat out the open window. "You a Mormon, now?"

"Hell fuck no," Edgar said.

He slid the real book out of the fake one. There were real people in there, Chief had met them. From these parts, could be anybody.

They hadn't said six words since Flag. Falling off the sky island into Indian land, Wupatki National Monument, Gray Mountain, keeping an eye peeled for Stoner, out there somewhere. They'd not hit it off, Edgar took it, Harvell and Stoner. Wouldn't be surprised if the two'd had words—Chief had somehow sniffed it out, what went on before they led Edgar from his cell into the hallway, the latches all click-clacking into the bright light of the room where they traded his old clothes for his new, clean washed, he hadn't worn dry underwear since August. He powered down the passenger window, fresh cold air stiff in his face, set the blue book spinning off into who knows where. Good riddance, he spat after it, his eyes watering, free, the last three days had been the worst. A sign said PAINTED DESERT, and DO NOT LITTER. At once hungry, thirsty, craving tobacco and chocolate, what he'd give for some Fritos. The pages of the real book fluttered. He rolled the window up. "There," he said.

Harvell drove on, stone-faced.

"You got a cooler back there."

"Yeah," Harvell said.

Edgar eyed the Pathfinder's rear compartment. Cook stove and a sleeping bag. Rolled up Paco pad. They going camping?

"I ain't no Mormon," Edgar said.

He smiled. For the first time ever, maybe, Harvell. Edgar tucked the book down by his feet, good socks on now, Redwings laced up, good to have something on his feet other than the K-Mart flip-flops they'd made him wear back there. Clean underwear, God how his balls had chaffed. This car seat the first cushion he'd sat on since the day he'd bought the mojo from the Indian woman, threw it at the devil bird like an idiot, DMF. Son of a bitch had swallowed it. The connection comes to him fully realized and unexpected.

"That was the shits," Edgar said, "Ronnie chomping off your finger."

The scarred red knuckle shines on the wheel, a little shimmy from the road, *Tuba City 46* a green sign says.

"Can't believe they was able to reconnect it."

A sage bundle, rolled in red yarn, lay on the dashboard. What Chief used to smudge everyone down with before entering lodge. Now and then he'd spot one, always east-facing, the blue doored hogans.

"He was better last time I seen him, Love."

The knobby tires made road noise at seventy miles an hour, barreling ass right on past the Tuba City turnoff toward Page and Edgar's truck, which he might just get in, fire her up and haul ass for California, don't stop driving till ocean, whales out there jumping and spouting off.

On the other hand, the one on the wheel without the angry scar, a wedding ring. The Harvell boy's got a wife and, oh yeah, a daughter, so maybe he'd bent his mind toward them, why he wasn't talking.

A family.

Edgar'd almost had that, with Tina. Three candles she'd lit on the German Chocolate cake that last night: Guess why there's three, Edgar, she'd said.

He couldn't guess. Why were there three? Father, son and holy ghost? Birth, death, resurrection? Up, down, sideways? "Why are there three?"

She'd looked him up and down, candle glow on her face. "What you want in this world, "You," he'd said.

"Us."

They'd left the cake burn on the table, back at Tri-County where he was caretaker in that other life, the one he'd driven away from to go west, come face to face with the black rider, and then Stoner and all that he stood for, jail time, then Chief and the inipi and the book with the answer somewhere inside its pages, locked up in there and waiting to get out, just like he'd been, back at Coconino County Detention Center, where he'd spend his last night in moonlight ripping out the pages of the book of Mormon, stashing them in the tank of the low-water toilet, an act that strikes him now as not the brightest thing he's ever done, it will come back to bite him in the butt, sure enough. He'd almost had a family with Tina, prettiest of the Casteen girls, back home in Arkansas, long ago and faraway.

"That's good," Harvell said. "That Love's better."

Why'd he have to think of Tina? She'd left him just before the whole goddamn mess, only to show up now while he was making his getaway. Why couldn't she just stay dead like she was supposed to? Damn woman, won't you just go on and die like dead people are supposed to do? Say. Can't you just die?

It's you keeps bringing me back, Edgar.

You.

He knew about the tides, J.W., had somehow studied them, how the moon and sun influence earth and everything on it, especially water. There was the Apogean tide, when the Moon was farthest from the Earth, and so pulling the least, high and low tides were lesser at this time of the month. The Perigean tide was when the Moon was closest and the pull was greatest, babies were born on this day, our water breaking so we felt it run down our thighs, all of us in time with the moon, how it moved day and night around our worlds. Twice a month the Moon and Sun are at right angles to each other and the Earth, and so the pull is lesser then on us and the sea and all watery parts of the world, boring, but necessary.

Syzygy. He'd throw his head back and say the word.

He'd say that word and shake his head side to side and smile, like it was somehow magic and saying it would bring us luck and money and a houseful of children to chase the dogs we'd one day name after planets, Pluto and Mars and Moon, who little Jack'd call *Dozo. Syzygy,* the word has some sizzle to it, can you hear? From a Greek word that means "yoked together" like we were in marriage, me and J.W. *Syzygy* was when the Sun and Moon lined up string straight so as to form a powerful gravity, one that hauled all waters to their heights, so the blood in our hearts would spring up and we'd feel it in our throats and say I love you, and believe it, and know it true.

I have not heard his voice in a long time now. But I remember the word, how he'd shake his head side to side when he said it. How I believed in all things being yoked together because that's how life is—the good with the bad, for richer or poorer, in sickness and in health.

Syzygy.

What yokes us together.

I am an old woman.

I have never seen the ocean. Not the one J.W. dreamed of on those nights when he'd be flying on a Cutter between Florida and the Grand Bahama bank, those days before we met when he'd worked the Merchant Marine, tied knots and read the water, learned tides and the salt water got into his blood, so he'd always yearn to go back, but he never did. He'd get this look on his face when he talked about tides, like they were holy and his love.

People have a pull on each other, I told him, I'll be your tide, your Sun and Moon, your Neap and Spring, didn't I tell him that? Love has that about it, a gravity. I miss him, my Moon and Sun. Starman.

For richer or poorer, in sickness and in health.

Wise words.

Down to the creek they're bolting a plaque onto the rock where Vina and I sat washing our clothes before the big walking west, Caravan Springs, they're calling it, dedicated to *the band of immigrants who, in early spring of 1857 began here an ill-fated journey to California, the shining goal of their dreams.*

We'll see it together some day, I promise you. That's what J.W. said, that he'd take me to the place I'd once walked toward, across the whole backbone of a continent. A *continent.* A *whole continent* we'd walked across.

I still can't believe we did it. Me and Georgie Porgy and Minerva, my faceless brother and sweet Vina whose hair shone bright. Made it damn near to Nevada Territory away from Deseret. Toward shiny California. A word with five stops in it. I'll take you there, J.W. always said.

No. I kept saying no.

He's out there now, a ways from the porch where the yellow rose grows. Sirius the dog star shining down on his face, me yoked to him there now, can't let him go. Can't. Not yet.

With my one remaining November, bright Venus to the east, and hunter falling west, sometimes this earth will open itself to you and your past meets up with your future in the present. The old tongue and groove creaks beneath the rocking chair and the wonder is fresh on me again, how the world opened up and fell away at the bottom of that canyon and we beheld the Great Salt Lake shining blue and real, clean from one side of earth to other. And it's only just come to me. I never told J.W. how I'd seen the inland ocean.

I'll tell him now.

This is Indian Country.

Late October, the cottonwoods yellow wherever there's water, scarce here on the Kaibab Plateau, Navajo land with Hopi First, Second and Third Mesas straight in the middle. They have this myth, the Hopi, that they crawled out of the earth down on the Colorado just east of where they were driving that second, out of Spider Mother's lair, a pink salt mine Hopi boys pilgrimage to for vision quest, Joey's tasted it, the pink salt from Spider Mother's passage to inner-earth. He'd rowed the Colorado in a sixteen-foot raft three times, first tasted the pink salt of Unkar Delta where the Anasazi ruins and kivas and pottery shards painted with exquisite trapezoids had stayed with him, and for some reason—maybe because he had no God save the universe itself— he'd gone Indian for a while, walked the red road, attended the holy ceremonies, *inipi*, *hambleceya*, sundance, ghost dance. When he'd danced in the moonlight for the world to come and seen Mama again, so tired from the walking, and she'd smiled at him and touched his face. It was her, ghost dancing with him in the moonlight.

There was no loss like that, losing your mother. How she'd carried you and felt you kicking, your life twined with hers, so she'd never be alone, not ever, as long as you lived. She'd told him the old story of him in her womb, how he'd hated onions, how he'd be still when she sang a certain song, how she'd asked the nurse if they'd castrated him yet, whopped on painkiller, getting her words wrong. It had been a foreign country to her, the west, where she'd been a runaway with Buddy Washer, dead now, both of them, gone.

Jimmy would have loved the river.

Six years apart, Jimmy was the closest thing Joey ever knew to himself, sweet boy with not a bad bone in his body, six-feet tall and sawdust bronze, he'd stuttered, but could sing like an angel in the First Baptist Church Choir loft, or when they'd drunk beer, him and Joey. He'd come off the river once with a split knee, and Joey'd driven him to the ER for stitches. Joey'd gone in with him and held his hand while doc sutured, somehow passed out and whacked his head on the ER floor so they had to sew him up too, and there was Jimmy when he woke up, only they'd switched places, him and his brother. He'd often wished it so, that it could have been him on that curve, that he could have eased off the gas, made the hard right that night out in the country, driving the short cut Joey'd taught him back from U.C.A., where he'd drunk beer at a party, and the words had slipped from his mouth unhindered.

It had killed Mama. For a while, it had killed her.

At the viewing, where they'd opened the jet-silver casket and gazed down on the thing they called Jimmy, she'd collapsed. Fell down and thwacked her head on the tile floor, a sound he knew it was bad luck to hear. Her blue-eyed boy, O.W.'s. Not a bad bone in his body. Six-feet tall and sawdust bronze, the angelic words effortless from his mouth. Or is that just a thing we do to our dead, bend them into angels? Bathe them in light. Configure their crooked ghosts to fit into our hearts? We can't help ourselves, can we?

The road to Page splits off Highway 89 at a place called Bitter Springs, just off Marble Canyon to the west on the Grand, the first camps for river runners about to put on at Lee's Ferry. Paris smelled like jail. It was in his scraggly hair, under his fingernails, on the pages of that book he'd disguised as the Book of Mormon, the cover of which he'd just thrown out the window, probably in violation of his release, throw in a littering charge and destruction of public property—was the Book of Mormon public property?

"You hungry?"

They could see the Vermillion Cliffs west, the afternoon sun full on them, Page one way, Lee's Ferry the other. Since he'd quit trying to get Joey to talk, his passenger had stared out the window and sulked. On jail food since August, it was a silly-ass question, no doubt about it.

Edgar said, "I could eat whole donkey."

I Stand With Standing Rock, a sign said. *Fighting Terrorists Since 1492*, another. "I know a place that way," Joey said, "Just over the bridge."

He still had folding money. Edgar said, "I'll buy."

Ten miles to Lee's Ferry. What he wanted, Joey, what he'd been thinking ever since the twin elders marched down on him high as Cooter Brown at Mountain Meadows, was that he wanted to see the river, wash his face and brush his teeth in the cold Colorado.

Marble Canyon Lodge, just up the road from the Ferry, was where river runners washed their last supper down with cold beer, bought an outfit for dress up night, or headlight or Chacos—whatever they'd forgot in the haste of packing—before putting on the river for the sixteen-day float. Edgar, of course, didn't know this, nor anything much about the culture of river folk, save from his Uncle Earl, who'd once pitched him and his cousins Butchy and Beaver, into the Mulberry River at flood stage, wearing those cheap-ass orange cloth life jackets, amongst the flotsam and strainers about to drown him any second, they'd bounced and bobbed thirteen miles, and at the end, Uncle'd whooped and hollered, said let's do it again, which is what they did, three days running.

They had to drive across Navajo bridge to get there, its twin running beside it, at one end the ten-foot plaque to the man of sound judgement and indomitable courage, and the other that Indian woman dressed in turquoise, twisting her mojos this second no doubt. And somewhere in between, out of sight but there, that ugly son of a bitch bird with its dinosaur wings and bald pink head. Give him the willies that second, seeing that bird look at him like he was supper, Edgar, where his bad luck started.

A gas station, restaurant, liquor store, post office, hotel—Marble Canyon Lodge—Edgar has a mind to hit all five, get him some stamps and fire off a post card to the boys at Tri-County, tell them what's up to the end of that bridge, how he got whopped in the head and thrown in jail for doing his sworn duty, come help him blow the fucker to kingdom come.

He hadn't taken three steps from the Harvell boy's truck, he'd only just thought the words *stamp* and *post card* and *blow the fucker to kingdom come*, when what he'd forgotten comes back. Hits him like a brick between the eyes.

It's in the book, the answer's in there.

Before the Harvell boy clicks his little clicker to lock the door, Edgar had it in his hands, the book Chief Joseph had given him, inside of which is tucked the envelope with the eight-sided star drawn on its back, the cosmos, Joseph had said, everything.

Inside—*I have your Chevy, ridiculous talk to bird peeing man. RB.*

In Navajo, he couldn't read a word of it. But he remembered. Chief had translated, called her "Sister." The return address said Dinnehotso. Where the fuck where was Dinnehotso?

Harvell hit the men's, told Edgar to get them a table.

Inside was dark, a bar with stools and a full shelf of liquor behind it, a TV with a baseball game on it, sound turned off. There in front of it, on a barstool with a mug of amber beer in front of him sat an Indian with a long black ponytail. The beer had bubbles rising from the bottom to the top. From twenty feet away Edgar could smell it, the hops and grain, the way it'd burn just a little when it hit the back of the throat, and the aftertaste on the tongue. Beer, proof that God loves us, somebody'd said. What Chief'd been canned for, beer.

"He'p you?"

The Indian's eyes were lit up by light from the doorway behind Edgar's back. He wasn't used to this, being free, spoken to, cold bubbly beer, baseball.

"It's a rerun. The World Series. Game 3. Boston and Dodgers. Longest playoff game in history."

Edgar held the book against his chest with one hand, letter with the other. He smelled corn meal. Fish and potatoes. The cut lemons and limes in the garnish bowls behind the bar. On the TV a batter lifted the ball into left.

"You know Rita Begay?"

The Indian said, "Sister."

"You know her?"

"She's Indian. All us Indians know each other." He was smiling then, the Indian.

Edgar walked across the hard wood, so different from concrete. Forgiving. Once alive. The beer had a salt shaker beside it, a bowl of peanuts. He held up the envelope, the eight-sided medicine star, the cosmos, everything.

"How can I find her?"

This time the sun shone on his teeth when he smiled. He raised a hand, pointed. And there in the doorway behind him stood Rita Begay in a turquoise dress and tennis shoes, the bright sunshine raining through the door frame, and behind that, just visible, the gorge where flowed the Colorado through Vishnu schist and Zoroaster granite that was four goddamn billion years old. A third the age of the whole universe, all the way to the Sea of Cortez and the great ocean the species had once walked across from the direction opposite of where he'd come from, seeking something that was missing from their lives. What was it all of them were looking for? Out of a shadow at the far end walked Harvell, so him and the Indian woman were both looking a question into Edgar's eyes.

It was the first letter he'd got since Tina, who drew little hearts above the *i* when she signed her name. All those letters wrapped in a red ribbon he'd burned in the Tri-County fire place. It was him kept bringing her back.

"Table for two," Harvell said.

"Three," said the Indian.

15.

Like the world on fire, J.W. That big wide open sky where the sun burned, turned the faces of the men on horseback pure-d gold, a holy light it seemed to me, as if it had the power of passing through our skin, our hearts, even, that first sunset in the Salt Lake Valley, the whole of our horizon ablaze, washed in that first light, my heart on fire.

"Do you think it's real?" Vina asked.

She was brushing my hair out, away from the fire, in a clearing where grew the most wonderful smelling bushes, silvery-green, sage it was called, blue sage. *Dog, cat, mouse,* she said when she hit a tangle, *dog, cat, mouse.*

It shone on goddess Minerva, full on her face, her eyes.

Vina braided fish tails into my red hair that would never swirl and shine the way hers did. "Are we even here at all?"

Ocean—I said, *Ocean.* And I still can't hear somebody say that beautiful word without tears. Joy, really, that moment in light. Oh, honey.

And then it was gone. Like a rainbow trout with those explosions of red and green and blue and yellow, yanked from the water so it flashes then fades right before your eyes.

Her fingers felt good on my scalp, sister's. I said, "It is real, isn't it?"

She laughed, a silver bell ringing. Dark came on us then, another night. "Know what I wish?"

"Tell me," I said.

Mama called us then, just a plain woman in shadow now. "Girls," she said. There was work before supper, three rabbits to skin, how the fur came off like gloves. Buckets to fill, potato peeling. Then the men had their singing and whiskey and we could see the far-off lights of the Mormons. Had they seen the light? Had it washed them and turned them gold, and got clean through their skin into their hearts?

And then there was bed, no fireflies in this strange land. Tell me sister Vina. For what did you wish on that first night in the valley of the Saints?

Tell me. Please.

Joey'd been there before, more than once. On the exact spot, on foot, on a mountain bike ridden from his own back yard where the slick surfaced stones lay beneath the soil, remnants of the glaciers that grinded down from the upthrust mountains. He'd cut willows from the creek, thirty-three of them bound with river webbing and hauled to Rose Park where they skinned off the bark and bent them over their backs for the skeleton of the sweat lodge. And the last time, many months later, he'd driven up Emigration Canyon on a Sunday before Thanksgiving, all the way to the top to see the blue reservoir, then over to Pinecrest, hiked the six-mile Miner's Trail back into the mountains, a fragrant canopy of Mountain Mahogany on either side of his path up by the caves where elderberry turns crazy colors in autumn. And there was this one spot, high up, where rock ribs were exposed on one whole bank, a wash seep some seasons, cedar and ceremonial sage growing through the seams. Lara liked to climb there, up on the steep rock ribs where lichen grew, the same yellowish-orange as her hazel eyes. An altar stone-shaded by the tree, he prayed for his people, gave thanks for escaping with his life. Said thank you for the privilege of walking on this good earth.

Only this time something was wrong. The tree was different, the shade over the altar rock. Piled in the wash were tree boughs, big ones broken from the canopy, four in all. The whole tree topped. Someone had to shimmy up that tree and try real hard to do harm, and for a long time to break that much down. *Why?* Why would someone do that? For what reason? Left their damage lay at the holy place?

Joey'd sat on the altar rock where he'd so often sipped water and looked out on the valley and the mountain, the bare knobs and sharp points, where he'd understand that he'd by god made it to where he wanted to be, that he'd hiked a trail near his home in the by god Rocky Mountains, in Utah, he lived in beauty. And so often these son of a bitches ripped Jesus out of it, the land. Just because they could.

And seeing the limbs ripped down and laying, he got self-righteous and pissed and cursed them out loud. He picked up one of the heavy boughs, heaved it off where the wash dropped ten feet to scattered boulders that fell to the creek below.

Heart beating, he heaved a second armful and a third, so they crashed down the rock wall. He threw the last one with all his might, so as to clear the rest. Only this time, he went with it. Airborne, the whole beautiful godawful nature of the place revealed.

And why he'd be thinking of the canyon where the Arkansawyers had passed down and walked out into the amber light of a first sunset, why it would come into his head the moment Rita Begay walked into Marble Canyon Lodge and Restaurant to hand Edgar Paris his truck keys, who can say?

But it happened, just like that, swearing to God.

The Indian brought them an order of chips and salsa, some fried cheese and a basket of fresh bread with butter. A pitcher of Dale's Pale Ale arrived with three frosty mugs and coasters with a picture of a raft that said *Keep the Right Side Up.*

The special was Navajo Taco, and this place had pies, three different kinds and a cake under glass, carrot with Italian glaze. Edgar'd hog-gobbled half the chips slathered in spicy salsa, buttered a piece of sour dough, washed it down with half a mug of beer in one gulp. He said, "Excuse me," belched a second time.

The Indian woman, Rita Begay, the one who'd called him *talk to bird pissing man*, stood at the table, the lucky rabbit's foot, green.

"Joey said, "Hi."

"Hi," Rita said.

The rerun of the world series had just entered the fourteenth inning, making it the longest running playoff game in history. "That's a good game," Edgar said. "Hi."

"These are yours," Rita said.

Edgar held out his hand. The ring jingled, just a little. Three keys: one to the truck, one to the front door of Tri-County Coon Club, and other to a padlock he'd once bought for Tina, painted both their initials on with pink fingernail polish and locked it to the chain-link fence in the cemetery where she lay buried, their love locked.

What he would have said if his mouth wasn't full: Thank you, mam. I just got here. How'd you know I was here? How come you to have my truck?

Joey poured beer. Outside, a truckful of rafters—you can spot them a mile away—in Chacos and river shorts, sunglasses strung around their necks and ball caps pulled down low, piled out onto the asphalt, come for their last supper.

Rita said, "No thank you."

"Water? Coffee?" Joey stood, pulled the chair for Rita. Edgar stood as well, when the when the river folk came in, smelling of weed and strong drink.

Rita said, "Everyone knows everything here. We have spies in the sky." She smiled. Her voice was soft, little puffs with her S's.

The Indian was pulling tables together. There were eighteen of them, the rafters plus the ranger, plus the bus driver from the rafting company that had that afternoon delivered six sixteen-foot Sotar rafts with diamond steel frames and dry boxes, marine coolers frozen solid for two weeks. It was a thing, putting on the Grand for the two hundred twenty-five miles from Lee's Ferry to Diamond Creek where the Havasu ran jet boats to Mead dam and back. An October trip, they'd be out there for Halloween, what a party that'd be. Joey wished he was going, that sweet burn at the end of a day pulling oars, the eddy fences and holes where hydraulics would flip your ass, suck you down to the bottom and hold you there till it thundered, that's what they said, till it thundered.

"Want to sit down" Joey said. "My name's Joey. Harvell."

"I'm Rita," Rita said. "Begay."

"Edgar," Edgar said.

"John, Sister," one of the river runners said, stuck his hand in for a shake.

"Harmony," said another.

"How about we all sit together," a tall one said, pony tail hanging half down his back, and before they knew it they'd been swept into the river party, ordering steaks and chops and Fettuccini Alfredo and pitchers of beer, shooters, baskets of fried oysters and onion rings. They were electric, these river folk, from all over, one—and Joey took this as a sign, told Renee later on the phone, when he said they'd be camping at the Ferry that night, home tomorrow by happy hour—from Arkansas. He had a look of Joey's brother about him, and they'd got happy and called the Hogs—*wooo pig sooie, Razorbacks*.

And they'd camped under the stars with the water shining off toward Pariah Riffle, Joey on a Paco with moonlight on his face, Edgar snoring in the back of the Pathfinder, Rita wherever she'd disappeared to, until first light, when the river party brewed coffee, waded into the water and pissed, the women splashing themselves off in the cold, breath steaming from their faces. Seven miles downriver, the twin bridges shone faintly, the one for pedestrians stained by the cross-shaped shadow thrown from outstretched wings, trembling a little in the new light. And the other issuing a slight moan as Officer Stoner's cruiser passed over, headed for Page and Lake Powell, named for the one-armed Civil War Hero, first white man to try the river, though it had almost killed him, surely it had.

The ox wagon sailed over the sage brush sea—The Great Basin, I'd learn, mountains in front of us and behind, on either side, so much wide open you felt it someplace inside that our kind must have known when there were no houses, when folk walked themselves where they would, and the world was theirs. It felt like that, ours. Faceless brother, did you know where we were going? Care? Had one of you given me a hank of hair, a rock, a bone? Did you know to be afraid? See signs? Something in the sky, in the wind? A smell? Dream?

I'd forgot ever having left the creek, the shady spring where Vina and I'd let our feet just skim the water, where the witchdoctors rode each other tail to tail and Georgie Porgy and Minerva skinny-dipped when they thought no one was looking. Of the evening I saw them in the creek, their skin all lit up and white. That dream we followed the river out of, the land always rising over the pass into the canyon of the sun on the inland ocean, to here, where the ox cart rocked on a sea of sage and we were queens of this new land, me and sister, our hair in fish braids, crowned in circlets of scarlet gilia, globe mallon, fire chalice and bluebell. The days and nights that bled together and who knew what hour or day or week or month it was, even, on an ocean of sage in a sea of time, where all that was floated tranquil on all that wasn't. That's who we were then. Can you believe it? Can you?

Every so often there'd be a place where the trail turned into a road that became a street that ran into a town and in that town there'd be a white steeple, and a bell would ring when they saw us coming.

Our harness bells would jingle. A girl waved at me once, and then I heard her cry behind a door that closed and the bolt slid shut. These towns had names Vina'd read when the bells were ringing: *Scipio, Kanosh, Beaver, Parowan, New Harmony*.

There was a deep dark forest growing on the mountains to our lefts, and sometimes there'd be horses, long-haired men with feathers laced into their ponytails. Shadowy things. Our mules brayed. All night long the mules brayed. Wolves made song. J.W., wish I could sing the wolf song for you this second, how Vina'd lifted her snout and howled so I joined her, the Dog moon rising.

A tree caught fire at first light, the leaf turning, and in that tree was a white-headed bird big as me, a Bald Eagle, daddy called her, and she made this shrill whistle—*shree, shree, shree*. In a nest big as a wagon. Its eyes on us, me and Vina, shining like it knew us, had known and waited for us our whole lives. Like it had news from another world.

And then it flew, a high circle above our camp where the breakfast fires were just burning down. *Shree, shree, shree* it went, *shree, shree shree*.

We were about to be famous.

She was knocking on the window, Rita Begay. His first night out, Edgar's, wrapped in a fleece thrown in back of the Harvell boy's SUV, first light pink on the windshield, chilly-willy, and have you ever woke up your first night out of jail and had that feeling in your stomach, that gut punch, somebody coming to get you, haul your ass back, lock you down so you'd never walk free again. Say? You ever felt that, Jack? Anybody ever told you about that? How the man was onto you, behind your back, about to rip your rompers. And where was he anyway? Chief? Rudolph the Red? Clickety-clack-clack. Whoa, his head hurt. *Wooo-pig-sooie, Razorbacks*, the kid had worn a hog hat. A goddamn hog hat. It's a full moon still out, bright son of a bitch. Hunter's. Water down there swishing, Colorado, the bridge up that away. In the dream had been an Indian princess dressed in white and green. A knife on her hip, a red rock in her hands. Called him by his Christian name.

"Edgar," she said, tapped one, two, three. "I see you in there."

Goddamn, these Indians got up early. Had good eyes to see you with. Been out praying to the rising sun or some shit. *Whoa*, his head, feel like he been in a fight. Has to pee like a Russian race horse. Drain the lizard, shake the pole.

People out there. The river rats. They're moving around. Women in the water, splashing they faces. It's Friday. Tail end October. He'd come west. Has not brushed his teeth and been a good boy. Had his ass thrown in Coconino. Just got out. Ate dinner with the rats, smoked hooter, played a drum by firelight. Somebody'd tooted on a horn. Professor smartass played the guitar. Down by the river. Six more weeks on good behavior. Then take his ass home. Put this place in the rearview. Ain't never coming back.

Edgar?

She was toting something, the Indian woman. Rita Begay. Who'd kept his truck. Why wasn't he in his own truck? Little bed back in the shell. How'd he get here? *Jesus*. He felt in his pocket, bladder about to burst.

"Missus Begay?"

Breath in front of her face. Cold out there.

"Yea. It's me."

He had his clothes on. Edgar was still dressed. "Gid me a second," he said. Slid on one Redwing, the other. Laced.

"Okay," she said.

And where was Harvell, whose charge he was in at that very moment? Probably already broke the rules, had it said anything about getting drunk and smoking hooter and calling the hogs with river rats? Or was it just peeing in public? What exactly were the rules of his release? Stoney out their snuffling around, waiting for him to fuck up.

He swiped a hand through his hair two times, got ready to meet his first full day as a free man. And what happened next was one of those things that roll toward you out of the fog that rises off the river when the air's cooler than the water, that slippery ether through which there is no seeing. Out there the Indian woman who could maybe tell him where his truck was, a bathroom, the whole goddamn river to pee in if he wanted, breakfast coming, get the hell out of Dodge. He was in back of Harvell's Pathfinder. Both rear seats were laid down flat. A door on either side, the back-door handles. He pulled on the one Rita Begay stood outside of, and when it opened and he stepped out into the fine October morning, an alarm Nissan's Japanese engineers had designed to wake the long-sleeping dead pierced the entirety of the frosty campground. A sound that would turn your pee blue. And it kept on bleating like that for what seemed like, to everyone listening, a very long time. Harvell heard it, and the calf-deep woman squatting in the river, the campground host and the on-call ranger.

Coffee drinkers back at Marble Canyon. From one of the twin river bridges, Condor number Four, who'd just stretched wings to sunlight, heard it and imitated the sound inside the throat of its featherless head. *Shree, shree, shree*, it went, a sound that put him in mind of another time and place, the ancestral feast of his lineage.

And from the overlook from whence he watched, Officer Stoner caught a trace of the sound and suspected no good.

That Harvell kid had taken something from the Meadow, no doubt about it if the dope head Elders who watched it could be trusted. And he had some skeleton shit in his britches, too, police report said. Small stuff mostly, DWI, failure to appear, a little of this and that and the other, maybe an uncrossed *t* and undotted *i* somewhere in there. Probably. University professor, think his shit don't stink. Professor peckerhead. He'd written papers, trusted his words to papers that he was fool enough to publish with his name on them, especially the one in Stoner's center console this second, the one that—if put into the right hands—could land him in a hole in the desert with the gentile kith and kin he so bemoans.

Stoner'd read it, the Harvell paper. The one that blasphemed the Prophet of God, and therefore the foundations of the church of the Lord himself. Back in the day you could take a son of a bitch out just like that for such a thing. Better to put him in a hole than let him live in sin. Spreading lies. Not being held accountable. And isn't that what this world cries out for—a little bit more goddamn accountability? There were some still thought that way. Important people in important places. Stoner's mama's people, fully redeemed, who'd fuck with a Lee now? They were still out there, avenging angels. Policing God's kingdom on Earth. They hadn't gone anywhere, had they?

Not a goddamn inch to the Arkies.

PART II

16.

Yakov wanted no part of the dynamite. It was shit. Even fertilizer was better. In Russia, they never used dynamite. There was not even name for it, maybe. It was old fashioned. Why on earth would they think to blow up steel bridge with toys? What was it about Americans to make them so dumb that they were blind even to their dumbness? With a Ph.D. in Physics from Moscow Institute for Physics, the goddamn chair, fully capable of rendering the good stuff, blow that son of a bitch and its ugly twin to China, and they ask him for toys? He had been approached about placing camera on the structure to watch birds, so he'd seen the plans, but such is the conversation when tainted with vodka, especially with the Americans for whom it goes to their heads so quickly, so they ask for this and you give them that. She was getting ahead of herself, Yelena. She was architect. Her part in all this was clear. Make the drawings, highlight support beams, show them fuse apparatus. Deliver the goods. Tell them burn the instruction book when done. Why had Yakov gone along with it? His eye flap twitching the way it does when he gets excited. Truth was, he loved to blow things up. More than anything. It was in his blood. His DNA. But he could have given them the good stuff. Make sure the idiots know that, Yakov said. He was capable of better.

Rudi came home for Thanksgiving. From Chicago. He left his skinny blonde slut there, in Chicago. How much weight he'd lost, smoking dope, the dark circles under his eyes, her baby boy, who should be home with his mother, they could go ice dancing, their blades throwing wisps, the way her and her father once had, the season of black crows squawking, when she'd lay in her room and count the floorboards to the shadow in the corner and hope to get away as bad as she longs now to go home, just up and take her family home. But Rudi was here now, from Chicago, and the Harvells had invited them over to dinner, and she was to do salad and brew tea, unseal a jar of mushrooms they'd canned over her birthday weekend in the mountains, when it snowed half a foot and Yakov'd set off surprise explosion to top it off and they'd built a bonfire.

It was good, Rudi coming home.

And now, this new thing, making the book, the twin intricate steel bridges, the weight-bearing beams and joist, they were beautiful and arched across the canyon, embedded in stone you could get your teeth into—isn't that what they said, get your teeth into? At Halloween, she'd invited them, the Harvell's because that's what she was supposed to do, keep a list, check it twice, interact, engage, become them through and through. There had been a derelict with them, a skinny, dirty man with a funny mouth. He'd dressed as Indian, fake black braids. She'd been Dracula's daughter, Yelena. And Yakov—he'd just been Yakov. The Harvell woman had been a sailor because her father was sailor and he'd given her the white suit. They'd got drunk. The phones were ringing. Rudi on the line—*Trick or Treat, Mama.* Little kids ringing doorbell. Ghosts and goblins and demons and zombies, oblivious to the fact that they were at that very second flashing across Yakov's camera straight to the motherland's remote screens, their faces being encrypted, their voices, the one who cried because her brother took her candy corn. What kind of holiday, Trick or Treat? In Russia, we don't dress as goblins and gorge on candy corn. Who could invent that, Trick or Treat?

And they wanted dynamite. 120 pieces with a fuse system and instructions for use. Yakov had been hurt. Deeply so. How dare they ask him for sparklers when he could unleash the Kraken, give them kingdom come, the seventh seal, all that Bible bullshit. Hadn't Papa detonated five-hundred Hiroshima baby doll? Won Lenin Prize? Got their goddamn phones tapped forever, so Yakov had come of age under the *gaze* that saw all, until he blew his eye out with nitro in Ukraine and the gaze turned inward. And now they are all part of it, the eye that sees itself.

The Harvell man, he is idiot, of course. They all are, with their *Dialing for Dollars* and *Bonanza* and *Quarter Pounder with cheese.* And then Trick or Treat in Magna, they'd sipped Stolichnaya from tall glasses while the miner's seed knocked again and again, *Trick or Treat, Trick or Treat,* their bastard and bitch progenitors looking on from the street, the golden seared mushrooms pickled now, just right with the vodka's bite, and they got happy, the sailor woman and the little funny-mouth, and Joey Harvell, who was history professor, he'd told a story she'd never heard, Yelena.

Underneath them the basement was strung with computers, hardwired together so they made one big one, the whole place a camera on the world, their voices translated at high frequency—his story, Harvell's.

She could smell the burnt jack-o-lantern, silly sailor woman drinking with them, little weasel man who talked like Beverly Hillbilly, *gonna' tell you little story 'bout a man named Jed.* Little Indian, fake braids.

But his story—that was the thing.

How his people had walked west from Mississippi to the mountains, and passed though this very valley, only to have every last one of them be killed by Mormons. Even the little ones. All dead.

It had reminded Yakov of Stalin, what had happened to an Uncle, his father's brother. Others. A whole lot of people. Siberia. Mass graves. No man, no problem, that's what they said. The party was a machine. Mother Russia or disappear your ass.

And that's why you're here, because the story reminded him of Stalin, what Yakov meant to say. He'd never got it down, the words, she translated for him.

Harvell told how one man had been executed for the deed. And then the Church forgave him and made his statue on bridge down river from the ferry that bore his name. Called him brave and courageous, who'd cut their hearts out with a knife. Left them lay.

"What can you do?" he asked, Joey Harvell.

"Blow it the fuck up," little fake Indian said. "That's what Rudolph the Red would do."

"How?"

Little Indian man had a snootful. "With a goddamn bomb. Dynamite. One stick for every one of them."

He was proud of himself, you could tell, little funny mouth, a stick of dynamite for each one of them killed by Mormons dressed like little Indian man at a place called Mountain Meadows down south.

Yakov wanted no part of dynamite. It was shit. Even fertilizer was better. But Rudolph the Red? Who was this Rudolph the Red who would blow up bridge where statue said killer man was hero? It had been the Uncle's name, his father's brother, who'd been sent away and killed, so that one of the children had grown up as Yakov's brother. Little Rudolph, so far gone. Yelena's father. Their son. Rudolph put skin in the game, for Yakov, it had.

And that was how we get here—to me making book, drawing pictures of bridge. Government had wanted permanent camera for birds down there over Great River. Big birds, black with bald heads. An extinct species, almost, they needed watching. So Yakov had the plans, had pictures of them, the weight bearing beams, how to string wire beneath the span, in the skeleton, tie the pieces into master fuse so they all become one, and then to a single ignition device with a double trip just in case. The bridge had twin. Blow one, maybe twin come with it. May be. It was simple, a child could do it, one of those brats ringing the goddamn doorbell every other minute, glutting on candy corn and Reese's Cups.

Dynamite was tinker toy. For Rudolph the Red, Yakov had said, his own face scarlet and the eye beneath the eye twitching in its socket, he could make bridge go away forever, both of them, real one and twin. In Russia they would never use dynamite. But here is how.

Here.

He'd never wanted to go as an Indian, Edgar, and now that's all she would call him, the Russian, little Indian this and little Indian that. "Can you lay off the little Indian stuff," Edgar asked on the sunny afternoon when she knocked on Harvell's front door for the Thanksgiving How to Explode a Bridge with Dynamite workshop.

She'd dressed up, her blonde hair shining. A red-haired boy was with her, Rudi. Rudolph the Red. I'll be goddamn go to hell.

"Okay, Jed. Go fetch Jethro. We got shit to unload."

And they did, more and more and more.

The boy'd brought hooter, sure he had. Little pipe made to look like a lit cigarette. And lord did these Russians scream bloody murder at each other, holy moly. When the good looker got sight of the fake cigarette full of hooter out in the backyard under the pear, those gold leaves a twirling down, she let fly on little Rudi Red to beat the band. Edgar'd thought he'd die, hauling the foil lined liquor store boxes downstairs into the basement, where his pallet had been made in a room crammed with river gear—life jackets strung with river knives hung on nails, the orange webbed net for tying over gear, a sand spike sharp enough to cut meat, and a whole slew of broken oar blades, each with the name of the rapid writ on it where the accident happened: 24 ½, Upper and Lower Disaster, Powerhouse, Lava and Skull, a wooden one signed one end to the other. Through the unfinished skeleton of wall hangs a pair of fishing waders like the kind Edgar once wore in the duck woods, flooded timber where old man Paris would throw his head back and let fly on the call, a whole bevy of decoys spread out in the hole, so the mallards would quack-quack down to the boom-boom of twelves and twenties, the sweet sixteens, and Buck and Boozer would jump into the black water with necks outstretched, gather the fallen birds in strong jaws, lay them on the half-sunk log just pretty as you please.

Only now, doing the last of his time in the Harvell House, the Harvell woman not at all happy to have an Arkansawyer living in the basement, one room over from where the dog that got put down over summer lived. He can still smell it, Edgar, feel it eyeing him from the doggy bed in the corner, both its bowls in there, one of which Edgar pees in sometimes, when he really has to go in the middle of the night, when the shadow from the fishing waders looks just like a man come after him from the dark, maybe the black semi ever parked outside thrum-thrumming, the way his old man's had those nights, out on the gravel leaking oil, a low growl.

And now, under the half-open life jackets laced with knives and red whistles, the foil lined liquor boxes duct-taped shut, with numbers *one, two, three* and *four* writ real funny, in cryllic. The pretty blonde one who could cuss and scream in Russian like a pig-skinner high on shine, Lord God, please don't let me cross that one who's going after Rudi the Red like no tomorrow, the turkey in the oven up there, old one eye asking Harvell to roll him another cigarette, and then Rudi red puts his fake cigarette away, and the mama quits her hellacious screaming and it gets quiet like the middle of the night when Edgar pees in the silver dog bowl and that's the only noise save the cars out on the road. Box one, open first. Do not smoke. Danger. *Peligro.* Funny word. No fucking smoke. Box two—same. Three, for beam three, same. Four, to be opened last: DO NOT SMOKE FUNNY MOUTHED INDIAN. The woman's writing. He can sniff perfume where her wrist touched, a good smell, puts him in mind of Tina, the Casteen girl he'd got pregnant, so she said they were three. He'd burned everything he ever had of hers, but the taint of her wouldn't let him be, visited in the quiet beneath the floorboards where the Harvells slept.

Just two more weeks. Jesus let him make two more weeks.

It's you keeps bringing me back, Edgar.

All quiet upstairs. Like church, before preacher Roy Dale Shoates went all hellfire and damnation, and the raven-haired choirgirl got down on the tremolo of her Flying V, sang "I'm in the Gloryland Way." And she was, up there praying like that, saying grace. The Harvell boy's funny that way, goddamn this and goddamn that one minute, prayer the next. That crooked scar all lit up and crimson Love bit him.

He was welcomed to come up for Thanksgiving supper, Edgar.

They'd set him a place, sliced dark meat from the bone, cornbread dressing and creamed onions, a bowlful of green beans with almond slivers cut in, fresh cranberry and he can smell the buttery bread through the floor. They'd slid the extension section into the dining table so it sat eight, only they were seven, and one seat was set to the T for all of them that were missing, food on the plate, gravy in the mashed potato divot. And out the front windows would loom up those mountains, snow on them now, freak backdrop of a foreign land, home way off that way, through the gap south they called Point of the Mountain, where the Fanchers had passed 161 years before, the empty place at the corner of the table—were they invited, the Fanchers and Bakers and Poteets?

Anybody you want to call? You can use our telephone, Edgar. Anybody you want. They'd all got happy, the Harvells and Kukalovs. Joey'd sneaked some of Rudi Red's hooter. The whiskey came out. Pulled out that sweet D-28 gitfiddle and sang

Russian folk songs—that blonde pretty thing belting it out. Yakov taught them all to say *I'll shit on you from the highest tree* in Russian, and they sliced the pecan pie, brewed the bitter Russian tea.

The Harvell girl put him in the mind of Mama Josephine, Joey's mother who'd grown up in Danville and shared kin with his Hector folks. She'd been four way back when, that Spring when Tina'd moved in with him for a while at Tri-County, and the whole business with the finger went down. Sweet girl, she'd grown up with the Mormons.

Yelena walked them through the booklet. Yakov pointed out hot spots, the eye socket aflutter, like a June bug was in there trying to bust out. They lay the woman's drawings of the twin bridges on the table while the Harvell woman cleaned and Rudolph the Red huffed hooter out under the pear. They inspected the ignition device, the shiny black handle you pushed down with both hands, just like the movies—which one was that where they blew the bridge?—and Yakov spoke broken English and asked for another cigarette with his tea. They went over it, and over it. The Harvell woman up and mopped the kitchen, started the dishwasher, she wanted no part of this and now that he thought about it, neither did Edgar. What was the point? Really? Why the bridge? Why not blow up their goddamn temple? How about them apples?

Impossible—they watched it always.

How about *This Is the Place*. It overlooked Salt Lake. There were statues up there—of the fat man and two others. Blow they ass to kingdom come.

Nobody went there—just boy scouts cleaning up used condoms and beer cans, stray tourists who took the wrong turn to the zoo.

The Capitol. Supposed to be a tunnel run from there to the temple.

Get real, Edgar.

Edgar took a turn under the pear tree. He lived in Chicago, the kid. Missed his girlfriend. His mother was a bitch. The Harvells had a meat thermometer that registered temperature across space and time—how did that work, across space and time?

Damned if Edgar knew.

I'm going to bed. Goodnight, the Harvell woman. He'd met her in Arkansas, but only for a sec. She was the one befriended Rhonda Love after Shiloh was killed, invited them to dinner after the finger mess. Some balls. She hadn't wanted to move back to Utah, Edgar thinks. Who would?

Could he bring them up here, the four boxes?

Edgar carried up the boxes. The Russian woman screamed at him. *Pozhar.* She gestured at the wood stove, the fireplace insert. Her voice rubbed him raw.

No, there was no fire in the fireplace stove. No fire.

Khoroshiy.

Good.

She said for him to open box number one, Edgar. He undid his side knife, sliced the duct tape, carefully, carefully. Inside the foil wrapping, the sticks are each wrapped in a sheet of newspaper, the Sports Page of the Tribune, how the Utes came back from twenty down to kick BYU's ass. They're shiny, red, he can smell them in there, Edgar.

Yelena unwrapped them one at a time, set them on the coffee table, gently. She said, "You mention names. To write on?"

Joey said, "Yeah. Here."

He opened a thick book to the page, took the cap off a black sharpie, made ready to write. As if it heard, the light shone in then, alpenglow from the setting sun on the Wasatch Mountains where glaciers had once plunged into an inland sea. Harvell pointed with the scarred finger, commanded Edgar *read, not too damn fast.* And so he did, his voice puny at first, then stronger:

William Allen Aden, 19.

George W. Baker, 27.

Minerva Beller Baker, 25.

Melissa Ann Beller, 14.

David W. Beller, 12.

John Beach, 21.

William Cameron, 51.

Martha Cameron, 51.

Tillman Baker, 24.

Isom Baker, 18.

Henry Baker, 16.

James Baker. 14.

Vina Baker, 11.

Larkin Baker, 8.

Nancy Cameron, 12.

Allen Deshazo, 20.

Jesse Dunlap, Jr. 39.

Mary Wharton Dunlap, 39.

Ellender Dunlap, 18.

Nancy Dunlap, 16.

James Dunlap, 14.

Lucinda Dunlap, 12.

Susannah Dunlap, 12.

Margarette Dunlap, 11.

Mary Ann Dunlap, 9

Lorenzo Dunlap, 42.

Nancy Dunlap, 39.

Thomas Dunlap, 17.

John Dunlap, 16.

Mary Ann Dunlap, 13.

Talitha Emaline Dunlap, 11.

Nancy Dunlap, 9

America Jane Dunlap, 7.

William Eaon, 42.

Silas Edwards, 44.

Alexander Fancher, 45.

Eliza Fancher, 32.

Hampton Fancher, 19.

William Fancher, 17.

Mary Fancher, 15.

Thomas Fancher, 14.

Martha Fancher, 10.

Sara Fancher, 8.

Margaret Fancher, 8.

James Fancher, 25.

Fannie Fancher, 25.

Robert Fancher, 19.

Saladia Huff, 27.

William Huff, 17.

Elisha Huff, 15.

Marion Huff, 13.

Weldon Huff, 11.

John Jones, 32.

Eloah Angeline Jones, 27.

Crystaline Jones, 14.

Newton Jones, 11.

Lawson McIntyre, 21.

Josiah Miller, 30.

Matilda Miller, 26.

James Miller, 9.

Charles Mitchell, 25.

Sarah Baker Mitchell, 21.

John Mitchell, 6 months.

Joel Mitchell, 23.

John Prewitt, 20.

Milum Rush, 28.

Charles Stallcup, 25.

Cynthia Tackitt, 49.

Marion Tackitt, 20.

Sebron Tackitt, 18.

Matilda Tackitt, 16.

James Tackitt, 14.

Jones Tackitt, 12.

Pleasant Tackitt, 25.

Amilda Tackitt, 22.

Richard Wilson, 20.

Solomon Wood, 20.

William Wood, 26.

James O. Poteet, 33.

Francis Marion Poteet, age unknown, survived.

Mary Elizabeth Baker, 5, survived.

Sarah Frances Baker, 3, survived.

William Twitty Baker, 9 months, survived.

Rebecca Dunlap, 6, survived.

Louisa Dunlap, 4, survived.

Sarah Dunlap, 1, survived.

Prudence Angeline Dunlap, 5, survived.

Georgia Dunlap, 18 months, survived.

Kit Carson Fancher, 5, survived.

Triphenia Fancher, 22 months, survived.

Nancy Huff, 4, survived.

Felix Marion Jones, 18 months, survived.

John Calvin Miller, 6, survived.

Mary Miller, 4, survived.

Joseph Miller, 1, survived.

Emberson Milum Tackitt, 4, survived.

William Henry Tackitt, 19 months, survived.

George Basham, Unknown.

Tom Farmer, Unknown.

James Haydon, Unknown.

David Hudson, Unknown.

Laffoon family, Unknown.

Charles H. Morton family, Unknown.

Poteet family, Unknown.

John Perkins Reed, Unknown.

Alf Smith, Unknown.

Mordecai Stevenson, Unknown.

Unknown.

Unknown.

Unknown.

Unknown.

Unknown.

Unknown.

Unknown.

Unknown.

Unknown.

Unknown.

Unknown.

Unknown.

17.

The men who built the bridge, who welded the steel and screwed the toggle jacks and set the pins, who suffered the hardships of the North and South rims, who fell the 467 feet to death off the tallest steel bridge on earth, they were from Missouri. Fancy that. Goddamn Missouri. The same Missouri that God had given to Joseph Smith so that he and his Latter-Day Saints could establish the kingdom on earth, Zion, God's own land with God's own people. Where they'd consecrate the Temple on the piece of earth and the prophet talked to God and God talked back, said take this one's twelve-year-old daughter, that one's little sweet thing for celestial marriage in the place they called *Promise*. Missouri, goddamn. Where they grew forty thousand strong so as to rival the governor, the President, even, and it was prophesied that the Kingdom of God was at hand, that Jesus Christ was its heavenly king and Joseph Smith the earthly, and the new temple would be built lying westward, near the courthouse in Independence. Where an army was formed, the Host of Israel, victorious over the lazy, illiterate gentiles at Crooked River, where an Apostle was martyred. Where the Garden of Eden had been. The lost tribe. Missouri, goddamn. Where Governor Boggs sicced the militia of 2000 on the Saints at Haun's Mill, and they threw the earthly King's ass in the pokey under threat of immediate execution. Who'd ordered those sameSaints to be the hell out of the state by April Fool's Day, 18 and 39. The men who built the bridge that would go by three names, just five miles below Lee's Ferry, they were from Missouri. *Goddamn.*

The place had history.

From the east, the goat trail descended from on high, switchback after switchback over hard rock scree to a place on the river where the water lay down in a shallow crossing the Indians had used—the only way west for some three hundred miles. The priest, Silvestre Velez de Escalante had walked across the water in 1776, seeking Navajo, Ute and Paiute for the slave trade in what would be California, so the place was called *Vado de los Padres,* Crossing of the Fathers. It was Mormons who first used it to ferry those who'd colonize North Arizona per command of the prophet back in Salt Lake, and it was there Bishop and Territory Legislator John Doyle Lee fled to seek refuge from federal authorities for what went down at Mountain Meadows. The church owned Lee's Ferry. He was persuaded to go there and run it, to lay low, keep his head down. The only crossing for three hundred miles, Lee's Ferry got popular, too much so. U.S. marshals captured him and he stood trial twice. Word was a deal was cut in Salt Lake for the second trial, trading a guilty Lee for Utah statehood, which it had been denied six times. Sold him down the river, fat man did. His buddy, John Wesley Powell, who'd loaned him the ferry boat Nellie Powell, named for his daughter, had his photographer shoot a last portrait of the Mormon Bishop sitting on the casket they'd execute him standing in at the very site where the Fanchers had tied their wagons together for the siege. Telling a joke, he was caught mid-laugh, Lee. The King of the Earthly realms adoptive son, and one time body guard of Joe Smith, Lee alone was ever punished.

The Mormon Church ran the ferry for thirty years thereafter. They excommunicated him for a while, and then they didn't. But the name stuck: Lee's Ferry.

O dark river of my mother's blood. To the stone world, then.

The Grand Fucking Canyon cut the new state of Arizona damn near in half, east to west, and that just wouldn't do, would it? What they needed was a whole bunch of Missouri motherfuckers to go netless, to blast Jesus out of the thinnest stretch of river, and build them a goddamn bridge, teach the river a lesson. Plans were drawn. Funding raised. May, 1927, Kansas City Structural Steel Company signed a contract to build Lee's Ferry Bridge. The great work began in June. Steel and steel workers rode cable over the gorge. They'd have their goddamn bridge.

The proposed and adopted design of the structure that some of the more stubborn engineers had taken to calling the Grand Canyon Bridge, featured a three-hinged deck, cantilevered into the canyon walls, a spandrel-braced arch of six-hundred feet at a dizzying height above the Colorado. There the steel workers went freestyle across the great span, arc-welding the twelve-ton piece lifted trembling by one of the great cranes that teetered over the cliff face, always on the verge of fall. Summertime in the desert, the Missourians stripped nearly naked, working at night sometimes, first light the others, the road cook barbecuing antelope on the south bank where the Indians had built a blue-doored hogan for prayer and revival, sacrifice. Mormons stayed the fuck clear. The Missouri roughnecks made them nervous, reminding them of that time not so distant when they'd tangled, been chased into Illinois, how their prophet was shot then bayoneted out of his second story jail cell, and his brother hit in the face by a .30 caliber carbine, holy moly what a mess.

On cool mornings as the desert is prone, a band of light shone just barely on the Vermillion Cliffs a hundred miles north and east, and there was one named Lafayette from Kansas City liked to sit beneath where the curve was the highest, see that pink light aglow, hand roll a cigarette and wait. Truly sublime, he could see a hundred miles, two hundred, the Navajo's drums boom-booming over to the fire, the smell of his tobacco, the dark shape of the river below. The sun rose up, and he liked to hold his breath that second when the first ounce of it, that liquid fire, oozed onto his right shoulder, shudder, the breath aching in his chest. Three minutes she was full up and he could feel the warmth of it on his outstretched arms, and he'd imagine flying the fuck away from here all the way to the salty sea. But soon enough the crane would squeal to life and the little fires from the arc-welders would blind you without dark glasses through which you could look at the sun, a man could stare straight at it and see spouts rise from the corona, and they'd get giddy and wild and high on the antelope meat the Navajo'd bless before slaughter.

And one morning this Lafayette from Kansas City, flung his arms out trembling in the new sun and fell that way to the river, 467 feet below. They never found his body, strange bird.

Missouri, goddamn.

The work went fast. Straw boss named Hoffmann was always there, watching through binoculars, passing word through the camp midget to the mule boy and back, the final superstructural measurement made on the first day of September, 1928, a year and three months give or take from when they'd commenced. And on 9/11, the seventy-first anniversary of the single worst U.S. mass murder, perpetrated on Arkansawyers by Mormons dressed as Indians, the last pin was inserted and the great shining span complete.

The Missouri steel workers went home.

Concrete boys set up camp to pour the deck, all the water for mixing hauled in from this holy spring where the flow was pure from mother earth, clean enough for Jesus, somebody said. The concrete cured three months and the highway boys drilled and bombed and grated hell out of the road on either side, made ready for passage. The opening was on a bitter cold day when the wind howled down from the Kaibab Plateau, snow in its teeth. Six laborers and an engineer were there for that first crossing, a yellow backhoe and highway dozer set to build the road north, up to Jacob's Lake toward Fredonia, Utah land, the Mormon Highway, it was called. The formal opening was set for June, a real hootenanny with the governors of the four surrounding states, congressmen and dignitaries, the President and Prophet of the LDS Church with members of the family for the dedication of Lee's Bridge which would marry the north country to the south, the east to the west.

For good and ever, hallelujah, Amen.

Since the time of Francisco Vasquez de Coronado who, in 1540, stood before the cathedral of Santiago, patron saint of Spain, who'd risen from the grave on a white stallion to slay the Moors at the battle of Clavijo and so became Santiago Matamoros, they had come to this wilderness, such a place as prophets went into seeking vision amongst the wild wreckage of earth and sky. With his fifteen hundred horses and noblemen and heavily armored foot soldiers, before which walked a thousand Tlaxcalan Indians, they raised a great dust walking to the sea at Finisterre, where earth ends. And so it did for all time up until then in 1540, when they'd try the great ocean for the new world, drawn by rumor of silver and gold to shores where Cortez had landed nineteen years earlier to steal the chariot of Montezuma who'd sacrificed 800,000 to prevent the prophesied conqueror from the East from ever arriving, so that the streets ran ankle deep with blood, no shield against the Spaniards. Lured deeper and deeper into the land of no return, they'd rise up over the Mongollon Rim and find the Zuni with clubs and arrows, whose mud huts held no gold, nor silver, nor precious stones. They pushed west over the three mesas of the Hopi whose holy medicine kachinas danced with rattlesnakes in their mouths, writhing and snapping in the great kivas which held not a trace of *cibola*. Who walked west into the *Dineh,* their horses dying of thirst, living on nuts and roots and cactus and out of wine, into true desert they'd walked and walked and then stopped abrupt. And at that moment, when they looked out over the great abyss for which there were no words, the unfathomable depth of this chasm, impossible, even to shoot cannon from one side to the other, *O wingless mother of Christ, what have you brought us to, this?* And at the bottom, as if to mock them, a silver band the Hopi swore was a mighty river, the mother of all rivers. He would not have it, Coronado, and sent his sortie down and down and down until they saw in horror that it was indeed as the Hopi said, more so, deeper than their tallest towers, a sea of emptiness between them and the painted rims where the army was nothing but a speck on the horizon. Here, where the old world came face to face with the new and could go no further, they'd come here and stood unbelieving that it could be so, turned and walked away.

Disgraced, the *Conquistadores*, they walked their footsore and starving horses back from whence they'd come, boarded their barren ships and were seasick all the way home, where they were neither honored nor remembered. *Pahana*, the Hopi had thought them, *the lost white brother.* But of course it was not them, or maybe it was? Remembered from a time before the ice melt, when they'd made across the north country on the trail of the great horned elephant and sloth and camel, a walking for which there was no return. *Pahana'd* forgot them, and they *Pahana.*

They would come, and come again, and each time the river and the gorge that was the wonder of the world would turn them back. The priests with their silver crosses, the men who sought fur, the lost and forsaken, for some 339 years none walked a step further than Coronado's sortie, stopped at the bank of burnt red river. It was just too fucking much.

A chunk of land the size of Germany was severed through and through, the Colorado hauling ass on a gradient thirty-two times steeper than the Mississippi, the drainage from the Continental Divide rushing through its veins, so that mighty trees were sometimes found five hundred feet above the surface of river. Surely, this was not true. Such a river would conquer all before it. Surely the river had never risen to such a height?

The Mormons came, prayed to their God for passage. The very last ferry sunk in high water and killed three. It was never replaced.

Until now.

Purple and yellow ribbons met and intertwined at the midpoint of the bridge, where stood the governor's daughter with a pair of silver scissors and a wine bottle full of Colorado River water for the christening. Seven thousand souls witnessed from the rims—there were a shitload of cars and trucks, ambulances and motorcycles. A bright bluebird day in June 1929. At one point in the festivities an airplane whose motor missed one cylinder came putt-putting up the river corridor, audible long before it was visible, echoing off the canyon walls, the river shiny and blue that day, the angle of repose giving way to vibrato and skittering off the ledges. The two-prop cut under the bridge, real close so the little girl got scared and spilled some of the river water, then, what the hell, just cracked it over a rail. A whoop went up from the crowd and a marching band received orders for the crossing, the deep tubas walloping off the cliffside, drums reverberating down the south rim where the Hopi and Navajo were camped, holding their own ceremonies.

In their tongue, the Hopi asked if this was *Pahana*, this new crossing over from east to west, did this herald lost white brother's coming, the shining river bridge?

For the *Dineh*, this breach of their ancestral walls was *koyaanisqatsi*, the world out of balance, not only the people and place, but their leaders, their high priests, all things. The world was fucked. Who knew what might pour through this new gap?

Governor got tinkled on, bystanders too. Wasn't the little girl a cutie? Done up like that, silver scissors and all?

"Today marks the dawn of a new epoch," Governor said. Man has achieved dominion over grim nature."

A fight had erupted over the name—*Lee's Ferry Bridge.*

"How on earth can you name it after *that* man?" some said.

"How on earth can you not?" said others.

Fisticuffs erupted. Tubas went silent. Drumbeat ceased to echo off far wall.

And so for a while, until the great debate in the Arizona Legislature of 1934, when it was concluded for good and ever that the miracle of civil engineering, this window from the old world to the new, should not be named for a convicted and executed mass murderer, this passage was known by his name, the John Doyle Lee Bridge. Six years later, they called it Navajo Bridge, *Koyaanisqatsi* in *Dineh*, though of course no one knew jack about that, the name the elders gave their pale face brothers as the right word.

A fire concluded the ceremony.

Back on the south rim at Indian camp. Rita Begay's grandfather, Sun Bear, was there, and it was from his lips in Navajo—the language that would be stripped from the people and forbidden by the generation of children forced thereafter to the white school, the ones adopted and sent to church and taught to pray, the language of the Code Talkers which neither the Japanese nor the Germans ever penetrated—they received the holy name for this place, this new epoch, this victory over grim nature.

Koyaanisqatsi, world out of balance.

They made smoke with the pipe, the governors and highwaymen and Sun Bear. Darkness came and the stars shone in the water. Their words then, they all came out smoke.

And the next day the place was empty and quiet, save the Dineh and Hopi and wind whistling through the guidelines and beams that curved into stone they'd painted the color of desert varnish, the color of time.

What had stood in the way, had become the way.

Seen from a distance, say from Pariah Riffle where one begins to understand that this river is not like other rivers, that it has its own personality and does not give two shits to have you on its back to Mexico, the silver span surprises—you just don't expect to see it there, of a sudden, a man-made thing out of nowhere. Joey Harvell had three times passed beneath it without ever having walked the concrete deck, which, subject to the approval of the Arizona State Engineer, and according to the requirements of Class A Aggregate, had been mixed with holy water hauled the four miles from Navajo Spring, which was said to come from the *Supapi* of Spider Woman Walking, the passageway between the third and fourth earth. From the water on a sunny day, the bridge shines, the great birds tucked up underneath, white numbers spray-painted on their shoulder wings for identification, and always the tourists who walked the span, waving down and hollering whatever their people said for *good luck* or *safe travels* or *hello down there,* the foreign vowels ringing off one canyon wall and then the other.

Five miles downriver from Lee's Ferry and all the boatload of shit one has to go through to unload the semi-trucks of rafts and frames and boxes and gear, the endless webbing and straps, food and liquor and a hundred cases of beer, then load it all onto the rafts, rigged to flip, a ball-buster of a job that will wear your ass thin, five miles from all that, pushing on the oars, making adjustments before big water, the fire igniting in the backbone, when the good pulling and spinning of the sixteen foot rafts begins to get into your blood, and there's the bridge, people waving off it at you, and you're on the river, the by god Colorado, floating the goddamn Grand, and these waving people, they're the last ones you'll see other than your own party, the hundred some miles to Phantom Ranch, well it moves your heart, it does.

And then you notice the twin. The other bridge. The mirror image of the first, only different somehow, in some subtle way, different. A perfect replica, the two in tune with each other, not fifty feet apart. They span the river in harmony with one another, and so undo the curse of *koyaanisqatsi*. Even the medicine chiefs admit it by the fire when their words turn to smoke. This New Harmony, maybe, the window of the old world to the new. Maybe it is so, the lost white brother, maybe he can change. Maybe he'll remember. Maybe the people will heal, their leaders, their high priests?

He'd felt the jolt of the second bridge, Joey Harvell. The one for driving, the one built twenty-six feet wider than its brother bridge, 352,000 pounds heavier in steel and concrete, though the differences meld, they looked the same, twin bridges from the water, the sound of cars passing invisibly above, the silent footsteps, east to west, west to east.

And what he could not know but would one day learn, as he passed under the shining window into the past, was that the twin bridge, the brother bridge had been begun on the very day of the very week of the very month of the very year he'd began his return journey west. He'd flown out from Greensboro, spent that first night on a grad student's floor, then rented half a duplex in front of which mountains rose up and went gash gold vermilion dusk and dawn, where it would snow a foot on an afternoon when he shoveled six times breathing in the fecund lake, where they'd start life anew, him and Renee, buy a house, have a child, see Nevada happy hours off the front porch. Where a thousand scornful eyes would turn on you if you lit a cigarette in public. Where he was given a dozen Books of Mormon his first semester teaching. Where shared traits cropped up tribe to tribe, the skin color of their tear ducts, the hue of red hair, eye colors, the length of limbs. They walked amongst those who knew them not their kind, a people united by blood and a harsh God who demanded every last one of them consecrate their right arms to avenge the blood of the Prophet for good and ever.

Who baptized the living as proxies for the dead.

Whose original temple plans included a sacrificial altar, and some houses, one particular in the Upper Avenues had stone pillars embedded around an alter with blood-red beads glued to its surface as goddamn lawn art. Decorated the fucker for holidays.

Where it was acceptable—perhaps even preferable—to kill a gentile rather than let it live on in sin, so readeth the Doctrine of Blood Atonement as sacrament.

Utah, where he and his wife and his one daughter were gentile, and therefore corrupt, living in sin for which they should one day be punished.

Whose was God's Kingdom on Earth, with Jesus Christ as Heavenly King and the Prophet of the Church of Jesus Christ of Latter Day Saints as Earthly King.

Where his heart and fate and whatever powers that be had led him.

Where the daughter who he loved was born.

In a state that touched Arizona, where he was born, where the father he'd never met lay buried. Where his mother'd run off to, the sage-fragranced desert air he'd breathed in her womb, the water that flowed in his veins, come down as snow-melt from those mountains he'd first flown across, their jagged tips flaming as swords.

Utah, where there were mountains.

Where his people lay buried.

Passing under the pedestrian bridge with its silver twin attuned at its side, he had not yet seen the plaque, the copper endowment announcing Lee's Ferry, *dedicated to a man of great faith and sound judgement and indomitable courage,* erected by the State of Arizona in the Year of our Lord, 1960, the year Joey was born, the year the Mormons reinstated the man to their church, and so granted him the status of God, whose own planet replete with wives and children—yay, children, sayeth the Lord—should not perish, but be granted everlasting life.

And then one afternoon on their twentieth-year West, before the snow storm that would drive them from Jacob's Lake behind a plow, he walked the 616 feet from east to west, turned the corner into the false alcove and saw. "One of these days I'm going to blow that up," he'd told his daughter. "Mark my words."

He'd spat. And that second one of those spray-painted condors flapping pterodactyl wings over the blue river. It had been number seven.

A lucky number.

18.

ON BEETHOVEN'S FIFTH:
The Fourth and Final Movement

Now I lay me down to sleep
I pray the Lord my soul to keep,
And if I die before I wake,
I pray the Lord my soul to take.

I.

Wherein is ascendant and triumphant that which has been withheld, namely the trumpet as initiate and terminus.

Isn't there one of your English poets who takes his waking slow? That one who learns by going where he has to go? That's what I go to University to study, you know, English Poetry—Lord Byron, Keats, Yeats, but especially the Americans, the old faggot Whitman and his *Leaves of Grass*, "I saw a live oak growing," all the jazz about Lincoln, "Oh Captain my Captain." They forbade us read the Beats for their decadence, Ginsberg—who was surely Whitman's legitimate son, Ferlinghetti, Snyder with his *Turtle Island* copped from the Indians. More than anything on earth, I wanted to be poet, to bring alive those percussive bursts from the mouth of *mamochka,* the brick walls of her garden shining sweet enough to taste, to say it in English, I don't know why. That's how they got on to me, that I speak English, and know the poets, especially the one who takes his waking slow, who learns by going where he has to go.

Of course, you ninny, you will not blow up steel bridge with dynamite. Yakov is right about this, it is shit, the dynamite. But this is good shit, the best we could get from the miner who stole if from the Rio Tinto vault where they've got enough to blow up the whole of the Ochers should they ever get the chance.

You will go to foundation stone, drill holes in the Moenkopi Sandstone, the red rock fissures—the engineers knew it to be the weak point, the underbelly of their beast from the word go. Isn't that what you say, *the word go?* You must drill deep holes in stone abutments on either end of the Lee's Bridge, in the Moenkopi—can't you hear the fissure in the word, even? There will go the good shit, in a deep hole dark as crows in winter. It is weakness, the abutments. You have enough of good shit to blow foundation, send the bridge f467 feet in one piece to river below where it will break into twenty-two panels and sink into mud and be gone.

Yakov got it approved. It is on radar. Help Americans blow goddamn Mormon Bridge on goddamn Mormon Highway who persecute us all over, turn them upon each other, let them draw blood. Yakov, my husband, with his bristly beard and stinking mushroom breath, he said make them book, the Americans, show them how. We could stay awake that way. No more sleeping. For a while.

This happens in steps. Step one is drill hole in sandstone on either side. In fissured abutment. Here is diagram. See Appendice A.

East side is steepest, hardest climb. You must drill there first. In dark, work with red light. Yes, be Rudolphos. 103 feet from deck to bottom anchor on either side.

You will find diamond drill bit with extender. You will work holes in places indicated on diagram to indicated width and depth. You will wear rope harness while drilling in dark with red light. Stars over your shoulders, in your hair, cold there. Little rat-mouthed beaver man to help you. Two nights, one for steep side and one for West. Camp at river. Be fishermen. Catch whopper. Have license. Catch and release.

Solstice.

Under fat moon. Cars will pass over and pluck the chords of bridge's twenty-two parts, she will tremble, and you will miss your wife and daughter and wish to be home. Do not be surprised.

Why have you come to do this foolish thing? you will be thinking. You will learn by going where you have to go.

II.

When we were young and not yet in love, Yakov took me in boat on Volga for whole summer. This was before he lost eye, before they calf-roped him into machine from which there is no escape, when he still fancied himself able to make a getaway, and I was pretty and could quote T.S. Eliot in English to tourists who passed us by in big boats and sometimes tossed chocolate or bag of ice. At night, we'd camp at places where he'd sent runners to stash coolers with lamb marinating for shish-k-bob, onion and potato, vodka sometimes, red wine, so we'd feast our way through that far off golden summer when we were young and not yet forced to love.

And at the end of it, when the flat bottom's motor—is it motor or an engine if it runs on gas?—was fried and there was no making it work anymore, Yakov had somehow connected the propeller to a hand drill that he held underwater at the stern end. And in that way, with a drill wired to a boat propeller and a marine battery we made it to Caspian Sea. So think of Yakov drilling our boat a hundred miles in dark while you hang from rope harness and wish to be home decorating Christmas tree, stringing popcorn and cranberry, fitting tin angel on top just so.

Only through time is time conquered.

You have by now studied diagram for drilling on east side then west. No easy work, no rest for wicked. Today is full moon. Full cold moon or Frost Long Night's Moon, or Moon Before Yule. The 22nd—day your wife's parents were married, we learned about it that one Thanksgiving. He'd been on Volga, her father, Renee's. Rock? Wasn't that the name? He'd been at Pentagon, knew the codes, the lay of the land, but Yakov could not get a thing out of him. He wanted to talk about wedding, how him and his Navy friends had taken bus from New Jersey to West Virginia, and the bride's family—was she Meg?—had waited into night and almost called it off when bus arrived. And off poured this plowed-happy Midshipmen, so wedding could go on, and she'd almost run away, Meg, she almost had. All of us we have that chance, to run away?

Tonight is West side, much easier. Saturday night, dancing with devil. The stone will hold the warmth of the day. You must tie on and rappel. Drill the holes deep in sun-warmed Moenkopi, stained to seem untouched by man. When I think of you there with dust filtering from cliff to river, the grit on your teeth and fine spray you feel on your face in dark, I think of my story, how I left my home in spring, to sleep and wake to sleep.

And miles to go before I bleep.

III.

Of course you must burn book.

Make fire of its pages like one you built on Green River where you'd taken us for river trip, when we showed up at camp at nightfall and Rudi had got sick and thrown up on his sleeping bag. When we rigged at dam site, ran the shuttle to Colorado, then put on—Mother in Law Rapid, Corkscrew, Skull, and you caught the brown trout that were supposed to be between thirteen and twenty, only you kept them all because you wanted to throw us Arkansas Friday Night Fish Fry. At primitive camp. We followed you to water with the board and fillet knife, squatted with you there as you sliced along backbone, separated pink flesh, illegal and translucent and beautiful. Eggs fell from inside of one, her bright eyes shining, red gills, we stood between you and water when another raft approached because no one ate these fish, it was as if they were holy and only rough beast would harm them.

You soaked the fillets and spawn in egg and mustard and Yakov played your guitar after setting tent, your vodka in his veins. He walked to river. Rudi wanted to try one. With fillet knife. You let him and he destroyed it. You threw whole of it into fire, began another, our feast, on Green River where John Wesley Powell had passed, right in front of us, on his way to where you are now, he would not disapprove, the one-armed scowling man.

You said to save guts, squeezed out the stomachs to see how they were feeding: scuds, flies, their own offspring. And I thought that odd, their own offspring, here in this cold water, circles like golden eyes glowing from their skin. Blood to your elbows. The guts sizzled in fire, smelled familiar, like something from my childhood, my *mamouchka*, the cabbage field beyond garden gate where black crows danced in snow.

You waded into river, shirtless, went under, under again. The water dripped from your hair. You swung it back and forth. Renee watched from folding table, making coleslaw, drinking wine. Rudi waded in and went under, he slung his hair side to side.

The guitar leaned against pine tree.

Yakov came carrying a bright green vine, and you yelled *No, No, No*. It is poison you said, poison ivy. And Yakov had put some in his mouth and chewed, and you called him crazy. You crazy fucking Russian, you said. He'd rubbed his chest with it, washed his face. You balled hushpuppies, little balls of cornmeal and flour, and fried potatoes in dutch oven. Then the fish and fritters. Sliced tomatoes and peppers. A cocktail sauce and tartar. We ate like queens and kings, the fried flesh thin and crisp and a delight to the taste. Arkansas fish fry. You cooked enough for twice our party. We'd have it tomorrow for breakfast, for lunch, fish tacos.

We drank vodka and sang to sky. Confessed. Told who we were and want we were doing, what it was like to sleep and wake and be made to sleep again. You told Yakov not to touch your goddamn guitar. Maybe you would not remember. Maybe not.

Become the enemy, right?

Place dynamite in holes, wired—*provoloka,* let tails be foot long from holes. Cover with liquid cement. See Appendix B, diagram. Sixty holes east, sixty west. Tail wires snaked from holes. Tomorrow night you will connect to master wire to detonator. Pizoelectric—quartz crystal.

Next morning Yakov was blistered head to toe. Hungover. Sunburned, he claimed, tongue swollen as summer sausage. In Russia we never carry our shit with us, he said when you strapped groover to your raft. We were American then. Rudi, too. Free on river. Carrying our shit. No cameras seeing though.

Like fish carcass, you must burn this book.

IV.

I dream in Russian. The colors are Russian colors. *Krasniy, ciniy, zhyoltiy, zelyoniy, oranzheviy, fioletoviy, beliy, chyorniy, rozoviy*—red, blue, yellow, green, orange, purple, white, black, pink. Beautiful green Siberia, the joke that it was a place where bad people were sent, a heaven on earth, beautiful green Siberia in spring time. Not unlike Uintas where we gather mushrooms on my birthday, King Bolete and Slippery Jack, the little scarlet ones for sautéing. Do you remember the snowfall? When Yakov set the birthday bomb that made sled hill? The bonfire? Drunk, stupid Misha? After you left we found where you'd peed your wife's name into snow. Renee. Yakov wrote Yelena. It took him two tries.

Day three is for connecting tails to master wire. See Appendix C. Does not take rocket scientist, and I've actually known one, little rocket scientist. Back in Moscow. Stupid as sackful of hammers. I used to write him poetry. Awful stuff about fall of Icarus, Phoenix rising from ashes. He was friend of Yakov. Little rocket scientist.

At Institute of Physics. He named one for me, a rocket. And on Mayday they shot them off above Red Square, rockets, the one named Yelena, they screamed off to blow up who knows what? Yeltsin was there. Gorbachev, that red splotch above right eye.

Yakov blew his eye out that summer. Turned inward. Who needed anymore poetry, wasn't there enough in world already? Give me bombs, that's what is needed. And your dynamite? Yakov is right. It is shit. He could have given you kingdom come, blow Mormons to smithereens.

What color would that be? Smithereens?

Not a Russian color.

Day Three is for rolling out wire, connecting tails, detonator. In afternoon the vermilion cliffs turn vermillion, a sort of red mixed with pink. *Krasniy smeshivat rozoviy.*

The color of buoys that wash in from sea.

V.

My father did not approve.

He never tried to hide that it hurt his heart, me leaving home for this—this dream of America. On the day that I told him he looked away, past *mamouchka's* garden fence to cabbage field with its grey horizon of sky dotted with crows, a murder of them. He would not talk to me. I said Papa, I love you, come see me and I will teach you to waltz, to ride horse, eat ice cream and sing "Take Me Out to the Ballgame." But his eyes were on complicated faraway spot, and he never looked back. Is that how I seem to Rudi?

Is it?

When he goes off to Chicago with skinny American girl, smoking dope and talking on Smart Phone? On day when we skated on frozen lake and he told me he goes to University in Chicago, did I look away. Past smelter and copper mine to deepest hole on earth. Were my eyes complicated?

I will not lose my son like I lost father. Not there to tell him goodbye. Papa? And Yakov with his cameras taking pictures from space, clicking and clacking on satellite, see through doors, through walls, but does camera eye ever see itself?

I grow tired of bridge, Joey.

They will catch you and throw you in prison and you will miss your wife and daughter and wish to be home. Or they will kill you and your eyes will be far away and complicated for the ones you love—their hearts will hurt.

For you, tomorrow is Christmas eve, Feast of Seven Fishes.

Night animals talk.

A messenger will come to you with secret blue as sky. You must choose east or west—one goes home, the other away. Set up high. Prepare detonator. Insert earplugs. Wait for rose pink light, color of buoy.

See Appendix D.

VI.

There is a photograph of Papa holding Rudi, one arm around him, pointing at something through window with other hand. Light on his face, Papa's, gleaming golden light. Rudi's back to the camera, on Papa's chest arms flung wide around his neck. They have same hair I see now, Papa and Rudi. Same.

You have never told me of your father, your mother. Your Arkansas. Do you miss it? Dream in its color? Is there place where your relatives lay to rest? How you say, buried? Is there a certain tree where raccoon once ate rose-pink persimmon globes and shit the white seeds in pile beneath? A flower? Smell? Is light golden in autumn so birds turn to light at sunset? Do bears waltz there? Are there bears? What are people named? No Yakov, no Yelena. Festus? Jethro? Uncle Jed? Are there music temples for afternoons when light has heft of cathedral tune? Drink? Eat? Friday night fish fry? Hushpuppy? What do you do there? In your land? Are there rivers and bridges and copper pit mines? Mushrooms? Mountains?

Is there a great ocean where sturgeon swim? How do they say *I love you* where you are from? Do you make two-headed beast? Your tombstones, what do they say? Are there days named for coming of age. For girl's first menstruation? Boys? Doctors, hospitals, medicine? What does it mean to throw salt over left shoulder? To leave tooth under pillow? Do you lay in bed some afternoons and count floorboards? Do numbers have personalities? Is there shadow in corner? Window? Light on fields that stretch to forever? Hope? Place to go when world sleeps? Crows?

What is your home? Do you miss it? Can you go back?

Can you ever go home?

Can I?See Appendix F. Burn book for warmth before first light.

The word for love, in Russian.

Lyubit.

VII.

In light of burning book, find lever of detonator. *Push.* We have not spoken of second bridge. What happens to first could happen to second. One thing causes another, or it doesn't. Yakov tells me to tell you.

For every action, equal and opposite reaction. Spooky action at distance. First one could take down second. Is possible.

Do svidaniya. Goodbye.

Spokoynoy nochi.

Idti domoy. Go home.

> *Behold, it is come, and it is done, saith the Lord God; this is the day whereof I have spoken. For they shall spoil those that spoiled them, and rob those that robbed them, saith the Lord God. Neither will I hide my face any more from them.*
>
> *EZEKIEL, 39-40.*

Blow trumpets—let them roar.

19.

Down into the green meadow we walked with the sun on our backs. Shady trees led to a spring with delicious chill water, and we lay down in the tall grass to take our rest, and there came the butterflies. On the verge of desert, this cool green place in September when the fall light was coming gold, and we were visited by butterflies. Clouds of them, they lit on Vina's raven sheen of hair, on our fingers, our lips. Came out our mouths when we spoke, our breaths mixed with the clouds of color that just went on and on. And of all the living things there, between desert and the cobalt sea that awaited us in our dreams, desires, what was hoped for and feared, what I want most for you to know, J.W., my love, the butterflies that descended on us at the mountain meadow.

I am an old woman. But let me tell you a secret. You. Who came to see me, who won't let me rest. Who've traced my steps, tracked me down and keep on tracking me like I'm some answer to the question on fire in your soul. So you've ended up here on my doorstep, offering what you've brought in trade for words, my words, for I alone survive to tell.

What is it you want me to say?

What?

Papa Georgy? Minerva? Sweet Vina?

You want their blood but I give you butterflies. That's right. Butterflies. As far as the eye could see, a great glorious swarm of them, that's what I saw, that's what I knew. Aflutter, they followed our wagons, rode the harness with its jingling, and I could hear the wings that first night with the stranger family. The girl who'd call me sister, who I'd snuggle to when cold winter came, butterflies. So you can forget chili and cornbread and "Blessed Assurance," all of that. The men who might have disobeyed their orders, and that tomorrow might never come, and we'd have topped a hill not so far from there and seen the sea spread out blue as forever and know we'd done right to walk west, that we'd made it home.

Butterflies.

Came following the man showed up in a wagon to haul us home. Flew loop de loops and figure eights around the family I'd tried with my whole heart to hate, but couldn't, I just wasn't made that away.

Followed us clean back across the Continental Divide, through the river valley and back up into Boone County, where Grandma Poteet and Grandma Jenkins recognized us by the knit work stitches in our bonnets, what they'd taught their daughters, the butterfly stitch, *mariposa*. Rest, Mary. Rest.

Last I seen them, the host of souls flying, they were down by the creek where I'll walk directly, show those men with the plaque the right place, where sister and I sat so long ago with our feet just skimming the water, snakes sipping water with their dark-forked tongues.

You came for blood, but I give you butterflies.

Edgar awoke with two thoughts burning in his head at the same time: one was the little pilot light dancing beneath water heater one room over; and the second was that a hundred and twenty some sticks of dynamite were wrapped in a cardboard box in the room next to the next room over where the yellow pilot danced. The two thoughts were congruous. They mattered. Did not cancel each other out. On the one hand, the Russian woman had gone into a conniption at even the mention of fire, and on the other, that was surely the fuck a flame he saw burning through the two-by-four skeleton of a wall. The room next to the next room over, where the dead dog slept before it was dead—Bear, thing was named. He smelled it, the dead dog before it was dead, felt it looking at him through the studs, spirit dog sniffing the strange new box, the diamond drill bit, the piezoelectric detonator. When pressure is directed to a specific point on a quartz crystal, a spark is produced, fire from stone, and such could be used to produce electric current, to initiate conflagration, to begin explosion. That's how he understood it, Edgar, there on the Harvell daughter's worn out mummy bag with its busted-out zipper and hand lotion in the side pocket. Today, the Monday of his first week of freedom. He should get up and go, put the whole mess behind him, get his ass back to Arkansas, or cruise over the Sierra Madre to California, that's where they were headed all along, wasn't it, the big blue ocean, gray whales blowing they spouts close enough to hit with a goddamn plug, what the Harvell boy said, hoss a Devil's Toothpick out and katy bar the door.

A broken oar blade is leaned on the concrete shelf, next to another broken oar blade and another, seven of the fuckers, each one with a nasty name writ on it in black: Skull, Upper Disaster, Hell's Half Mile, Up Yours, Disappointment, Satan's Gut. There's life jackets and river bags, netting, a sliver sand spike with HARVELL printed on it. They're river people, these Harvells, like the ones taken him to the Navajo woman's hogan to retrieve his by god truck, parked out on the street, all he needs is gas. He still had folding money, they hadn't taken that. And the book, Chief's. Rudolph the Red, blow the man away, don't hold nothing back, give it to'em full throttle: *Resist much, obey little. Now or never.* How he'd smuggled it out in a hollow Book of Mormon, no words on the cover, just a gold man blowing on a trumpet, the ripped-out pages under a stone in the tank of the toilet that doubled as a water fountain at Coconino County. Frisbeed the cocksucker into the Painted Desert, let him blow his horn the fuck out there, rooty-toot-toot.

He *should* haul ass. Piss on them. Just like Tina Casteen had done to him way back in that other life, the one that could have been—*guess why we're three Edgar? It's you keeps bringing me back.* How could the living harm the dead? Or put another way, how can the dead harm the living. The answer, Edgar understood, that moment when he woke with the two thoughts on fire in his head, Navajo princess riding him on the black bird to who knew where, twin sides of the same thought, joined at the hip.

Fool—not letting them die. And for them, not dying.

Let be, Edgar.

From the room of the dead dog before it died, each of their names as articulate as breath, they wait and go on waiting for the living fire that ends all.

Now or never.

A man called their house from time to time who hated his own mother. Dial up the land line from Texas and disguise his voice badly, say *evenin' gringo, como esta?* Sometimes Renee'd answer and the pass the phone off straight away—she had no patience for this bad actor's shit. "Whew," the guy'd say to Joey, "who pissed in her cornflakes?" Other times Lara'd answer, if she was home from University, and she'd go along with the shtick for a while, then pass off to Joey, say it was somebody named Big Tex who was a bill collector about to kick down their front door or some such. This guy's mother, who he'd hated while alive and detested in death, had ridden with the Hell's Angels, and never really knew which one had fathered her son, so she was all the time inviting twenty or thirty of them over and having him stand on the coffee table so everyone could get a look, but they never ever figured it out, which one was the father, and mother and son held it against one another. Now he hated all women, especially those in the Me, Too movement, and he'd call up to rail at the top of his lungs about how he'd married a stripper, who'd stolen everything he had, his money, job, retirement, manhood, children, even his dog, Dexter. The bitch. Only this night, in December, on the eve of everything about to go down, Joey'd picked up and listened through the first bout of vitriol, and then the guy said, "Just how are you doing, anyway?"

"Good," Joey said. "I'm doing fine."

It was night before Renee's 59th birthday. She'd bought Dungeness Crabs and Scallops, the steaming was about to begin. Lara'd baked a carrot cake that day while Joey and Renee'd skied. They'd opened wine, a Syrah she liked. He'd bought six bottles. It was the official beginning of the hollerdays, what they called them, all of their birthdays and Christmas rolled up in three weeks.

"Just what makes you so fine," the guy, who Joey'd somehow met because he edited a history journal where he'd submitted. A guy who'd published Joey's work, who was all about the piss and vinegar in his Mormon vendetta.

"It's my wife's birthday. We're cooking a feast."

"So fucking what. She'll end up boning her divorce attorney."

"We've been married thirty-one years."

She came into the room, Renee, raised both brows. It was him on the other end, woman hater from hell. Big Tex. Want to have some fun with me without him knowing? he'd once said to her.

"Don't mean a thing."

Joey said, "I've got to cook."

"You'll hate her someday."

He put the receiver in its cradle, the hard words flying before the click, and the phone ringing immediately after, until he unplugged it and let it die. A long, long time ago, before the stories that would come to direct his life had ever happened, he'd listened to his mother and father fight through the bedroom walls. They went after each other, murder in their hearts. And it took a long time for him to learn, and only then through his own marriage and life and life, that it was only possible to hate someone in the same capacity as you could love them. What you felt in one direction was equally true in the other.

"Who was that?" Renee asked. She'd bought new curtains, insulated black outs to block road noise and cold.

Yellow ones came fluttering the November J.W. went to be with the Lord. Isn't it strange how our life passes right before our eyes, and we don't even know it, don't even notice the Sunday afternoons when the dogs bark down in the hollow and a hard rain comes that floods the basement again. Clouds came down from Canada, tornadoes in their time. There's a frady hole out by the second barn J.W. dug, laid cinderblock and fitted the wooden door on hinges. We'd go to it when the big wind came, and this one time when the sky got the color of a bruise and the sweetgum turned loose of her spiky balls and it got so quiet you could hear the rattle in his chest that would take him, J.W. All down the path we ran, climbed down into dark onion-smelling quiet, just me and him. That's when we heard it, just a little at first, then so loud it got under my teeth, there where the memories are, I swear, and outside that freight train came rolling round the bend, and somewhere inside with me and my love, the snake. In springtime. All the apple blossoms blown down when we came out, the sun full on us. Butterflies came that May, tasted blackberry bloom on the fence lines around the plot where I buried him, J.W. Terry, who I married January 25, 1874, when we were 22.

Walk with me now.

Down to the creek where the cool shade takes us home. The butterflies will come to the water where witchdoctors ride each other tail to tail. And I will tell you the last thing, what you've come to hear, what nobody knows, what I alone survive to tell.

The wild roses grow there and we can dance in the meadow, the sun will shine on our faces and we'll be young again. Won't we? Like the winter when it snowed and you peed my name off the tongue and groove porch? Isn't it strange how your whole life goes by and you don't even know it, don't even notice the bright angel morning when Georgie Porgy Eagle goes *shree, shree, shree* and you lay down in the tall grass where the cool water flows from a spring you'd just die for a drink of again, this day, I can tell you, I can.

He killed the rattlesnake, J.W. did. Strung it from a dogwood tree, and died not long after. A hard rain came, flooded the basement. So any time now the rains don't come, folk go to killing snakes, stringing them up from the forks of trees, tease the sky for clouds. There weren't none that day when the fake Indians come running on us, when the men tied our wagons together and dug the trench. Daddy said goddamn and Vina give me the look. "Hold my hand, child," she said. It was September, and the butterflies came. They lit on us, sipped our sweat.

We breathed them, and they us. It's time now, Lord. Walk with me to the creek and we'll dance in the meadow, the sun on our faces. We'll be young again, love in our hearts.

I'll tell you what you come to hear.

Just help me down the step, I can see the path now, right there. Vina, faceless brother, Mama. Daddy. Father. Sister.

How exactly to tell your wife, on her birthday, no less, that you plan to blow up a bridge with dynamite stolen from Kennecott Copper Mine, and that if you get caught, to kindly post bail and give a call to Captain Len Elderege, a Mormon attorney, who can maybe intercede with the bishops and whatever other warlocks need to be consulted to keep your ass out of the pokey for life. Should you wait until after cake, say during clean up, while loading the dishwasher, just haul off and say, "Oh yea, I forgot to tell you, I'm driving down to Lee's Ferry mañana, remember that bridge?"

How about, "You know that fellow living in our basement, he and I we're going to Zion to avenge Captain Fancher."

Or, "I need to go to the river. Just a few days. I'll be home for Christmas."

After thirty-one years, did they even hear each other anymore? Was it even possible to get the word across from one side to the other? He had people in that party. The son of a bitches had never said sorry, kiss my ass, nothing at all. Their whole world wide religion thing, the missionaries going two-by-two bullshit, learning every language on earth, preaching the gospel, celestial marriage, sealed for eternity, the Jesus jammies and secret namings, consecrating their right arms to avenge the blood of the prophets, the Tabernacle Choir and "little piece of Paris," General Conference twice a year and golden tablets, that gold Moroni on the top of their temple blowing to beat the band, it was all one enormous buttload, wasn't it? built on a foundation of outright treachery and murder. Somebody was going to bygod pay. Or some *thing*. The bridge would do. Kill the goddamn way west. Window to the new world. That was enough. Wasn't it?

That would be enough.

Lee's Ferry Bridge. He'd be home for Christmas. They'd spend their honeymoon anniversary in Castle Valley. The New Year would be a good one. Trumpett would go to jail. The Russians exposed. Lara had that trip to Argentina to study whale lice, and they were set to bike the Camino again, Puente la Reina to Santiago de Compostela. Retirement just down the road. Their golden years. Renee had booked a VRBO in Sooke, British Columbia. Salmon swam that inlet, big-ass kings and boats to fish them from cold waters.

Their whole lives lay out before them. Didn't they deserve this?

Didn't they?

It was just a bridge, a man-made thing. Built by Missourians, if the story be believed. Missouri, goddamn. Built just downstream from J.D. Lee's hideout, where Brigham had sent him so as to be protected from Federal Authorities, because Brigham's adopted son was a by god wanted man, having perpetrated at the fat man's order the single greatest loss of life on the whole goddamn manifest destiny migration westward. He'd led the massacre of 120 emigrants from Arkansas, and word was it was right brutal, women and children and rape and mayhem and that kind of shit. Under the white flag of treachery. Part of the plan. They left the bodies to rot where they fell, the women's long hair wafting from sagebrush to this day. Word was the Arkies had cheered when the Nauvoo Legion soldiers had marched them toward their deaths, thinking these soldiers in uniform had come to save them from the fake Indians. That they'd come to the rescue. Only the word was given, a gunshot, and each of the escorts turned on his liege, men who'd been under siege for five straight days, who'd buried kith and kin in shallow graves, who'd shit and pissed and vomited and bled into cat holes dug into the thirty foot circle, their children, women. They shot the men first. Then the women and children. Down to the youngest able to tell the tale. Left them lay. Wolves, it was said, preferred first the youngest girls.

Had not the land opened itself up to him and showed him the sign, green for life and living, a strand of golden hair woven into the clasp. Had he taken something from the monument? You're goddamn right.

The bridge was history. Blow it the fuck up.

And so in his mid-fifties, when there was nothing keeping him from escaping Utah which anybody with half a brain would have done about then, Edgar T. Paris found himself once again driving across the vast sage ocean of red land, down and down and down, and he knew that it must be true, the prophecy of the jailbirds who'd pressed his license plate—Arkansas 956 DMF—he was *Dumb Mother Fucker* for life, surely he was. Solstice, sun stands still, a seven-hour drive Harvell said. They'd split the goods, half in back of Edgar's camper, and the other in the Pathfinder he follows just now, a pocket full of cash, he'd gassed, a paper sack filled with sausage biscuits for the road, homemade, they smell like home. Not yet daylight, they hit Beaver, the little cameras click-clicking above the pumps, recording oil checks and top offs, thirty-six pounds even in all four tires, the windshield washer tool dripping fluid on the hoods of their vehicles, everything okay. Back home the boys'd be barbecuing backstrap venison for Christmas dinner, glazing the German Chocolate cake and stuffing duck callers in stockings. Back at TriCounty Coon Club where he should be now, where he'd spent that one Christmas time with Tina, naughty elf, who'd let slip that she was preggers, that Edgar'd be a father, that they were three now, a family.

Goddamn. DMF. When would she finally let him be? What would it take? Maybe he'd never get free, Edgar. First light, just a little to his left, the freeway flies south through New Harmony, Toquerville—what they do there, sit around toking it?— Hurricane to Arizona, a town called Mad Rabbit. Hello, I'm from Mad Rabbit. What were they thinking? They all crazy, all of them who'd come west looking for something they never found, a part of themselves they missed, lost, just like Edgar, like the sad Indians he'd jumped on the side of the road way back when, that woman selling mojos on the bridge, son of a bitch bird who hog-gobbled one he'd thrown in disgust, brave, courageous good decision maker Lee, Stoner who'd whacked him upside the head, Harvell, the Russians, the whole lot of them, looking for that lost part.

Tina, too, was that what took her away? Was anything ever enough?

Roadside, a run over deer's eyes glow Christmas red, just before the turn off for a rest area, empty save the lone black semi, its galaxy of signal and danger lights conjoining with sunrise.

Edgar's not surprised.

It's all of us has to face our demons.

20.

Stoner smelled rat. Roadside in the Painted Desert, *ratty, rat, rat.*

The blue book cover missed its inside pages, they'd been ripped out. It was the same as jail issue, the ones handed to all prisoners so they'd have something to do other than meanness, maybe some of it'd sink in and they'd stay clean for a while. Not likely, seldom seen. But this book, it was trying to tell him something. Here on the triangle of space he ever drove into the earth, from Page to Flag to the Ferry, how exactly did a Coconino issue Book of Mormon come to be shining bright as a blue hogan door for his eyes to see on a Friday, Winter Solstice, the long night after a short day. He could dust the fucker for prints, run them *mañana* at the Page facility, bunch of derelicts. What he really wanted was to get on home and put an end to the week, the whole damned year, all of it maybe. He could do it, deserved it, only no one would be home, just like last time, and the time before that—it was what it was. He'd end up at the hotel restaurant eating chicken fried steak smothered in white gravy, pie on the side, coffee. The season full over now, only a stray fisherman or river rat. They let him keep a trailer there at Jacob's Lake, next to the snow plow driver from Salt Lake, whose wife had run off and left him too, so the place had a feel to it, sort of a Heartbreak Hotel thing, though Stoner's heart was not broken, thank you, mind your own goddamn beeswax.

He turned the book cover in his hands, the solstice light falling on Angel Moroni, embossed in gold, trumpet grasped in his right hand, to his mouth, cheeks puffed, blowing the good news of the gospel—of how merciful the Lord hath been to his children, that living men might be sanctified, perfected in Christ, that they might become holy, without spot.

His father had spoken so, and his father before him. Stern men of faith with the holy ghost power to consecrate certain spaces as holy and sanctified and without spot. It had been a hard way, not answering the call. They'd never be pleased with him no matter what he did, not on this earth and not on the next. His brother held Father's blessing for good and ever. Fuck it. Stoner's lot was to be exiled to this desert of stone and sand, life with the Lamanites, exiled Tribe of Israel, drunks and addicts and lowlife scum.

A semi blew by, speeding. Black as an Ace of Spades. Likely high on crank. Out here in the goddamn middle of goddamn nowhere, first day of winter, alone.

Somebody'd torn the pages from the holy word—someone he'd had doings with, had spoken to, arrested, maybe. Who?

He turned the cover over and over, as if he had the gift his brother possessed, the beholding of angles and ministering of spirits. It was speaking thusly to him, the good book, testifying to the truth.

Someone had passed this way and thrown it out an open window. The insides had been ripped out beforehand, and so the cover was used to conceal. Stoner sniffed. His wife's wrist had lain on the sheet of paper as she wrote those words in blue cursive. Her goodbye, he'd sometimes held it to his face, and could so breathe her in and make her home again. He regretted burning that last letter, if only for that, losing what little she'd left.

Sometimes a man could smell a herd of elk on a hidden ridge before he saw them. Like a dog, like a wolf.

Stoner lifted the defiled word of God to his face, sniffed.

The scent came sudden and distinct.

His heart quickened, Stoner's.

Even as a boy, he'd been quick to anger. It would come on him, so that he quit thinking, went into some other way of being. He'd lost his temper with the woman, the last time worst. His weight to carry.

Stoner was aware of the great space around him, between him and the Vermillion Cliffs, the ferry named for his far-off forefather, come from the meadow where they'd slain the ancient enemy, not an innocent soul among them, and so avenged, if only for the moment, the blood of holy prophets.

A second time, he breathed the scent.

Rat.

He could taste it.

Out in sage and earth-hued dirt, blue sky so big it hurt on a day the government was shut down, and he was no longer handcuffed by the laws that protected the guilty, shielded the corrupt, and so postponed the blood atonement that had been commanded by Christ the King through the lips of his Holy King on Earth.

There'd be prints.

He'd dust the fucker later for prints, but in his heart, he already knew.

In a stroke of synchronicity of the sort that had occurred so often in Joey Harvell's life that he was no longer surprised, but rather felt the kind of recognition which accompanies coming upon a loved amputee at a family reunion, familiar and strange, the bloody idiot President had shut down the government that very day, so there were no rangers to meet them at the campsite gate, to run licenses and record their plates and tags and have them rubber band a certificate noting their campsite number and payment stub around the rearview mirror, rather just a flyer noting that the toilets and showers were closed, there was no trash pick-up, and that the trout limit remained two per day, one over twenty and one under fifteen. Artificial flies and lures only, possession limit equal to three days maximum.

Fisherman's camp was above the put in, where the day's rafting parties were now in charge of policing themselves, and so having the most kick-ass party that Joey had ever witnessed at Lee's Ferry boat ramp. Winter Solstice, 2018. They'd broken their groovers out, were pissing in the river, just like you're supposed to do, a hot-wired stereo on a baloney boat howling. Folk wearing boas and dog suits and one boat captain in a wedding dress danced the hoochie coo. The smell of meat grilling a hundred yards away.

Best to steer clear. That kind of thing could draw the heat in a heartbeat. A busy night ahead, he backs the Pathfinder into the parking slot, number twenty-one, lucky number.

Paris killed it in the run over lot, cardboard duct taped to the little windows on the camper in his truck bed. The afternoon was clear, warm for December, it felt that way. There ran the Colorado, green, darker in the tongues, flat here, rolling out, The Crossing of the Fathers, it had been called before Lee came, a Federal Warrant out for his arrest. He'd brought some of the wives, the older kids for labor. The Church had claimed the land for the Latter-Day Saints of Jesus Christ whose kingdom was to be manifest on earth just as it was in heaven.

Between them, they've got enough juice to go to the pokey for life, maybe, a thought that Renee had weighed with him before they left. *Is this worth us? Your family? Thirty-one years of marriage? What good can it possibly do for anyone?*

Lara was a third year Sophomore, home for break. They'd put up a Christmas tree, decorated. She'd stamped out five hundred hearts from colored paper and had set to work on a 58th birthday card for him. Christmas, when he was born. All those years ago when his mother heard the sound of the tin angel candle ding just when her water broke, and she'd hemorrhaged, and they'd both nearly died. He'd been given this life, Joey. The miracle of it.

"Don't do it, Dad. This is stupid." Lara'd said last night. She'd turn twenty-one in January—good God.

And in the five minutes it takes him to stake his tent, roll out the Paco and mummy bag, to place a filled water bottle where his head will be and make sure of the headlight, to place a photo of them two of them together, Renee and Lara, everything he knows of life in this world now—his whole life really—he sees the whole thing, the whole hot mess for what it is—stupid. Foolishness, utterly so.

Paris joined him at the picnic table where they each cracked a beer. "What do we do now?" he asked.

Downhill, they'd lit a fire—a real doozy—in a grill pan on four legs, the yellow flames mixed with blue and orange, the smell of pinyon on the breeze, a good hard killing frost just around the corner. A good night for sleeping in your own bed, in your own house, the three stockings hung already.

God, he was stupid.

"We're supposed to be fishermen," Joey said. "Guess we ought to fish."

And that's what they did till dark, cast Rapalas into the green water and jerk jig, having a time with the cutthroat whose scarlet slashes shone through four feet of river water, strong enough to snap six-pound test.

They'd fried their fish gold back at camp, balled hushpuppies, and so reenacted the Friday night fish fry that bound them as kith and kin.

Night one—drill the east side. Steepest, the hardest climb. In fissured abutment. Here is diagram. See Appendice A.

They called them "the hollerdays" him and Joanna. She was from Vernal, the daughter of a bishop, wild thing, though tender-hearted with a temper like his, so he'd say something, she'd say something back, and before you could say *pig shit* they were throwing the ornaments off the Christmas tree at the picture window above the kitchen sink, and they'd find little bits of silver and gold glass in coffee mugs and fruit bowls, in the sugar and freezer ice. It's just who they were, in their DNA. His mother'd told him that it was a good thing, him and Joanna fighting the way they did—it meant they loved each other, because you could only really fight in a meaningful way with somebody who you loved. And the fight, she claimed, was only equal in intensity to the love, or potential for such—that's what his mother said, and Lord knows she should know after fifty years with God's own son of a bitch his father. You could rob a bank and not get that much time.

The thing about being from Vernal was that it was a redneck town where, before everyone got hooked and rotted their teeth out with crack, there was heroin, and before that speed, and just plain jane wacky weed, and if that didn't work, the Colorado border was spitting distance and you could just hop, skip and jump on over and get whiskey frisky. And that thing about a preacher's daughter, true.

Probably he had his own crutches, Stoner. Didn't everyone? Even his righteous-ass brother the church warlock. He'd take Joanna and her bourbon breath any day of the week over what his brother had—the house, the cars, the kids with multi-colored braces. There's always a pimple and a bad smell somewhere, isn't there. You could fart through silk, but the smell was the same. Bro had a skeleton or two under his bed, didn't he? Best not go there, sniffing up that tree.

And now the government shut down. Which meant all the park rangers were kaput. The trash and toilet services. The North and South rims where the yahoos climbed class three cliffs in flip-flops summer, spring, winter and fall, and it was the rangers' job to haul their dead asses out on pack mules, after the condors had had their way with them. Where the rats down at the put in were no doubt up to no good that very second, and poachers were going to town on the trout fishery, and all manner of everything the fuck else was going to hell too. Stoner's territory had just tripled and quadrupled and whatever the fuck five times was.

Friday night was coming, he was lonely, Stoner. He'd thrown away Joanna's number so many times he knew it by heart, how her voice would ooze through the phone, say *I know it's you, it's always you.*

The twin Navajo Bridges shine when he crosses, rose pink from the Vermillion Cliffs to the north and west, the longest night of the year. He wishes Joanna could see it that second, that she was in the truck with him then and they could go home and lay down and laugh at the silly-ass things they'd worried themselves sick over for their whole lives.

And she'd say *you, it's always you,* so a little wisp of air'd come through the gap in her front teeth, the mark of Venus, she called it.

She smelled like oranges, Joanna.

That's the goddamn trouble with living in your head, next thing you know you'll be hightailing it the back way to Vernal, redneck capital of Utah, knocking on the Bishop's door despite the restraining order.

The Navajo's wrapping up her table now, Rita Begay—she's a good egg, quiet, has a daughter over to Monument Valley, a teacher, graduated from the U. Up in Salt Lake where that Harvell was in History. Professor Smart Ass—they'd let anybody teach. Goddamn. Who he'd sent that fish-faced Arkie pisser home with as custodian. Sixty days. Drove this way toward

Salt Lake City.

The gold angel on the book cover in the plastic evidence bag has the slightest sheen in the last sun of the shortest day. He fights the urge to make the turn back for Marble Canyon and Lee's Ferry where the rats are no doubt having a shit fit.

Stoner smells rat. *Ratty, rat, rat.*

He'd head on over to Page, dust the fucker for prints, have the warrant for both those Arkie's asses by Monday morn, Christmas Eve, here come Santa Clause. He rolled his window down, let the good air get him in the face, wash away the road stink.

Back in the city his brother'd be presiding over the Festival of Lights, have him a couple naughty young elves against the cold. To hell with it. Uphill to Page and Glen Canyon, he'll take a room there, order some wings.

Maybe call Joanna.

The Moenkopi grit has a taste to it, wordless and foreign, though remembered from somewhere so deep inside it must be his soul, if such a thing exists. Did he believe in the soul, Joey? It was a good question, a good place to be, the banks of the Colorado River at Crossing of the Fathers, *aka* Lee's Ferry. Ten hours of drilling, a thing he'd only done in stone once in his life, when he was gifted the piece of pipestone for the canupa that leans against his prayer blanket back home in the study he built off the north side of the house where he has burned so many hours agonizing over the past that was truly neither dead nor even past. There was something, surely to God there was *something*. A trace, energy, a thing that spoke to you and was you in lodge or vision quest or in the hottest hour of Sundance when the tree shimmies and the heat comes on and three go down in a second, the wind whipping, the spirits come on you and there's no doubting, they make the hair on our arms stand. Though you can't see them, they're no less there than the air you breathe, the spirit people.

No?

Mama'd tried to contact him after she died. The phone would ring out of kilter, and he'd hear her voice. *Joey,* she'd say. *Joey?* Surely to God if there was anyone that would want her near, it was him. She'd be there in his dream, real, asking him to help her, that she didn't want to be in that place alone, to *please oh please oh please help me.* Jimmy'd never come to him that way, asking for help. Somehow, going through the windshield at eighty miles an hour had left him quiet in the dreams, embarrassed, maybe, six feet tall and sawdust bronze, kindness in his eyes, they'd walked a roof ridge together once, a house they'd framed together, and after decking he'd taken Jimmy up and they'd walked the crown, careful not to slip on the sawdust where the cuts had been made. They'd held hands out, walked like tightrope walkers in their nail aprons, their twenty-five-foot tapes with their initials carved on the metal casing buried in a pouch with eight penny nails and a utility knife, pencils for scribing. In the dream, Joey's speed square fell out, skittered down slick plywood then fell the thirty feet from decking to concrete, pinged, went on ringing like a bell, so that every time Joey ever heard a bell, it took him straight there, holding his arms out on a roof ridge in Lonoke, Arkansas, with his one brother, Jimmy, thirty-two years dead. His maternal grandfather, Marion Weldon Poteet Stepwell, spoke to him in the language of a duck, right through the walls of time, usually something about the garden or whiskey, how the Big Boys had a touch of blight that had to be cut out, Tobacco Mosaic or Nematode, that the okra grew faster if you picked it every day, how Joey needed to follow the blood trail back into the wood, where the doe deer the old man'd shot lay dying illegal as hell. They'd get the warden drunk, he'd stamp the tag.

Back strap venison, fresh meat for supper son. Sometimes he'd blow his duck caller out the back study door at daylight, wake the whole neighborhood, have them confused with duck language. They could hear him from the Dean's Office, the dome of the stadium, Joey blowing the duck call Mama'd given him, with a note saying that this was the very last physical thing she had remaining of her father's, that maybe it could connect them through the generations, maybe it could?

Grandmother Dee tried to get him to accept Jesus Christ as his Lord and Savior, up on a bridge, the very same bridge, Joey realized in his sleep, as the one he'd just spent ten hours drilling under, so the fine dust got up under his teeth, his nostrils, in his ears and belly button. He remembered the silver water shining below and Dee begging him, pleading from her side of eternity to follow Jesus. Like that story in the Bible, where the man in hell begged to be able to tell his brother. And when he said no, she turned loose, fell backward and the sound of her body breaking on the rocks below would stick with him for all the waking and sleeping moments of his life.

He'd run into Mama walking one time. In this huge vast land where everyone was walking and their feet were dirty and swollen and they'd forgotten everything they'd ever known, and Joey was walking, and he'd seen her at the same time as she'd seen him, and they'd hugged as strangers do and wept and were happy, mother and son.

And she'd forgiven him for yelling for her to *please just goddamn die,* just as Lara would one day to him, what the newly dead don't know but learn. The living need for their dead to stay that way.

One night on the river, after too much whiskey, he'd somehow wandered into the current, got caught up and swept to the other side where he had a vision of walking in a field of light, only he didn't want to keep going, he missed his wife and daughter and it wasn't the time for him so he'd turned around, Joey Harvell, come back to the bank, where he sank back under water, and there was an Indian in a raft waving his hands back and forth above him. The Indian had expected him to be afraid, but Joey wasn't. For some reason, he wasn't. His headlight shined up through the water, a shaft of light, and then he was out of the water, breathing. He handed the light to the Indian and the Indian let him be. He'd broken ribs. From the other side, they heard him yelling. *Help*, he screamed. *Help me.*

Two river runners, a man and a woman, ferried across and had a time getting him on board. The woman had fallen into deep water. It was cold, in the twenties. The next morning he hadn't remembered a thing. The boats were different. He'd shit in his pants. For a long time, it came to him in pieces. Being under water. The Indian and the light. Walking. Deciding to turn back.

Mama'd drowned in her hot tub. She hadn't been ready to go. There were extenuating circumstances. Dumb truck driver, O.W.'d said, stared him in the eye.

Mom Dee was worried about his soul. Si, he wanted the tomatoes covered with a blue tarp, night of the first frost. Jimmy was silent, sunshine in his eyes. A bell was always ringing, *the jewel is in the lotus*.

Of course he first tasted the red dirt of this desert when his mother carried him here, in that beat, overheating car across the heart of Texas and into New Mexico, where the light changed and the taste of the earth came as a voice never heard but recognized, the way it was when Renee called him out of the blue, when he was obituary writer for the Democrat-Gazette and they'd rang her through to him from Capitol Hill in DC and he'd heard the pieces of her words and they pierced him to the root. Went through his heart so that he knew this was the voice he'd been hearing his whole life, since before his life when he'd tasted the dirt of the desert in his mother's womb. Like the instant he saw the quarter size splotch of brown hair as Lara breached into this world, and she came screaming so the midwife said, "She's a feisty one." All while they sutured Renee, he'd held her and rocked her and hummed to her the sad song of humanity, and knew that this was why he'd come west, that he was home, that she'd tasted the red dirt and he would never be alone again in this lifetime.

On the other side of the river, just below Ledge Rapid on the San Juan, on the morning after they'd found him screaming in the cold and ferried him back to his tent and his clothes and his life, Joey Harvell had spotted his coat, the useless arms crossed on a boulder where, he'd learn in quick time, the three ribs had been broken.

He offered it his rowing gloves, Joey, so there he lay, strange effigy of himself. He's passed it since, in the boat alone, with his wife, his daughter, he always offers something to the place where he crossed over. Tobacco. A sage bundle. Jerky. Reading glasses.

And he thinks of what the newly dead don't know but learn. To be born flesh, depart the great mystery and be free of this earth. The Moenkopi dust he'd drilled up from Earth's bones tastes of that great walking.

Of course he must burn the book.

Down there by the river, he could hear it in his sleep.

Two stories here: running away and being run away from. And there was, thanks to his fucking warlock brother, the name business. See, it's like this—if you are married in the church, say you and sweet thing go in for a temple endowment, well get ready, and try not to get laughing sickness with all the washings and anointings and talk of blood and more blood, lots of blood. Our arms intertwined for the anointment by which we swore to defend Zion to the death, and, of course, the part about avenging the blood of the prophets. There was the sword business, a long, shiny sharpened fucker, that got Joanna giggling, and the scape goat thing—Billy *bah, bah, bah our sins away*, and then the naming. Brother whispered it in my ear, said out loud that I was never to forget and never utter it to a soul—her holy name. That we were sealed for all time, and in the beyond I would call her by that odd word, and she would join me and I would be her god. In God's own image. Me.

And here's where it got tricky. She'd grown up a Bishop's daughter, and knew the whole rigmarole, or I thought she did. Joanna said to brother, all dressed up with the silver sword dangling at his side, she said, "Tell me his secret name."

He said, "Do what?"

"His name. Tell it to me."

Our wedding day, how we were solemnized. My father watching, my mother. Her people, they were all there. After, a feast prepared. Desserts on top of desserts on top of desserts. Only Joanna wouldn't touch a thing. Nada. And even later, she didn't feel like doing the thing we'd been married for to begin with, but I was her father now. My will.

"Tell me your name first," she said.

I said, "No."

I mean I couldn't. I didn't make up the rules. There were punishments. Eviscerations. Gruesome things. It wasn't my fault.

"Leave it alone," I told her.

The running away started that same night. I see that now.

She said, "It's not fair."

"It's not supposed to be fair."

"Well, fine."

I said, "Fine."

"Go ahead and fuck me."

It was always there, that godawful name brother'd whispered into my ear. Now that the divorce is final, why shouldn't I tell her. And oh yeah, the other thing. That I can have as many names as I choose whispered into my ear—as many as I desire, a whole goddamn notebook full if I want—but she can only ever have her name whispered once. She is sealed to me for all time, and there is no breaking that seal. When I'm a god, I can call her out. She *has* to come. That's how it is.

Two stories: running away and being run away from. And they both end the same way. I didn't make the rules.

It's part of the deal.

Sorry.

Sixty holes east, sixty west, their names incandescent under the full Cold moon, the heft of a Sunday night with the last of the buoy-red light dying on the Vermillion Cliffs, Edgar unrolled wire just under the six-hundred-foot span of pedestrian bridge named for the Lee who'd once hidden here from a Federal warrant for the murder of emigrants from Arkansas. The stray car, pick-up come sneaking across the twin, headlights a kilter on the canyon walls. He hears snippets of music from the windows of some of them, and sometimes they stop mid-river and take a long arcing piss off the side so Edgar stills, pulse in his neck. The Harvell boy back there tying each stick to the main line, Fanchers, Poteets and Bakers, unknowns and unaccounted for. And the moon was just something to behold down in the canyon, slashed on the water and house rocks, alive almost. About to speak.

He worked east to west, passing the rolled coil through the top line of spandrel braces, so it caught in the Vs, invisible from above. That Navajo woman, Rita Begay, she'd sniffed them out first thing, finger weaving her mojos, a younger one there with her that afternoon, a turquoise skirt against earth-colored skin, raven hair snaked down her back—a daughter? Sister Begay, Chief Joseph had called her, and the daughter a teacher over to Monument Valley, they'd buried her birth sack in the school yard so she'd come back. He could feel their eyes from the Indian side, the canyon underneath him for so long their wall of protection, four hundred miles of impasse until the Missourians came to build the Mormon bridge, Missouri goddamn.

The Russian woman's book was shit house crazy. Filled with everything but what they needed to know to blow the bridge. Finally, he'd taken over the drilling, the stone good on his hands, laying the pilgrims to rest, sealing them in with candle wax, the ceremony of it, what the heart understood.

But the Russian woman was full of shit. Burn the book, goddamn right. But her pictures were good, back in the back, the Appendix. Her drawings were right on, a dotted line in bright red where wire went through the Vs, hard work, slow going.

Back there, one of the Indians is smoking, the red eye aglow.

Edgar could use some tobacco himself, a shot to warm his insides, but the light was pretty, the flicker and shine. Whatever came next in his life, Edgar had not one hint, it could go this way or that, south likely. But for now, there he was, unrolling wire under Lee Bridge, side to side, a messenger on the way, the crazy Russian said. Be on lookout. A messenger would come. They'd have to decide.

Stoned on vodka, likely, when she wrote it. They drank it for breakfast, the sons a bitches, Edgar'd heard. For lunch and supper. They got paid in vodka instead of a paycheck, he heard somewhere. Maybe it wasn't true, getting paid in vodka.

The stars were out, Venus big as a beach ball. Paris stopped, set the roll on the deck. He unwrapped a fish taco from his knapsack. The tabasco burned his throat and the cabbage cooled it. He sipped water from the bottle. It was good.

Rolling down from the west, a galaxy of signal and danger lights, he saw it coming, no doubt about it, a rolling black hole in the night come home to him at last. Onto the twin steel bridge with the moon on its back.

Edgar faced it broadside.

The semi stopped mid-bridge, just like he knew it would. There was no sound, no snippets of song or cigarette smoke or golden arch of piss, just his heartbeat, his breath.

Had he ever even told anybody about this truck, dragging demons between states? All of them suspended between sides. He thought of Stoner whopping him upside the head when he pissed in Lee's face, of Chief Joseph and Rudolph the Red. He'd never actually read the book, but Chief had told him about the good parts, especially there at the end, where old Rudloph'd held up a scarecrow of himself for the cops to blow away, then shimmed off the cliff side, down to the river below and swam away to the rest of his life. *Hayduke lives*, Chief had said, and it was true, even if it wasn't.

"Hayduke lives," Edgar said. "Rudolph the Red."

He could see the cab, the rolled down window. Six hundred feet, one side to the other, he was halfway home. Indians' eyes glowed from the other side. There was the drumbeat of his heart.

For some reason, he thought of the Russian's sewn shut eye. He closed his eyes, Edgar, and he could see flickers of ghost moonlight, hear the truck's idle, very real on the twin bridge, harmonious, the exhaust from its stacks. A man in there, lit by dash light.

Or was it a woman?

The weight of the realization dizzied him, so one foot slipped, then the other. It was him kept bringing her back. Tina. He'd followed her down out of the hills where they'd once loved. Nearly killed him in Oklahoma. To here. This second. What the living could do to harm the dead—not let them die. He knows it in a heartbeat, Edgar does.

The spandrel caught him between the legs. Honey babe, Jesus. He took the roll of wire between his hands, set to work. It was a lonely sound, the air brakes hissing, before the thing began to roll and go away. Headed east, toward home. The signal and danger and taillights coalesced into a single red eye that blinked, and then blinked at him again, and was gone.

In the dark, a single snow flake touched his face, strange that Edgar would think it a butterfly.

From high on the western side looking east, awaiting first light on Christmas Eve, wire all run, the thing waiting to be done, Joey Harvell remembered talking to his blood father's sister, he'd got the number from information and dialed her on a whim. The red dirt's in his mouth, under his nails, has worked its way into his ears and under the callouses on his fingers. He missed Renee, Lara, should be home that second wrapping last minute gifts he'd given thanks for being able to buy, having the money, haunted a little by how his mother must have felt at Christmastime when flat broke, nothing to spend but food stamps for him, Jimmy and Trace. O.W. run off to Florida or somewhere to get sober.

She'd told him, his blood father's sister, that there were others like him, children born of mothers who'd been brought here, to Arizona, under false pretense and runaway. She called some of them by name. Boys and girls long grown into men and women. And by now they would have had children, and those children children, so that a whole tribe of wandering Washers inhabited the desert, living in trailer parks from here to Las Vegas, pumping five dollars' worth of regular at a time into cars that overheated and ran on threadbare tires, whose tags were expired and inspection stickers had been razorbladed off in the parking lots of bowling alleys where some of them had been hit in the head with tire tools and never had the wound stitched so there'd be a pink welt on the scalp just under the hair line. Whose crooked teeth had never been straightened, whose cavities went unfilled. People to whom the dentist would say, "You're dooming your child to dentures." A vast wooly-headed feral people who wouldn't know each other from Adam. That's what he's thinking about while burning the pages of Yelena Kukalov's book, and waiting for first light so he can explode the fuck out of John Doyle Lee's goddamn bridge, Joey Harvell, and go home.

Waiting for the far-off cliffs to turn the color of buoys that wash in from the sea. *What is your home? Do you miss it? Can you go back?*

Can you ever go home?

In light of burning book, lever of detonator.

When he was a God, he'd call her out, and she by god *had* to come, Joanna. Then he wouldn't have to spend his time lifting fucking prints off the Holy book, chasing around every low life between Page and Flag, and there were plenty of them, believe it, a whole derelict slew. Take the two Arkies whose vehicles have been double-parked the past two days at campsite twenty-one down to Lee's Ferry, now what in the world would two grown men—one with a job and a family—be doing down there day before Christmas with the government shut down, pretending to fish? Pray tell. Sleeping all day and up to who knows what at night? And the fish-faced one's gone and vandalized state property a second time, ripped pages from the good book, and wasn't there something in there about if any man takes away from the words of this book God's own shit would rain down on his head? Didn't it say that, the good book? And the other one, the one who should know better, he'd gone off and left wife and daughter so he could go sleep on the dirt with river rats. What kind of man does that? Ph.D.—piled higher and deeper, what he'd always heard, Stoner.

He'd prayed—yes he had, in a moment of weakness he'd cried out—for God to help him stop thinking about boozy-breathed Joanna, and Vernal, her Bishop father and what had happened that last night together, and this is what had come.

The Arkies.

Prints all over the place, front and back cover, on the tank of the toilet back in Flag where they'd fished out the missing pages. And just to make it double-down good-time fun, Harvell'd been somehow connected to some *Russkies*—who were suspected of theft and sundry other crimes.

Merry goddamn Christmas, boys. Here comes the judge.

A big-ass semi bright lights him on the steepest part of the fall toward Bitter Springs and the river. He heard the grind of a dropped gear, rpms squalling as she busted her ass uphill on a road not made for commerce. Ordinarily, he'd of flipped on his bubble gum machine, let the siren scare piss out of trucker boy. He'd inspect the load, find what was hidden, there was always something hidden with trucker boys. And there was something about this black one, high balling it the hell out of Dodge. Ordinary night, he'd put trucker boy in his place.

But not tonight.

Stoner'd smelled rat from the get-go, Angel Moroni cast out into the desert, left to lay like a dog. He'd sworn an oath to avenge such, that afternoon with Joanna and the shining sword of Eden. How many of his kith and kin had paid with blood to keep that book safe, to bear it to the most holy place?

Far away down and down near the canyon, tongues of flame, fire. Full moon splashed the road before him, shines on the semi disappearing in his rearview. Christmas coming. He'd driven with Joanna once up into the high Uintas, where they'd sawed down a blue spruce, and got stuck in the mud hauling it out. Or was it Hell's Backbone? Muddy snow. A farmer'd pulled them out with a tractor. The smell of that tree had filled their house, and she'd fished out a bird's nest, bits of pale blue egg, good luck, she claimed. And they were a family then, him and Joanna. Fuck with him at Christmas?

He'd treat with the Arkies, they ought to have known better.

Camp broke, truck packed, he could leave if he wanted, Edgar. It's the right thing to do, haul the evidence off somewhere and stash it, ice the three-day possession limit of cutthroat down in a good way, make it look like they really had come to fish, for the Feast of Seven Fishes some eat on this very eve, when animals were said to talk out loud, say who knows what. Hello, I'm Mister Trout, heard the story about me and the loaves? How about Jonah? Fuck 'em and feed 'em fish. Fish on Friday. Teach a kid to fish. Fish gills. Fishing expedition. Fish for me, where it all began. He was delirious, Edgar, been up too long, breaking camp, sweeping out the fire pit, hiding everything he could under a blue tarp like the kind you string up from tree limbs at deer camp down near Carthage when it comes a rain and wind. Last night was now this morning—he'd fallen asleep while driving here, the West rim, the blue woman, Indian Princess, who was she? Why'd she come to him, the flapping wings, turquoise on her neck and thigh.

"You should go home," Harvell told him. "It only takes one of us now."

Edgar said, "Where's that?"

"That what?"

They'd parked a good mile off on House Rock Road, a hidden moon-washed hike to the flat spot where the wire hooked to the detonator. Sixty sticks drilled into stone on either side, all their names printed in block letters, Harvell's hand, the right one with its sewn-on finger pointing to the scene of the crime—the words they'd been known by.

"Home," Edgar said.

Joey pointed toward the other side. "That a-way," he said. "Go home."

He could. Why the hell not? Would they even know he'd done this? Would they care? Give a rat's ass? Had Tina joined them now, safe on the other side?

"You don't have to do this. Go on home," the Harvell boy told him.

Starved for sleep, 4:30 now, maybe, he ran through the room scheme of Tri-County where, in another life, he'd been caretaker, a grave digger on the side, of Easter Sundays at First Baptist where they'd stand up and sing "Up from The Ground He Arose!" and it was almost possible to believe it true. He didn't live there, not anymore. Did he?

What had he ever done in his life that mattered. Made a difference? Wasn't this something? What would Chief Joseph say? Rudolph the Red? The boys back to Tri-County? Hadn't there been a prophecy that one day one would rise and take revenge, right the great wrong?

Was that him? Was it?

These Mormons, they lived in Salt Lake protected by mountains, and all down the goddamn corridor like they owned it, as if it had truly been given them by the hand of God, so they could kill who they would if they decided. Fuck you, Jack, if you didn't like it. If their prophet, the King of God's Realm on Earth commanded it, then it was right and good. Blame it on Indians. Trade John D. Lee's head for statehood. Bring on the Olympics, the brotherhood of man. Pardon Lee. Reinstate him to the church, his nineteen celestial wives. He'd be a god, own his own planet, sew seed up one side and down the other. As if nothing had ever happened at all. No kiss my ass. No nothing. The book of the past was closed, their prophet said.

Well we'll just by god see about that. We'll just goddamn see.

Just beyond what might be the blast perimeter, with what any moment will be a view for the ages, Joey Harvell feeds what's left of the Kukalov woman's book to the fire: *for they shall spoil those that spoiled them, and rob those that robbed them, saith the Lord God.* She'd written that for some reason. He'd thought that they were atheist, the Kukalovs. How Yakov looked at you with that hollow eye socket like he could see the part of you you thought you'd hidden, how he'd got them drunk on river vodka and they'd confessed to being sleepers. He has not forgotten. Egging him on, were they? Why?

The moon was going.

A lone car sailed over the vehicle bridge, twin of the one they'd wired, for pedestrians now, people on foot who'd look down on recently departed boaters and wave, say last words. They were tourists, the walkers. Likely nobody from these parts, their roles in this story had been played out a long time ago. It was over. Done deal. Navajo Bridge, tourist money, Rita Begay crocheting her mojos. It was not a thing anymore, not for the folk of North Arizona, Coconino County, butt up against the Rez.

Let me do this in a good way, Harvell prayed. Let no one come to harm by what we do on this day. Let me leave behind those things that do not serve me in this life, *Tunkasila. Omakiya yo. Omakiya yo. Omakiya yo. Omakiya yo. Help me. I'm suffering.*

Blow the trumpets. Let them roar.

The next three things happened at once: the lone car that had sailed over the bridge returned, the first rose-hued light struck the Vermillion Cliffs to the north and west, so daylight was on them, and a great dark shape rose up above the twin bridges, glided down to the perfect center, the eleventh panel of the spandrel-braced arch. It was suddenly cold, terribly so. His hands shook. Cold spilled down his shoulder blades. Off to the side, Paris said, "It's time." The car parked in the lot on the east side. Somebody got out, walked. They were on the bridge now. A pedestrian. A man. In uniform. Stoner.

Paris said, "Blow him the fuck up."

Light was coming, quickly. Flying from the east, chasing the dark from every crevice. Now or never. Lit by the burning book, *push.*

Joey took the glove off his right hand, let fingertips touch the cold handle.

Only a feather-weight of pressure, it moved, just slightly, who would have guessed the hair trigger? Buck fever—he hadn't had it since those Arkansas days when he'd sit shivering on a tree stand till his butt froze to it, feet on fire, and then from his periphery slipped the buck, new sun on its horn tines, and time would stop, the shaking and heartbeat.

In his right front pocket, the green hair clasp, a strand of strawberry blonde hair wound around the silver clasp. It had shown itself to him, Joey Harvell, the green of living things on an early fall day when butterflies swarmed. Monarchs and Painted Ladies, Aphrodites and California Sisters. She'd been there, the girl witnessed the siege. Helped bury the dead, tended the wounded. Thirst had made them crazy. You forget food, the smell of blood, other things. But the butterflies had found the cool spring a rock's throw away.

She'd died thirsty.

Some Indians were said to have the power to stop time. To postpone sunrise. Geronimo. Cochise and his warlord sister, the Navajo and Hopi who watched them from the other side. This bridge had allowed their ancestral enemies to cross, the crossing of the fathers, Lee's Ferry, day before Christmas. Rita Begay unfolding her roadside table, blue mojos for luck, pink for love, red meant a hunger salve, and green for the ones who were thirsty.

The sun rose up, just as it always had, a sliver at first over White Mesa, then the fiery circle ascendant. On his face, the warmth, immediate and real. In his eyes, blue like his father's.

Somewhere was drumbeat, prayer, a shrill voice making words of the death song.

Dead in the middle of the steel bridge nearest, the one with wire stretched beneath the chords of its braces, roosted on the handrail so the sun struck fully, a black bird stretched wings to their full span. Caught in that first instant of daylight, the great wings shuddered and throbbed, were imbued from the inside out with light, it seemed to the men who looked down from the Western rim where the lever of the detonator was already in motion. The great raven-hued wings of an obscene angel, they bore a white stripe on the inside, so it seemed as if the bird had flashed a pure white cross, which now shone so brightly that it hurt the eyes, trembling, sure, on fire, holy. An angel, before them, white cross wide as the bridge itself in the first light of morning, shaking wings out on the pedestrian side where a man was walking.

"Goddamn," Edgar said.

Stoner carried the hollow shell of the Book of Mormon—there was nothing inside—brandishing it as if to confront the Arkies with the heft of their sin, and the great beauty that Heavenly Father was willing to forgive, that it would be best for them to embrace the way toward life eternal.

He did not see the angel bird, its outstretched wings, golden shudder and throb, the cross so white it hurt to see. How the transom was electric beneath its gnarled claws. The head bald of feathers so as to plunge into the body cavity and emerge clean of carrion. Nor was he aware of the men on the Western rim who just now held his life in the palm of one five-fingered right hand. The Begay woman and her princess daughter had withdrawn in the distance, were a mystery to him now. River below, sky above.

Thinking, when he was a God, he would call her celestial name and she would come to him and he would be whole again, that great emptiness in his heart would be healed and he could go on with it, life and living.

Just as the wings shimmered and throbbed and the great white cross shone across the desert land where the Saints had once pushed handcarts toward to make it their own, as the lever reached that moment wherein the 120 names would loose their vengeance and so be revenged under heaven, sayeth the Lord, as Stoner wondered why on Earth he'd ventured here to begin with, a microburst wind of the sort that sometimes happens in the west when cold air confronts the warmth of sunrise came over Lee's Bridge, an instantaneous hand that yanked the hollow book from Stoner's grasp and sent it spinning the 467 feet to the river below where a green tongue caught light. Time stopped and the spirit wind came howling. Joey Harvell's right hand was taken from the lever, of his own will or not, and because she'd died thirsty, he took the green hairpin from his pocket, blew the grit off and sent it spinning to the river: *water of life, water of death.*

Swim home sister.

And all this before the deformed angel who shuddered and throbbed before them, throwing the white cross which could not be denied. Ashamed of themselves for what they'd done, the men did their best to clean up their mess, and went home as we ever have, whatever and wherever that might be.

The condor withdrew its shimmering wings, sought shade and food for its young. Just as condors have since the first of them flew down to join the trek of our kind across the great ice bridge of the north, driving before us the beasts we'd slaughter to extinction.

Butterflies would migrate south, the sun warm on their blood-soaked wings so they would lift and flutter and fly toward light.

PART III

21.

Of course he'd never get it right, none of them would, what it had been like to go west. Chasing the sun over the continent's boney spine, see mountains lift saw teeth from a hundred miles off, and think that's where I'm going, that's where I'll be, and never, finally get there. It was an idea, the West, and is there ever any attaining an idea? Walk out in your backyard on a Sunday morning in springtime, the tulip and daffodil and forsythia just going apeshit and in blows a blizzard with thunder and lightning in its teeth and a foot falls before you know it, and then the sun comes full-out and the glimmering world is beyond dream, beyond words. The sort of space that gets into your being, look west off the front porch and see Nevada in the nuanced shade beyond Antelope Island where buffalo roam, and whales were rumored to have once swum in Salt Lake, remnant of ancient Bonneville, freshwater gushing down from the hard cut mountain glaciers to the Sea of Cortez and beyond. They'd lived on the lake banks of the great flyway, fed on birds of every color, woven the feathers into crowns and owned the land, disappeared, the bone heaps of stork and heron and swan fifty feet tall in places. Where the cutthroat evolved and woolly mammoth walked ruts into the ancestral highway south, the one the emigrants walked, where the black snake highway runs now. *Utah,* a vowelly name, *place where there are mountains.* They'd try and go on trying, but they'd never get it right, what it had been like to come here and believe oneself to be Lord and keeper of the realm. Where anything and everything at all was possible, the future a clean slate, wiped bare of the gore and travail it had taken to get this far. *This is the place,* they said.

And it was.

Know where your water is, the Hopi elders said from Oraibi. Big fucking dry desert of the west, damn well best know where your water is. The upthrust Wasatch Front, the ring of fire tipped mountains around the Salt Lake valley gets 500 inches of snow a year, 750 or 800 in a real good year, the snowiest place on earth save somewhere in Japan that gets the Siberian freight train moisture dump. That's upwards of forty, fifty feet of snow shining on the mountainside when June snowmelt comes and that clear clean water comes hauling ass down into the Mormon-built reservoirs, so when you turn on the faucet to your backyard water hose, say to water the chickens or tomatoes or spray dirt off your patio, out comes the coldest, cleanest most delicious water imaginable, so you bow down to this water, spurt your head off, drink long and hard and it is good.

The dogs drink this water. The wharf rats that sneak the chicken's pellets while they're not looking. Know where your water is—damn straight.

And Joey does. He knows the water.

After Mama died, he got hooked up with these white Indians who practiced sweat lodge and vision quest, and even the bloody Sundance Ceremony where grown-ups lashed each other to a cottonwood tree, hurled themselves on ropes till the flesh ripped free and was offered in swaths of red cloth to the treetop and therefore the sun and Great Mystery, *Tunkasila.* People did such, out west, some of them did. And Joey'd agreed to *hanbleceya* up in Croyden on Johnny Tune's farm, where an *inipi* was built beside a cold running creek, and you could crawl out the sweat lodge door and roll in the pool they'd made and it was like heaven, the cold water.

They'd put him on the mountain, inside a grave plot made of sprinkled tobacco, a choke cherry bough in each corner. A Mandan woman sang his death song, high and aching and real. "Don't look at me," she said. "You're dead."

The heat came on the second day without food or water. He could hear the creek running, the cold water trickling. At night the stars went crazy, and he prayed for a vision, but mostly for his mother, and how it must have been for her, drowning in her hot tub. Had she thought of him, wished to say goodbye. He'd never met his blood father. She was all he had.

And on the third day he would've traded the finger, and then a hand, and finally an arm for a drink of the trickling creek water, he was wild for it, wrecked. In his grave plot was a purple rock, size of a heart. It was his vision. Hummingbirds dive-bombed his tobacco bundle, like gladiators, they held forth. A dark shape passed behind his back—he felt it there.

On the fourth day, he'd trade his life to drink the water. This is the truth. He would have traded his life for a drink of water, clear and cold and holy. You won't believe it, but it's true. *Mini wakan,* they called it, the first medicine.

The rock exactly matched one dug from Mama's grave back in the Solgohachia Bottom, the Trail of Tears, Stepwell land the family'd sold in hard times. The son of a bitches clicked together, interlocked, two pieces of the same rock.

How about them apples? what Mama always said.

He never forgot, Joey didn't. You forget food. Fear subsides. You can pray and sing and give thanks and piss your bright yellow water-starved piss in the bushes. Cover your ass with the eight-pointed star blanket at night. Go crazy with the stars.

Flip the bird to the red-headed hummers. You could do what you would out there on the mountain, your death song ringing in your ears. But finally, everything came down to a drink of water. What alone was worth your life.

It was the holy secret he'd learned from *hanbleceya.* His vision. Know your water.

He didn't know this when he got there, to Utah, him and Renee, when they'd moved into old man Hacke's house next to an apartment where Mexican boys peed rainbows off the catwalk, so it splattered on the driveway, and you could smell it from the front porch that overlooked mountains to the east, where they had happy hour that first week, with not the faintest idea of how their bodies had begun to dry. By September, their nails had cracked, their lips and faces and fingers and hands. They'd slathered lotion on each other's' backs, stocked up on Chapsticks and lip balm, cuticle cream, cotton gloves for sleeping. To no avail. The desert air dried them top to bottom. And who would have ever known such? This great drying out?

It happened.

Just like it happened to the Mormons and the Arkies and Okies and stone age hunters who'd traipsed this way after the giant sloth and camel, how the foreskin of their penises would shrivel and drop, and the women's menstruations would sync with a day when the rain blew in, and then went away.

They watered the Jesus out of their yards, near the college campus where Joey took the Ph.D. in the *History of Conflict Between Mormons and Southerners with a Focus on Mountain Meadows and New Harmony.* They'd been thirsty, the Fanchers, it was the water, the lack of it, had been their downfall.

On the day he drove downtown to have his electricity turned on, his phone and utilities, Joey'd got nervous, let's just say there were certain events in his wild Arkansas time that were not entirely resolved, the sort of things that can cause trouble, especially when you're turning on your electric and they run your name, give you the trace, ask for previous addresses and next of kin. He'd flown in from Carolina where Renee was packing their house, and there'd been this huge discussion about whether or not she really wanted to pack it up and move away from the East Coast, all the life and family and friends and everything else she'd ever known on earth, for Utah and the west, which she knew next to nothing about save there were mountains and Mormons. It snowed. It snowed a goddamn lot. She'd never particularly liked snow. It was slippery. She'd wrecked a car in it at Assateague. Mormons had horns, didn't they? Tails?

It had been a real question, whether or not she'd come. Rock and Meg, her parents, had just moved to a big-ass place on an island off the Florida Coast, there was a lot of room down there, ocean on one side, river on the other. What was in the

west for her, cactus? Men with nineteen wives? The Tabernacle Choir? What gives?
Renee had asked.

All this is to say that on the eve of entering grad school at the University of Utah
in Salt Lake, of taking up residence in a new life with a clean slate and wide-open
possibilities, it was not the sort of time you'd want your name and an old Arkansas
address to go ringing bells, and shut everything down, get you sent to the shithouse.
So yeah, Joey Harvell was nervous turning on his electric, just like he should be.
They ran his North Carolina license, not a problem. Typed in his Greensboro address
where they'd never missed a payment, not in six years, the house where they were
newlyweds, where they'd consummated their marriage. Not a problem. Had he ever
committed a felony? No. Had there ever been a warrant? No. An alias? No. People
want to believe the best about you, even in Utah. They ran his deposit checks. No
problemo. His phone would be turned on the following Monday. Would he be home
for the gas and electric connections?

So it had all gone slicker than shit, the full height of the Rocky Mountains
between him and any place he'd ever been in trouble. Just like the Saints. He was not
the first to feel such protection, nor the last.

Outside, still shaking a little, he'd lit a cigarette, inhaled deeply and let the smoke
out in breaths. And that instant he felt the burn of a thousand scornful eyes fall on him.
For smoking a cigarette? What gives? They grew the goddamn shit in North Carolina.
What's with these people? That's what he thought. Look at me that way for *smoking?*

He'd learn. What it meant when the man who came to measure the kitchen
cabinets would not shake Renee's hand, said, "I am *not* a coffee drinker," when Joey
offered a cup from fresh ground beans. As if he'd been offered a hit of heroin. And
he *meant* it, there was something *corrupt* about coffee. Stop in Price down in Carbon
County on the way to the river where liquor was medicine for those who'd rowed
sixteen miles in a day, ask somebody, anybody, directions to the liquor store, and
they'd give you that look, say, "What is that?"

"Liquor Store. The DABC," you say.

"Never heard of it."

"You've never heard of the liquor store?"

"No," this person, anybody at all, would say.

And so you'd ask again and get the same thing. Finally, a woman in the 7-11 will
tell you that they all know exactly where it's at, they just came from there yesterday,
and don't want you to see them there today. And when you find it, sure enough
she's right, one of the *never heard of it* people asking for a bag so no one could see
whatever evil lurked inside.

The fetish for desserts, utter disregard for speed limits or slow lanes, and if you did go the speed limit in the slow lane how they'd flip you off, veins standing out in their necks invective on their lips. How they wouldn't eat your food because they believed it unclean, nor invite you for a sleepover if you were an eight-year-old on the soccer team who brought chocolate covered strawberries for the snack nobody ate, and four girls put their arms around one another and talked about the movies they'd watch at sleepover, how they'd get to stay up late, and your daughter would look at them, and then at you. She'd end up faking it and get caught, which was even worse, the exile of stinking gentiles.

And the Jack Mormons were the worst: they got to be wild and wooly as all get out, drink your liquor and smoke your dope, then get self-righteous because they could—they could always go back. They took their shoes off in class, made themselves so utterly at home, because this was their goddamn world and weren't they cute? The bee's knees?

That feeling of always being an outsider, in your car, at the DABC, at the airport where they stood in droves holding signs that said WELCOME HOME ELDER JENSEN or RASMUSSEN, or HANSEN or PETERSON or SUI SUI because a whole tribe of Pacific Islanders had joined the fold, migrated to Zion to live in Heaven on Earth. And when you went to the dentist, the hygienist would tisk tisk when she saw you were a coffee drinker, and not hesitate to hurt you with the hydroponic tool that burnt like a motherfucker when she spied tobacco stain, hit the porous spot on your tooth root, smile and say *sorry*. Do you drink? the physician at University Clinic would ask you at your yearly physical.

"Yes."

"How much?"

"Five, six."

"A week?"

"A day."

"A day?"

"A day."

He'd write in his book. Sometimes speak into a recorder. His tone betrayed him. They'd ask if you knew that it was bad for you, drinking, listen to your lungs when you confessed to smoking. Would you like to quit? Are you willing? They'd talk heart attack and stroke, ask about your PSA screening. Had they found polyps in your last colonoscopy? Did you have a family history? Where were you from, that accent? Texas? Sounded like Texas. They had a cousin who'd done his mission in Alabama. Sweet home, they'd say. Somebody went to Med School in Virginia. Did you want to see the diploma? And no more than two-a-day from now on, okay?

Cigarettes or drinks?

Both.

And you'd lie your ass off next time, because you really didn't want to let them down, Virginia Med School and all. And one of them, your dentist river rafter friend, maybe, he'd bring you fresh baked bread on Christmas eve, still hot, his smiling daughter at his side. This is for you, he'd say, see the wine glasses and bottle on the table with dinner, but it was okay, only two. He'd offer to work on your boat trailer, grease the bearings and replace the lights. Invite you on the Middle Fork of the Salmon, do Dutch oven peach cobbler, taco bar, birthday party for one of the four daughters, they'd brew your coffee, heat water to wash your face at daylight on a morning of big water, rapids that had taken lives, float sweep to rescue swimmers. By their big-ass fire they'd talk about fireworks and water filtration systems while splitting wood with a hand ax and never know any songs you played on the guitar. You'd go to your raft, turn toward the water and drink your bourbon, hand roll cigarettes. They'd leave you be, go goofy when you returned, have a spare toothbrush when you couldn't find yours. Need some super floss? Fingernail clippers? Check outside your tent with a black light for scorpions.

And just when you were about to come around, when you'd turned loose of whatever wasn't serving you in this life with the Mormons, one of them would die. Say the mother of your daughter's best friend, who she'd ask to her senior prom years later, a woman born on Valentine's Day with a heart big as your mother's and her sweetness to boot. Someone you'd made Minestrone and fresh bread for after the double mastectomy, who'd fought this thing hard to the end, and had a party on the night of her passing. You'd cross the street on a September day that corresponded to those other dates, the ones you tried to turn loose, and her husband, who it turned out was a high priest, would consecrate the earth where the hole was dug. He'd perform magic rites, claim authority over earth and sky. All things in between. The photographer would be there shooting, *click, click, click*. He'd arrange the family in front of the casket, big smiling, all teeth. Individual shots with mommy's casket. *Say cheese*. Everybody now, around the casket, she's not there now, *cheese*. She's in her new place, Terrilyn. The husband will call for her on the appointed day. And the girl, the one your daughter'd take to the Senior Prom, she'd be smiling and crying at the same time. And her father, the high priest, he scolded her, questioned her faith. Straighten up there, he said. Be happy.

And you and your wife would walk back across the street, both of you with that sick to the stomach feel, because you'd both buried mothers, you'd grieved their passing, missed them deeply, and knew that some deep part of your life had gone away, that it wasn't coming back, not ever. It wasn't true. She was not on a new planet awaiting the sound signal of her celestial name to wake her sleeping beauty. She was in the ground with both her breasts sliced off, cancer-starved and dead. She would rot into that hole, and the girl who'd have her picture made smiling on your front porch with the sun lighting up her hair on the evening of her Senior Prom, a white corsage wilting on her wrist, she'd never see her mother again, not ever.

Not ever.

And vice versa.

Be happy my ass.

And the whole mystery of these people would start all over again, and you'd think about those hundred and twenty sticks of dynamite, sixty on one side, sixty on the other. Waxed into holes, each with a name written on it that corresponded to a sentient being that once drew breath, who'd loved and been loved and died. Killed. Heads stove in. The moment to moment capacity for great violence there, in that stone on either side, always possible. Because it wasn't over. No one could make it be. The *Book of the Past* would not be closed until those with skin in the game decided to close it. So help him, God, Joey Harvell'd think.

So help him God.

22.

For three days that summer they drove cross country, the three of them, up through Brigham City into Idaho, Boise with its Basque flags flying, crossing into Oregon at Farewell Bend where Lewis and Clark had waived goodbye to their pasts, the Snake flowing into the Columbia and the series of magnificent locks and dams, over the silver bridge to Washington state, north to Olympia and the long, desolate stretch to Port Angeles and the ferry to British Columbia. Renee had secured a VRBO in Sooke, which was known for its King Salmon, and for being the ancestral home of Spirit Bear. What she wanted, Renee, was to get him out of his head, her husband, and besides, the heat was oppressive, the hottest July in recorded history. It would be cool in Sooke, breeze blown in from the Strait of Juan de Fuca. Sixty-five in the daytime, or something. There was a hot tub at the cottage. He could fish. Let him fish. And Lara needed to get away as much as anyone, more, fried to the gills with school, whatever friends she'd ever had off on gap years or out of state schools, just like they should be. Anyone who'd grown up in Utah owed it to themselves to get the hell out, at least for a while. Two weeks in this case, they left on a Sunday.

Between La Grand and Pendleton, Blue Mountain rose up and the temperature fell from ninety something to seventies, so they could camp, given that they'd brought the whole shit load of gear, earplugs to knock out each others' snoring and the marine cooler full of road meals, just in case. They found a slot at Emigrant Springs. A loop under trees with no motor homes and their noisy-ass generators. There was a flat spot for the tent, a picnic table, good sunshine with a nip in it for happy hour. Joey grilled cheeseburgers, and they ate them on buns with sliced pickles and onion, crisp lettuce and ranch beans. After the long day's drive, the food was good, and breathing fresh air with the tent standing crisp against the background of trees was pleasant. There was the vacation in front of them, two weeks away from what had already turned into a trying summer. Lara had come, twenty-one now, she'd ridden crashed in the backseat of the Subaru, earbuds in listening to who knows what.

Their bags were laid out side to side inside the tent that was flyless to the stars. Emigrant Springs camp ran parallel to the Interstate, so they could hear motorists cresting

Blue Mountain where the land opened up and you could see clear to the Columbia Gorge cutting east to west where it gouged into the Pacific at Cape Disappointment.

They'd forgot Lara's camp chair, so Joey'd unfolded his for her, sat on the cooler knocking back vodka tonic. Her hair was in a ponytail, Lara's. She had Renee's mother's eyes, staring out of Joey's face, a widow's peak from MaMa Josephine, who knows what from Joey's blood people in Arizona. From Renee's father, Pops, his sense of ease and grace and messiness, the sweetest of manners when warranted. Meg's way with people, they loved her, strangers even. Something of Joey's long lost brother, Jimmy, that's what Joey said, a sweetness. A walking conglomeration of them all, their Lara, with her millennial tendency toward social justice and mistrust of institutions. Mixed with Josephine's inclination to believe someone's word, not a suspicious bone in her body. Last summer she'd studied whales on the coast of Argentina, and here she was now, the three of them on the road, camped at Emigrant Springs on the Oregon Trail, soon to crest Blue Mountain and see the forever beyond.

"Those emigrants you studied, did they come here, Dad?"

The company had parted at Fort Bridger, some of them had no doubt walked this way and escaped death and dismemberment, seeing their children in that wagon with the jingling harness, the older ones headshot.

"Probably. A few of them. Why?"

Renee'd read the interpretive sign outside the restrooms, how the companies had left behind the most amazing things, sewing machines and fine china, silver and oil paintings, bedsprings and hardwood dinner tables, their whole lives strewn along the rutted way.

She was older than his mother when she'd run with him from Arizona, blood father not far behind, threatening kidnap. In her third year of college, Lara, she'd only just chosen a major, Family Studies and Human Development, though Renee still wasn't exactly sure what that meant. Something to do with counseling and studying why teens and old people acted the way they did. Whatever, it had clicked with her, finally.

"They liked it here. The shade. And the creek. Would the creek have been here then?"

Joey hand rolled a cigarette. Five hundred miles today, he was on one.

He said, "There's a spring here somewhere. They'd need water after a climb like that. Don't you think?"

"For their oxen?"

The light was going. Maybe he wouldn't snore so tonight. With the plugs in, she can hear her own heart beating, which keeps her up for some reason, the *thump, thump,* the space in between.

"For their thirsty daughters and wives so they wouldn't be cranky."

She had to arrange these kind of trips fully on the sly. Otherwise he'd never come, all eat up with the tomatoes and chickens, and all that business behind last Christmas, whatever he'd been up to with that Paris man.

She had this dreamy look in the golden light fading. "Do you think I could be one? A pioneer?"

Renee said, "We've got to get up early and go. Marshmallows or bed?"

"We never do Smores—it's so *mo mo*."

"Don't forget your headlight if you want to read. I'm brushing my teeth. Want to come?"

Their neighbors had built a fire, dry pine popping. And there was the smell of them, marshmallows, the ones they never roasted. The 4th of July came twice in Utah—once with the nation, and a second time for Pioneer Day just now going down back home, the hootenanny with its parade and rodeo and state wide days off work and school, liquor stores closed, celebrating the day they'd walked out the mouth of Emigration Canyon, looked over the Salt Lake Valley and said *this is the place,* though it was rumored those words had never, in fact, been uttered.

"Of course you could have," he said, just as the two walked off to brush teeth in running water. "You've been a pioneer girl all along."

"You're just saying that," Lara said.

"No I'm not."

That night, the summer triangle overhead, bright Vega in the delicate harp of Lyra, the one Joey'd told her was the dolphin, Hercules off in one direction, between the staccato bursts of Joey sawing logs and the generator just up hill, Renee'd listened to the sound of diesels climbing Blue Mountain, how the pitch got higher and higher as they dropped gears. Like a heartbreak some writer said, a westerner Joey knew about and quoted. To her, it sounded like the boat motors she'd grown up with, how her father'd throw it into reverse at the last second to keep them from crashing into the dock at the end of their pier.

Dad and Mom argued about a tire. A *tire*. We'd crossed the Columbia which was kind of beautiful with tugboats and windsurfers who'd catch twenty feet of air, the state of Washington flaring behind their backs. It got crazy outside Portland, Mom behind the wheel, Dad navigating her this way and that, take this exit, no that one, you're speeding, can you take it easy on the brakes, watch out for the semi, its got its blinker on, that was a good jazz station you just turned off, you're not supposed to use cruise on the Beltway, do you want me to drive? That kind of stuff.

We needed gas. *Before* Portland, we'd needed gas. The little message board said we had twenty miles left before empty. Dad said that was low as it went, twenty miles. It was past lunch time. Mom was hungry. You know how it gets, that queasy feeling. The first place we came to was a truck stop. Super J or something. Of course, Mom hated truck stops. Dirty truckers blowing their noses in the bathrooms, the condom machines, prostitutes knocking on semi doors in the parking lots where diesels idled. Bad food. Farts. Truck stop coffee. I could go on. And grandpa, Dad's dad, he was, of course, a trucker. And Daddy'd first seen the western states from the passenger seat of a long-nosed Peterbilt, that's exactly how he put it, and that he was maybe kidnapped, and you'd see one antelope ear twitch, then a hundred would appear. So the first place we came to outside Portland, just off the 205 Beltway at Battle Ground Exit, was a truck stop, and their old argument began again.

Mom preferred premium. Dad pumped regular. He checked the oil. Nobody checked the oil, what in the world was he doing? He squeegeed off the front and back windshield, what the gas attendants did in Oregon because it was a state law that no one could pump their own gas, or check their tires, leftover from the New Deal, a guarantee people'd have jobs as gas pumpers.

Dad had worked at a gas station. Grandpa had owned a small truck stop outside Lonoke at one time. Him and his brother Jimmy knew how to fix tires, how to use the machine that took the tire off the rim, how to use soap to find the leak, cut and plug holes, mount and balance. He'd done that for money, Dad had. He'd stashed a tire gauge in the driver's side door compartment before the trip, only he hadn't used it yet. It had been smooth sailing so far, until after Portland.

The left front needed air. Could she pull around to the compressor island?

The windshield was clean. He'd paid at the pump for the gas.

If the tire was low, she said, the computer system would say so. It wasn't saying so. The tire wasn't low. She didn't need air. I needed to pee. I'm going to pee, I said.

Behind me, as I walked, his voice.

It was thirty goddamn psi, he'd gauged it. The tire wall instructions called for thirty-six minimum, hot. Her computer didn't know shit. You take a car to a mechanic, he isn't going to ask to see your computer, he's going to pull out the tire gauge he keeps in his front pocket where his name is written in goddamn red cursive and gauge your tires. He'd air it up if need be.

And so we didn't eat, not at the truck stop. And we didn't get air in the tire that would later go flat. And though my ear buds were in and I faked sleep when she asked if I wanted to drive, they didn't talk a lot on that flat ugly stretch between Battle Ground and Olympia.

At first sight of the Puget Sound, just at the exit from the main road to 101 which skirted the water and would take us to Port Angeles and the ferry, they rolled their windows down. We'd crossed the salt line, and breathing that good air made them okay again. Strange how the sight and smell of salt water was medicine for Mom and Dad, me too, I guess.

I don't know. It happened.

We made sandwiches at a rest area. He hauled out dripping lemonades from the cooler, one for each of us. Ice cold grapes and Doritos. Somewhere along the line we grocery shopped while Big O mounted and balanced the new radial. Welcome to the world of grown-ups. I'd have my share of fights about sillier things than tires, no doubt. But still. It's like the fight wasn't about tires at all. It was about who they were, where they'd come from, who their people were. Dad's were gas station people, they changed their own oil, fixed their own flats. Pumped Mom's people's gas, washed their windshields, and yes, gauged their tires.

That's what they were talking about, who they were. Defending that. And me a perfect mix of them both. He put a gauge in my car, too. I keep it there, driver's side, thirty-six psi minimum, hot.

They got lucky. The last room in the Port Angeles Inn, with a back porch overlooking the blue Strait of Juan de Fuca, two queens, free breakfast and WiFi. Straight up happy hour with plastic lawn chairs on the cliff face where wild flowers and blackberry bloomed. Blue water as far as you could see, the earth's curve. Ships, freighters sailed the open water, far-off and shining.

The town itself ran along the foot of a cliff, a fishing village with colorful Victorian woodframes, tin-roofed with shutters, Main Street with a few fish and chips places and an Italian that the hotel clerk had recommended. At the dock that was built out of the estuary, the ferry was loading for Victoria, motorcycles first, then cars and trucks and RVs, and then semis and delivery trucks, a whole boatload, who could believe the son of a bitch could float. The scene played out on the water before him, the horns and signals, mates whistling, shutting the ship's holds against water. The engine whirred to life, and men worked ropes onboard, their arms flashing with the coils. She sailed past the Coast Guard island and let her horns blast north across the strait. The wind came whistling and clean, a bite to it. What better medicine on earth than to sip vodka tonic with tart lime and watch such a show, the seabirds squawking over the colorful real world? Renee came out and sat with him there for a while with her bourbon. A captain's daughter, the sea was close to her heart. She missed it in Utah. He knew that. Lara'd sacked out on one of the queens. What was it about youth and sleepfulness? With the world up and alive like this?

A bright red Russian tanker was docked off the causeway jetty—a thing to behold. The size of two, three football fields, she sat there taking fuel and supplies, the biggest ship Joey'd ever seen. How much oil she must hold? Men walked the deck, a few of them, he could see them moving, just barely. How many of them standing on top of each other's shoulders would it take to make one of the fierce red letters: NO SMOKING. A river, no really, two-hundred CFS, gushed from a hole ship side, and all sorts of pipes and hoses and cables were lashed to her. A supertanker, he'd later learn, in letters white as the mutant angel's cross, panted across both her shoulders: MOSCOW KREMLIN.

What he'd give to walk down there and knock one back with these Russians. Say *I'll shit on you from the highest tree* and chow down with them on pickled mushrooms. Ask them if they'd ever heard of old Yakov Kukalov whose father'd won the Lenin Prize for founding the Russian Nuclear Program, yes, the one who missed an eye with pretty architect wife, Yelena. Who worked this second, no doubt, for the very name painted on their ship, hacking our computers, the blizzards of messages sent out to stir our collective shit, get us all fighting and blind and crazy, the subterfuge to distract us, all the sleepers awake and then not, awake and then not.

He knew explosives, Yakov. That dynamite shit, it was for dummies.

His cameras seeing all, *click, click, clicking* at us from satellites, the moon, the red railing and Captain's tower of the MOSKOW KREMLIN.

It was too much, really, these Russians. And now with the ship the size of a stadium docked at Port Angeles, where they'd come to get away, to fly to another country and escape the heat and Mormons and whatever it was that drove Joey to be the way he was. He hadn't thought of it for a while now, how it had been on the canyon when he'd burnt the pages. Yelena's story, for every action, an equal and opposite reaction, what happens to the one thing must happen to the other.

Renee'd called him in at dusk. Where should they eat?

Fish and chips, Lara's fave.

Not as fresh as the cutthroat him and Paris'd horsed out and pan fried from the Colorado, but not bad, cold beer, on the wharf, with his family, a baseball game on all the strung-up televisions, boat lights blinking on the water, horns blowing and more whistling, the Coast Guard cutters always moving in patrol. Their 9 a.m. ferry loaded at 7, they'd have to be up early for breakfast. Clear and brisk, the forecast said. Lara folded her paper menu into an airplane, wrote a message on both wings and wouldn't let them read.

It was cold, the steep walk back, a stairway up the cliff face, one hundred steps exactly, Joey counted. From the top, Lara launched the paper airplane and it flew like a champ, down and down, she flew and landed next to the solitary black piano in the plaza below, the ebony and white keys clearly visible from above, as were the dark letters on the airplane's wings, indecipherable from the height, but there.

It would be there the next morning at daylight, the plane, its cargo of words. YOU ARE LOVED, his daughter'd written next to the daily special on one side. DON'T GIVE UP, on the other—words used to ward off the epidemic that plagued her generation.

You are loved.

Don't give up.

Mama'd given up, when he was only a kid, four maybe, and he'd been best man in their wedding, her and O.W., and they moved to that house on Thayer where the Magnolia bloomed and there was a wrought-iron staircase painted black up to their front door. Across the street from Arkansas School for the Deaf, and the football team would practice on the field across their street. He'd watch them on the afternoon when O.W. carried her across the threshold, out there grunting and harrumphing, hauling in ninety-yard touchdowns, the bomb. The deaf cheer squad doing *Funky Monkey, Satisfied,* making themselves into a pyramid. Only something had gone wrong and Mama went inside of herself. She quit smiling. Her laugh disappeared. It had been October, the ball season full on, crowds of the deaf and hearing, blind and berated making a joyful noise across the street on game day, a Saturday when dust motes floated in the honeyed light, and Mama slipped in the shower and cut her wrists. That's what she said, that she'd slipped. After, back from the hospital, she'd held him and said everything would be okay. Everything would.

Her white casts smelled like sugar.

23.

She paid their money and they drove on board, into the hole, the ship's belly where vehicles jammed head to foot, a hundred, more, for the twenty-four-mile ferry to Vancouver Island and British Columbia. There'd been a dog to contend with, Joey'd given it a biscuit from breakfast, and the thing slurped it up, let them pass to the upper deck, where they bellied up against the bow railing for departure. She'd grown up around shipping yards from Norfolk to Charleston, a stretch in Monterey and the War College, the smells and sounds, the ruckus of launch, it took her home, now where might that be? Navy was either up or out, and up meant the constant moving from one post to the next, her Captain father saluted by enlistees who went into conniptions when they drove onto base, the ports where her mother and brother and her would stand with the stiff breeze in their faces waiting for his Destroyer to come sailing, flying the Number 1 flag, code for *I Love You.* He'd be in his dress whites, clean shaven, and the ceremony of arrival, the folding of his flag as he disembarked, would all have to happen before they could finally hug and restart their lives, if only for a month. All those first days in new schools, always being the new kid, a year ahead of her age, there were 12-step programs for people like her, rootless, who'd grown up military. And now, twenty-five years in Utah, and still she said *I live there, but I'm not from there.* The longest she'd ever lived in one place times five, was it home? *Utah,* where she'd die? Should they make arrangements, her and Joey? Their bones be interred there? Bright light in her face, the sharp wind cutting through her fleece like it was nothing, with her family on a Wednesday between places, white capped mountains gleaming on the state side, and the blue width of Canada on the other. The thought is inconceivable, and so she let it go. Joey asked a stranger to photograph the three of them on the bow of the ferry, sailing at 20 knots, big smiling, their hair crazy.

After an hour to Sooke in traffic, trying to both drive and read directions off her phone because Joey was useless, and Lara with her earbuds inhabited another world, they made wrong turns and ended up at a house with a busted-out screen door and a car jacked up on concrete blocks. There were goats, two billies that *baahed* at them from the gravel drive.

"This is our VRBO?" Joey said.

"Goats!" Lara rolled her window down, pitched out a fistful of corn chips which they crunched between yellow teeth, the one slit-eyed and bleating.

"There was supposed to be water. The rental's in sight of water."

She was trying, Renee. Had planned it all, paid in advance, rental insurance and cleaning fee, $185 a night, a hot tub and fully-stocked kitchen. She was goddamn trying.

"I don't see water," Joey said.

The owner was returning her text. They'd made a wrong turn. This was not the place. They needed to get back on the main road. Head south.

"You paid *what* for this?"

Lara said, "*Dad.*"

"Will you just give me a chance?" Renee said. And that's how they arrived in Sooke, B.C., day after Pioneer Day, 25 July 2019. Make a right at a pole by the elementary school where a child had been run over, they were told. There were plastic flowers hanging there, and you could see them a long way off. Down the road, past the boat works and marine repair on the inlet, find a white gate coded to 2019, just like the year. They moved in, walked the path to the bay which was at low tide, had their dinner and went to bed. Joey'd sat on the back-porch smoking, the stars were good, he said.

She heard him brush his teeth, turned to face the wall.

The path hugs a wood fence in shadow, little fat Buddha at a fork, one way to the big house, the other to the gate that opens onto a rock beach. A real deal chill is in the air, the smell of spruce, cedar, salt water. A white-headed eagle shrill-whistled from a place he couldn't see. Flat bay stretched before him, on the other side a white house, wood, with a pier and a boat, another house on stilts, the light just coming. The water had a gleam to it, *seiche*, it was called, the one word Mama remembered from his blood father, a man he'd never met. He'd seen the bear sign on the way in, the foolproof trash can at the gate out front with its combination set to the year of the Lord, 2019. He brewed coffee in a pot he'd never seen before, in a kitchen he'd never stood in before, in the dark he knew all too well. Little lights going off here and there, the WiFi box, time on the microwave, a sliver from Lara's phone beside the pull-out couch where she slept. The sound of her breathing was a comfort to him. He was glad she'd come, so many other things to be doing when she was twenty-one. Would he have traveled with Mama and O.W.? Once, on the way to a family portrait, him and O.W. got in a screaming match in the front seat of the Pontiac. The old man had lurched off to the roadside, thrown it into park, said for him to get his ass out. Mama'd cried and cried, Jimmy and Trace white-faced in the backseat. You could see it in their faces in the portrait, the pretend smiles.

He heads right, past the plastic lawn chairs the owner's set up for clients, up beach. Blackberry bushes are head-high on the bank, where the red sun just then cleared a silver Air Stream with a front porch built onto it, another house trailer in the space, next door, and beside that, another. Their "seaside vista amidst outrageous beauty with hot tub and immediate access to beach" was next to a trailer park, a goddamn trailer park, like the one Mama'd rented when O.W.'d run off to Florida to get sober. It lifts his heart right then at sun up, good hot coffee steaming in his mug, to have come to live the week at a hundred-and-eighty-five a night beside house trailers. Renee'd shit, the car tires thrown up on top to keep the roofs from blowing off.

At makeshift stairs up to the grass lot in front of the trailer park, a sign says *T'Sou-ke First Nation* above a colorful drawing of a bird perched atop an equally colorful fish with a hinged jaw. Rez land—they were living next to a trailer park on Indian land, bear country, land of fish and eagle. It's a good morning, a good day to be alive, near the water, the ocean, the seabird squawk full in his ears now, he knocks back a jolt of strong coffee and says Thank You to no one in particular, heads off toward the far point where a spit of rocky shore reaches out to the deep channel.

In another lifetime, he'd lived with Indians. Cherokee out on the county line where a shot up sign announced *Welcome to the Authentic Trail of Tears.* The Mayfields had taken him in when Mama finally lost it and ended up in Charter Vista, and the kids got farmed out to whoever'd take them. Rocky Mayfield was school janitor at Joey's Junior High, and had offered one afternoon in fall when Joey was waiting for a ride from Deacon Spenst and his three Bucky-beaver teethed girls. "Come stay with me if you want," Rocky'd said, smiling that goofy

Indian smile.

"Where do you live?" Joey'd asked.

"Under an apple tree," Rocky'd said.

It was true. The house Joey lived in all that winter while Mama got well and O.W. sobered was under an apple tree, the mismatched shingles stolen from as many job sites as the men had ever roofed, not unlike the ones he walks away from toward the spit where a deep channel rolls, mussels down there shining, oysters, the gleam of otter and King Salmon, Dungeness crab, probably, he can smell it, the sound full of life.

An old Indian walking a dog laughs when he walks by, points at his back, says "Way to go."

Joey looked at him.

"Your cat," the man, who was missing a front tooth, said.

Joey came from people who missed teeth, who walked around like that unashamed, saying *way to go* to strangers at sun up. His back? Cat? On the way out he'd thrown on Lara's East High Leopard sweatshirt over his flannel, the black cat spotted with red dots.

He walked as far as he could, Joey. Right out to the drop off. From there he could see, way out in the distance, a much larger spit, and beyond that, past the jagged cliffs off Sooke Point, open sea, blue water. He'd read that sailors got addicted to the horizon, that far-off curve of earth. Chased but never caught. That hole we keep trying to fill.

When he turned back, far down the beach near the *T'Sou-ke First Nation* sign and the house trailers with the tires weighing them down on top, he saw Renee, walking his way. He saw her see him wave. It was her had brought him here to this place. How many times had she saved his ass?

How many?

They kissed when they met, hugged. She held the front of her flannel in a bundle. "Look,"

she said. "Can you believe it?"

Inside the fold, with the chill and slightest whiff of salt air on them, blackberries, ripe and leaking and tart to the taste. They sat down together on the rocks in the sand and ate the purple berries one after another, slurping coffee and making the sounds that mean *this is good* in any language.

She threw a rock, a skipper, one, two, three, four, five. Thirty years ago they'd met by chance, a stray phone call to the newspaper where Joey worked in obits, her the congressional aid for an Arkansas legislator, calling about watermelons the size of Volkswagens, Hope Melons, she'd called them. They'd exchanged addresses, written each other for five years. Now they'd crossed the by god country, come west, were joined at the hip by Lara. Three decades had passed. Time. They were going grey. What on earth?

They ate the chill berries, the sun warming them now, rising to the treetops across the bay, shining on the white pier where a family loaded gear into a fishing boat.

"I dreamed of Mom last night," she said on the walk back, the slick rocks clacking when they stepped on them. "Her hair wasn't dyed anymore."

Back in Florida, Cap had married the island's hairdresser. The one who'd done Meg's hair. Finally, they'd got along, Joey and her, Renee's mom. A West Virginia firecracker, she brooked no shit.

"What did she have to say?"

Eagles nested in the high spruce above the cove, and at his feet that second, a white wing feather, the length of a forearm, shining and pure.

"Jesus," Renee said.

They'd reached the Indian sign, *T'Sou-ke First Nation*. He buried the quill in green grass next to the sign, so the feather shone there, seemed right. Next day when they made the walk, there were two, and the day after that, three.

A heavy fog blew in on them, rain, and when it finally lifted the world seemed raw and new and surprised at itself, and they drove to the marina to look at boats because you never knew what would happen. Lara wore her Leopard hoodie, the sun in her hair.

Tail end summer, school in three weeks. A woman sold crab out of a shack flying the red, blue and black Salmon flag of the *T'Sou-ke First Nation*. Her husband had a boat, she said, and flashed teeth. He's the best Salmon man on the water. Did they care to try?

"How much?" Renee said.

The woman threw both dock-rough hands out, separated by four good feet. "About like that," she said.

From the deep dark of sleep she heard him rattling in the kitchen, making coffee, getting the bacon going, beating eggs into a bowl for scrambling. Mom moaned from the bedroom. There was juice on the table, a cut orange, the sour blackberries they had with every meal. He'd baked biscuits. Biscuits? Grated cheddar straight into the eggs, a slosh of milk and lemon juice, salt sprinkled from the palm of his right hand, a grate of pepper. She watched him, pretending to sleep, the smell of it on her now, doughy biscuits steaming hot from the oven, bacon draining on a paper sack, and here came Mom, dressed already, her fishing clothes, what earrings had she chosen. Three times they'd risen this way before going on the ocean in chartered boats, the three of them with a Captain, a mate sometimes, Armando once, in Mexico, a cutie, he'd helped Daddy land the Marlin with its terrible bill, leaping twenty feet in the air before they'd landed it, an awful beautiful fish. *Corte, corte*, the captain had screamed, and the huge fish had taken one of the mate's white deck gloves with it when it went, so you could see it waving down and down through the blue water.

It's how his grandfather used wake him, with muscadine and buttered bread, out on the john boat with a kind of lure called Devil's Toothpick for bass on Lake Ouachita where you could see veins of quartz crystal shining sixty feet below, where he'd gone those summers to get away from their fighting, MaMa Josephine and grandpa's. He reinvents it, I guess, on mornings like this, feeds us scrambled eggs and pork, hauls us in the dark to the docks, where boat captains wait idling, rigging the lines, whetting hooks, having a leak off the starboard side. There'd be the smell of whiskey on board, tobacco. And that fish smell, the boat rocking in its slip, the slurp and swish, waterline dark on its underside. Diesel smoke would hang in the air and we'd swallow Dramamine, me and Mom, and vomit off into the water, sometimes. Chumming, Daddy called it. "Wait till we get out to start chumming," he'd say.

Harbor seals would swim up sometimes for our fish guts, fat as water pigs, and one had belched once so she'd smelled its breath.

He'd sing, *What do you do with a drunken sailor?*

Why you throw him in bed with the Captain's daughter, he'd answer himself.

On the water before light, the seat ice cold on the head in the cabin. The three of us, he'd take us fishing, that look on his face like we were about to do something holy.

And this time we were, I guess. About to do something holy.

We had our breakfast in the strange kitchen, a door opening to the bathroom that wouldn't stay shut, push it in and it would drift, only you couldn't tell when. And in the bedroom, on the shelf above her suitcase, a black spider, the size of a silver dollar, and fast, so fast. Daddy tried to catch it in a wash cloth when she showed him, but it disappeared. Who knows where?

She wore her knife, Lara, *para corte*.

Yesterday, they'd driven to Port Renfrew, her and Joey. On a curvy road that rose up through horse pastures and then woods and then deep woods, turn a corner and splashed in front of them the Pacific Ocean sweeping left to right, far as you could see, forever. A few houses and then none, run over animals, how dark that road must be at night, the logged sections like missing teeth where starlight poured through, the moon. Joey'd found a jazz station with static in it, a trumpet like an elephant bawling. She drove and the road took forever. The radio went out, the road turned to gravel. And then it was like we were driving to this place nobody had ever been. And when they made the port, it was just an old wooden hotel with a huge wrap around deck where girls in bikini tops against the chill drank champagne and hikers napped right on the sidewalk. She had to pee, and hanging in the hallway were photographs of all the ferry ships that had sunk in the straight, and hand typed cards noting how each had happened. One told the tale of a Captain who'd brought his wife and daughter over for the first time, and the ship had sunk and they had drowned, only he lived and had to watch it happen.

Why did she read that?

They stayed long enough to walk to the end of the pier, a snag of land out to a deep channel. No man's land. Honeymoon Bay, it was called. Why was it you drive and drive and drive to get somewhere, then drive to some new place from the place you'd just driven to, then stay there ten minutes and drive off again. The girls behind you sipping their champagne with freezing red skin?

Now, the boat, a shining aluminum thirty-footer rocking in its slip. Not quite daylight, and bone-cold. She'd forgotten how the wind cuts straight through fleece, Joey'd worn long-johns, long handles, he called them, good thinking. Lara'd freeze.

His name is Elden, the captain. He motions them on, walks into the cabin and fires the engine. Backs slowly from the slip, then motors around the spit jetty into open straight. He's her father's size, every bit of it, quiet, those grey eyes gazing through the blurry glass, looking for who could guess, a sigh, shadow, moment when light looked right. Joey stood in the doorway. They met eyes. Strange how they'd got to reading each other's minds.

She'd think something, and he'd finish her thought. Vice versa. Fog, he was thinking that second. The boat had motored into fog. Heavy, you couldn't see a thing. As if floating in dream, in some place in between. Saturday morning in a fog bank off Sooke Point, she'd learn, this holy place for the Indians, a place where you could see forever.

He killed it, Elden. Went adeck. The first rod he placed in a holder on the right, let out the line and clipped to the downrigger, sank it sixty feet, a fluttery green jig around a dead sardine. As a girl, she'd watched her father send the downriggers to deep water, just as Elden does, the left one now, not talking, taking hold of the steering wheel on the back transom and slipping it into gear, setting the troll.

Daylight was barely visible when the first fish hit, a King, Elden set the hook then handed the rod to Joey. Lara's eyes widened when the netted fish hit the deck. He whopped it on the head, the beautiful salmon whose green stripe shimmered, threw it in the hole. Lowered the downrigger and reset the troll.

There were other boats on the water. Off Sooke Point, ghost lights, the growl and troll. Outside the cabin, a fore deck chair on either side, she in the right one, Lara nodding in the left. Real cold, the kind that got into your bones. Worthless fleece. The bile in her throat. Dramamine? Had she taken hers? Was it any good to take more now?

A second fish hit, big salmon, twenty-, thirty-pounder. She reeled one in, so both forearms burned and she almost passed the rod off, but didn't. Lara lost hers. Elden made commands. *Go there, take the fish fore, keep the rod tip up, he's a mean son of a bitch.*

They moved in a big circle, daylight now, heavy fog, couldn't see a thing out there. A fierce Coho was released. The diesel was getting to her. She'd chum, for sure. Lara said, I'm cold, Mom."

"Me, too."

The head smelled of piss. Try peeing in a moving boat, trying not to touch the seat, the cold when you do. Elden yelled. And that's when she first heard it, that *sound.* A monster. That's what she thought. There's a monster out there.

They'd circled around to face a monster.

The next King hit like a freight train, dragged out thirty yards before he could reel once, tighten the drag, kiss my ass, anything. The Captain was screaming at him, and he felt their eyes on his back, and something else, a sound he knew from his other life, the one before Renee.

He turned the fish.

And then he ran, the fucker. Elden screamed. Lara was on her feet beside him, full awake. Up on Sooke Point, not fifty yards aft, the sound of earth's back breaking. Stone eaters, something heavy. Backhoe? Dozer? Rock crusher he'd shoveled powder-fine dust from under back at Freshour Concrete outside Lonoke, eleventh grade summer when he'd come home and blow the dust and snot and blood out of his head, and Mama'd found a glob of it in a balled up sock and made him quit. A great howling grated above them.

"Take her fore, goddamnit. She'll tangle in the stair."

In the Captain's hand, the gaff gleamed. He could see the sky in it, himself, far off, both of them behind him now, Renee and Lara, who he loved. The colorful flash of the fish that had been holy to these people, in the deep, deep hole a hundred yards off Sooke Point where they'd prayed for him to return, that God might send him back again for the people, just as he'd come since they remembered, since time began, since stone on stone. A fire man high-up on the jagged point. Singing the word for return.

His arms burned, his legs, he didn't have enough heart, maybe, to stop the run one more time, and even if he did, it's just a fish, dead soon, and what's that worth?

"What's that sound?" Joey asked, the eyes flashing, ten feet down. He'd cut the motor, Elden. Other boats materialized, coming their way. Up on the cliffs, he saw it turn in its tracks, crunching rock, hacking it to hell.

Next day, they'd drive round the bay and find the place, the holy point, place of prayer, the luxury condominiums, decks with gas grills overlooking the ocean, hot tubs, glass walls, a road down the cliff for walking, one unit an open house with one free Cabernet by the glass. They were shooting for a Christmas opening, the rock wall encircling the sky units all done by then.

This one was something, no stretch to see why they'd call him a God, get down on their knees and pray to it—fish brother, fish sister, take care of the people, let us do things in a good way, let us give to you the things that don't serve us anymore, Great Mystery, father sun and mother earth, the seven holy directions, above, below, on either side, front and back, inside, we are grateful. We are. For you coming to us, for giving us the Red Road, canupa, inipi, hanbleceya, brother fish, sister fish, swim home.

Swim home.

The king lay there trembling, seeing our world through his. And for a long time he'd wonder how it must have looked, washed up against the stone cliffs whose fissures ran up and down, sea to sky, the family of them on a thin-hulled craft, the fingernail of sea, earth, air, fire and water.

Everything, really. All there.

24.

The black spider came back. Of course it did. Why wouldn't it? Or maybe it never went away. This was her home. Where she'd birthed her young, six generations of little black-eyed monsters staring at oblivious guests, like that second, the eight legs still on the hardwood bureau, eye-level, staring. They were messengers, weren't they? Spiders. Or was that snakes? Some book of Dad's, all those Hopi people emerging from Spider Woman's house down on the Grand, a salt mine with real salt she'd tasted, passage to the other world, Spider Woman's world, where they'd come from, where they'd go. What did she want from Lara this morning, Spider Woman, their last day, a Sunday. Just over there, on the pillow, her phone, she could do a search for black spiders, they were all poisonous, weren't they? One *that* size? Jesus. She could call Dad, in there sawing logs. Mom with earplugs in, the pharmaceutical kind so your heart thump-thumped, how could anyone sleep like that? *thump-thump, thump-thump.* Maybe it lived under the pull out couch. She was sleeping in Spider Woman's bed, wasn't that a fairy tale, waking up in Spider Woman's bed?

Next time she woke up, the owner who lived in the big house by the beach was crunching gravel in her golf cart, the hum of the gate that opened onto the street that fell down from where the first grader, a girl she can tell by the flowers, was hit by a car, maybe a tourist, maybe someone who'd driven this road, poked 2019 into the control box, and driven in to park where they'd parked, walked inside to sleep the night in Spider Woman's bed, the black eyes shining and alert, the message telegraphed through space and time and whatever else there was, the next time she woke up it was gone, the black spider.

"Did you kill it," the owner'd say when told about the spider's presence. "Did you *get* it?"

"Of course we didn't," Dad would say, the last hour before leaving. They'd been surprised when she knocked on the door, said they were supposed to be out an hour ago. There was cleaning to do. Another party was scheduled to arrive. How long would it take?

"Why not?"

Dad'd get that look in his eye. Once on the river, camped below warm springs where rare frogs lived, they'd walked up on a party of rafters who'd carted a styro-cooler up so they could drink beer and soak, get the kinks out. And this one kid, a fat little boy, he was catching the frogs and throwing them against a boulder, smashing their brains out. Daddy'd said for him not to do that, it was bad medicine to hurt the frogs, this was their spring, where they'd come from. Only the fat little boy laughed in his face, looked up at his beer-dazed parents who'd clapped him on, said *you da man, froggy boy, you da man.* And he'd gone back to catching the frogs between his hands, bashing their brains out on the boulder. And a night later, by firelight after steaks, they'd seen the flicker of headlight far up river, the screaming when they got close: was there a doctor, was there someone who could help? Please. Someone help them. Little fat boy'd inhaled too much albuterol during an asthma attack and was now suffering a violent seizure. Every three minutes. He had one right in front of us. I thought he was dying, the little fat boy.

"You don't know?" Dad'd say to the owner, loading our gear into the roof rack, looking down at her in the golf cart.

"I guess I don't."

She was looking at me, what I had in the plastic bag, the two-gallon ziplock. Three salmon heads Dad had saved for bouillabaisse looked out at us, Mom inside, cleaning furiously. She grinned. "What you got there, sweetie?"

"Fish heads."

"Whatcha gonna do with them?"

Three fingers of blood swished inside. Over in the trailer park someone was roofing a front porch, the nail gun rat-tat-tatting. "Is there a bin for compost?"

She said, "Take it to the beach. Throw them to the eagles."

And that's what I did, walked down the ferny path, out ono the tide-slick rocks, past the *T'Sou-ke First Nation* sign where three white wing feathers seemed to have sprouted beside the bird god. The heads were slimy. Almost before they hit the water, the eagles had them, talons shining from their unfurled claws. They screamed *shree, shree, shree,* disappeared as suddenly as they had come.

She watched me from the golf cart on the fern path. Beside little fat Buddha. All along I could feel her eyes on my back.

On a curve in the road just before the river bridge on the way out, a building with a ten-foot statue of a white bear, its right paw held up as if in greeting, Spirit Bear, it was called. They had time to kill. All day, really, now that they'd had to bust it to get out so Miss Priss could clean the cottage for the next guests. What kind of time was eight o'clock for check out? Where had it said anything about that? She'd planned on leaving at noon, Renee, taking it easy to Victoria and the ferry back to Port Angeles where they'd booked the same room as before, the one that looked out on the bay, the steep steps where Lara'd flown the paper airplane, *You Are Loved.* It was a museum, where Spirit Bear stood, and inside were photographs of what the place had looked like a hundred years ago, when the fish trap was still running out off Sooke Point. She should have demanded a discount, getting kicked out like that, the mess with the spider, Lara could have been stung.

The museum's free, doesn't cost a dime.

Joey'd found a video of the fish trap. In a little room with three wooden chairs. Lara slept in the Subaru. They'd left before breakfast. No one was all that happy.

On the screen was this gigantic work with the petroglyphs of a seal and a salmon faced out to the Strait of Juan de Fuca, a thousand years old, somebody was saying, where they'd prayed, where the fish trap had been built to operate on tide fluctuations. At high water, ten tons of the torpedo shaped fish swam round the curved dome of the point, stalking schools of sardine and menhaden, anchovy and shiners. The trap was a series of pilings that formed a maze the fish naturally swam into, and when the water fell they were trapped. A black and white video showed the salmon men hauling them up from the dark, piling them high beyond belief on a bleached dock that shook beneath the weight of what had transformed into a single body of color and beauty and terror.

They smiled, the salmon men. Someone sang a song about what a hell of a way to catch fish in a trap, manna from heaven, the time of your life. It was a park now, with the Fish Trap Beach Access and Scenic Overlook Trail. *Could we go? Did we have time?*

In the parking lot, a man was screaming at his son. Tourists just like them, the father was red-faced, screaming that his boy had a bad attitude, that he was sick and tired of his shit, that they should just go home and forget about it. His mother was *hecking* fed up. He would take no more of the boy's *hecking shit. What exactly was the hecking problem? Did he need his hecking butt spanked?*

Lara's eyes shone from the back seat, smile on her face.

Hecking? What on earth was *hecking?*

Lara photographed the three of them with Spirit Bear, holding their right hands up in greeting, going to meet the *hecking* day, to live their *hecking* lives. *Take care of us, oh Spirit Bear, give us safe passage, we pray.*

A Utah word, it was what Mormons said instead of *fuck* or *shit* or *hell* or *damn*— no getting away from them, *hecking* everywhere.

"They're real, you know," Lara said. "The spirit bears."

"Maybe we'll see one."

Their car had Utah plates, sure enough, the boy with a bad attitude and his red-faced father, the mother who was fed up.

"Maybe we will," Renee said.

On the way out of Sooke, British Columbia, past their road with the sad flowers tied to a telephone pole with red ribbon, past the marine yard and the *T'Sou-ke First Nation* pick your own produce garden and the river bridge that ran down from the glacial potholes on the mountainside, he'd sweet talked them into one more thing before the drive to Victoria and the six o'clock ferry back to the states and home, and this is how they came to park under a shade tree at East Sooke Historic Shoreline Trail Park which advertised a short hike to the best view on earth, with a stone seal petroglyph to boot. Lara of course did not want to hike, she'd be sweaty for the ferry. She was hungry, why the heck couldn't they have lunch at the place that served French fries with gravy over the top like normal people, hadn't they done enough already?

Joey made their sandwiches, smoked turkey and Muenster on wheat with mayo and sliced pickle, sprouts for Lara and corn chips. A cookie for each of them. "It's the best view on earth," he said.

They strapped on day packs and filled water bottles at a fountain where someone had scribbled *fountain of youth* in red magic marker. There was a map, the trail lay out in front of them where blue ocean shone, open water, silver boats rocking on the horizon.

"It's always the best view on earth when you want something. Isn't it?" She set out in front of them, fully as tall as he was, Joey, every bit of his weight, blood and bone. From the back, he could see both of them in her, Renee's Rockerson thighs, and the shoulders he'd inherited from his grandfather, Si, who would have been a hundred years old now.

"Do you know where we're going?" Renee asked.

The trail fell a half mile through pastureland, apple trees growing next the ruins of a farmhouse. Lara was busting it, hauling ass.

"That way," he said after her.

Low tide, a whole lot of people'd brought lounge chairs and barbecue grills on wheels. They were grilling hamburgers and hotdogs, sausages and chicken breast, their babies crying and some of them digging gravel from a bank with plastic shovels and rakes, little red buckets. The tidal pool was ice cold. Joey waded in, splashed some on his face.

Back on the bank, Lara rolled her eyes, shook her head side to side.

Renee pointed up the shoreline trail. *This way*, she mouthed. And he followed them, river sandals dripping, saltwater burning where he'd cut himself shaving.

"Wait up," he said, the women disappearing into heavy wood, trees that if they could talk might say the unspoken.

There are signs. Warnings of bear country, rip tides and cliffs, a historic cabin and petroglyphs. The Scenic Shoreline Trail is marmot habitat. Easier Route and More Strenuous. Falling Danger, Becher Bay, Whale Watching Point, About the Park. She could feel the cool of her sandwich and grapes through the backpack, chocolate back there, phone, friends, freedom. Twenty-one, everyone she'd ever known was somewhere doing something infinitely more cool than walking a trail heavy with tourists to see a seal carved on a rock. Reina was in Ecuador studying mummies. Kayla, Argentina, whale lice. Housemates in Ghana with World Health, and Barcelona for language immersion, IT Training in Paris, Theater Abroad in London, and whatever on earth happened to the gap year everybody else got to take. *Jack?* Who knew about Jack. Jack Smack. The heck with him.

A ways off through an opening in the trees where these lovers were just then kissing, the first of the overlooks. She could hear Mom breathing behind her, how far back? He held her, his hand just on the small of her back. The girl's eyes met hers. *There,* she was thinking. The kissed girl. The silver of her laugh.

But the view, it was serious business.

If ever there'd been a place to be in love, it was here, on this rocky fjord jutting into the blue swath of ocean, hundred foot firs—or were they spruce? Cedar?—growing right out to the cliffs, jagged and sharp with waves the size of houses crashing into them, the sound of it, the violence, lace-white foam flung skyward.

The embarrassed lovers retreated to the shadows, into the periphery where they blended in and went away. Her own little sky island. Panorama. A place to take your breath, to die for.

"Nice spot," Mom said, huffing up behind her. They sat on a flat spot with a table rock before them. "Best seats in the house," she said.

Gleaming salmon boats trolled the blue water, one sometimes invading another's territory so horns were blown, warning shots fired from pistols. But not now, peace out there, pretty as a picture from a friend's vacation, the one that you'd always been jealous of—how they loved to talk about it, let you know how much you'd missed in life.

"Where's Dad?"

"Behind us. He'll be here any second."

Who was it said the sunlight on a Sunday afternoon has the heft of cathedral tunes— one of Joey's poets? Not today, not on this Sunday, end of July, August just around the corner, back to ArcTec, all those kids in lock down, the cutters and the pants puller downers, abused and addicted, the crazed and infirm and afflicted of the Salt Lake Valley, she'll sit at a desk in front of them, the wide picture window with its shatter-proof glass, look past their faces, over the crowns of their heads and see the Ochers, named for how they turn red at sunrise, the lake itself, flat and serene with its Antelope Island where buffalo roam. She'd be sixty in December—*60*. How on earth did she get to be sixty? Living so far out on the edge, mountains and mountains between her and home? Two time zones between where she'd first been kissed, Friendly High, Virginia is for Lovers, the dark man who massaged her feet in Adams Morgan, *baba ganoush,* DC Space, Lou Reed's smoky voice in the loft. She'd retire. And then what? Joey's colleague was paralyzed from the neck down the week after his retirement party, riding a mountain bike down City Creek Canyon.

The lettuce is cold, crunches, the mayonnaise with a bite to it, all that blue splashed out before them. Too close to the cliff, she can hear it, the water bashing its craggy face, a far-off island with a lighthouse flashing, she can barely make it out, Joey says they passed it on the ferry.

He sliced apple for them, his flannel laid out on the rock that overlooked Becher Bay, salmon water, boats out there trolling. Lara's earbuds are in, her head nodding, munching corn chips. What could she be thinking? One thing appearing, another disappearing. It'd been a forty-hour labor, Lara. Her head had been misshapen. She'd pretended to be Mormon in school, the only way to get invited to jackshit. She'd been found out. Should they be horsewhipped, her and Joe, raising her in the Salt Lake Valley that way, pretending?

Would she be scarred for life, their one daughter?

She slides two apple wedges under her upper lip, Lara, makes this goofy face at them, nodding, the music in her head, her mind. It's enough. Isn't it? She wasn't going to let it happen, not today, a Sunday lunch on a cliff with the best view on earth. She wouldn't let the light have the heft of cathedrals, not today.

Joey held the water bottle up, his face warped behind the green.

"Here," he said. "It's from the Fountain of Youth."

Each of them took some. The love bugs had flown. They had the place to ourselves. The three of them ate in peace, snippets of Lara-song mixed with the surf, their last day on Vancouver Island. Had they found it here?

Had they?

The seal petroglyph faced open water. The patina had faded. That was how to tell the age, how much of the original patina had come back to the stone. Desert varnish, they called it in Utah, this artist ancestor, a relative, maybe, of the ones who made stone spirals back in canyon country. Paddling the north coastline of the continent.

A sign instructed them to avoid trying to understand what it meant, the seal, sprawled there on the rock, big as a cow, a buffalo, a sea turtle like the kind that crawled in to lay eggs of Melbourne Beach on the afternoon of Mom's funeral.

Now why had she gone and thought that?

Daredevil Lara monkey-climbed the pitch above the seal—A Utah girl, no keeping her down. And Joe? Joker? Where was he off to?

The seal trail had ended, but they'd kept going, Lara high above the precipice, the stone temple music pouring from house-high waves. Doing her father's trick, standing on one leg with both arms thrown out, framed in a moment of ocean and horizon, Joey picking his way to where the land fell away to nothing. Motioning Renee to come.

Dizzy, full alive, one more time she followed.

The cove lay hidden behind the bald face of the petroglyph stone. It was the size of a small house, their backyard, maybe, boulders and riff-raff and flotsam circulating in the pull and push of waves. She's above him, his child, his baby, what Mom Dee had called Mama in the butterfly poem—the one that said *we love you baby,* and *precious in the sight of the Lord is the death of His saints* and *In loving memory of our precious Josie who went to be with the Lord.* Her face flashes before him now, Mama's, the sound of how she'd said his name, how she'd dreamed of flight, her up there arms flung out. *Be careful,* he wanted to say. *I love you from here to there. Don't give up. You are loved.*

The thing drew his eyes to it.

What had brought him here today, to this place, wild with wave and light and tree scent? Across the flats of Nebraska along the Platte, where Mom Dee's people had once retreated to the green Ozark hills stayed put with the Poteets and the Stepwells and the rest, *why leave,* why?

Of course he didn't know this then, couldn't. The pieces needed time to fit, time and forgiveness, weren't they the great healers? That the red and white buoy just then bobbing amongst it all was somehow moored to what the trees spoke with no words. Lara watched from above, saw him bouldering into the deceptively deep pool, reach for it, if only he could have this, shouldn't he, didn't they deserve the buoy, after all this?

"Dad," she said, "Be careful."

He smiled up to her then, held it shining in his right hand, the one that had found the green hair clasp with her strand of strawberry blonde wound into its core, the hand that had held the lever of the detonator, the one that had cradled her the dark morning she was born, while the midwife sewed up her mother, when he'd hummed for her the sweet sad music of the universe.

Looking back, through the odd lens that time makes, it shouldn't have come as a surprise, what happened next. How he'd snatched what was a very real buoy from rough water, held it dripping as a prize to his daughter, who, of course, was no longer there. Renee came walking, smiled to see him make it to the cove's mouth, the thing between his hands, how pretty it was, how it might look strung from their back deck, a souvenir from their travels, a thing to talk about on afternoons when happy hour stretched into the shadows, this was from the day we lunched on cliffs above the ocean and had the best view on earth, when we found the seal petroglyph. When we suffered ourselves to the elements and were healed.

But it doesn't work that way. That's not how the moment will come to be remembered, is it? Love, the one buoy, what remains when the world quiets?

"Where's Lara?" he asked, unstrapping the daypack, unzipping its hole.

She said, "Lara?"

They turned eyes upward to where she'd just been, climbing, doing the leg trick, daredevil Lara, Joey in her blood. That Stepwell flare for the dramatic—she wasn't there. She'd flown. Or gone into the water. Like Mama. Who'd drowned in Arkansas. Who lay buried there on a hill of brown-eyed Susan overlooking a lightning struck tree, where Joey's spot was, Renee's, plotted, named, all of them, *there*.

He'd see it on the ferry ride home, the place where he'd thrown down the pack, fought his way up to the edge where she'd last been seen, searched the knife-toothed cliff face and the violence of waves below, nothing. Renee behind him then, her sob a lone note. From the deck of the east-bound ferry, they'd see where she was lost, their one daughter who they loved more than themselves, how they'd sprinted up trail and so startled the two women, lovers, on honeymoon, maybe. Had they seen a girl? *Yes,* she was waiting by the petroglyph sign, the one that instructed them not to attempt interpretation, not of the seal, the buoy, none of it. Mother, father, daughter, they'd see where she was lost, only different now, a whale breaching in between, stiff wind in their faces. Where they'd been at the exact moment in their lives when all was lost, and there was nothing left for them to do but become the pathetic people they were about to become. What they'd been saved from by that one affirmation, that one *Yes.*

photo Austen Diamond

About the Author

Arkansas native Michael Gills is the author of eleven books of fiction and nonfiction, including the novel *New Harmony*, Book 4 of the Go Love Quartet. A fourth collection of short fiction, *Burning Down My Father's House* will be published by Texas Review Press in 2023, as will a sixth novel, *Before All Who Have Ever Seen This Disappear* (Madville Publishing). Other work has been nominated for the PEN/Faulkner Award for Fiction, awarded the *Southern Humanities Review*'s Theodore Hoefner Prize for Fiction, *Southern Review*'s Best Debut of the Year, recognition in the *Best American Short Stories* and *Pushcart Prize Anthology*, and inclusion in *New Stories from The South: The Year's Best*. Gills is a Distinguished Honors Professor at the University of Utah, where he lives in the foothills with his wife of thirty-five years, Jill.

www.ingramcontent.com/pod-product-compliance
Lightning Source LLC
Chambersburg PA
CBHW020605250626
47154CB00004B/1375